SWING 12

Swing 12

Sisters Dancing the Nazis Insane

PJ FENTON

Silver Arrow Publisher LLC

Edited by Roberta J. Buland.

Dedication

This book is dedicated to my nephews: Seth, Matthew Patrick "Packy," Sean, and my niece, Madison.

This book is also dedicated to the Swing Kids who partially inspired this book.

Acknowledgements

The author would like acknowledge *Grimm's Complete Fairy Tales,* "The Shoes That Were Danced to Pieces," now commonly known as "The Twelve Dancing Princesses," and the Swingjugend, or Swing Kids, that inspired this story.

The author would also like to acknowledge the works of Alison Owings, Lynn H. Nicholas, Ruth Andreas-Friedrich, Lucie Aubrac, and Mitchell G. Bard and their respective works: *Frauen, Cruel World, Berlin Underground 1938-1945, Outwitting the Gestapo,* and *48 Hours of Kristallnacht* for the historical insight they provided into this time and place in history.

Thanks also to Roberta J. Buland, Editor, Right Words Unlimited, for her professional editorial guidance.

CONTENTS

Cast of Characters

Swing 12 a.k.a. the die Fürstin Sisters

Wanda die Fürstin – one of the four youngest members of the die Fürstin sisterhood and the youngest overall. Arrives at Linden Academy with her sisters Karma, Vita, and Christine and is introduced to the life of a swing kid by her elder sisters. She possesses a strong desire to stand up against the Nazis. First to come up with the idea of *Swing 12.*

Karma die Fürstin – one of the four youngest members of the die Fürstin sisterhood and the second youngest overall. Close to Wanda and talks with her often, she arrives at Linden Academy with her sisters Wanda, Vita, and Christine and is introduced to the life of a swing kid by her elder sisters.

Vita die Fürstin – one of the four youngest members of the die Fürstin sisterhood. Arrives at Linden Academy with her sisters Wanda, Karma, and Christine and is introduced to the life of a swing kid by her elder sisters. A natural dancer and actress and can act her way out of anything.

Christine die Fürstin – one of the four youngest members of the die Fürstin sisterhood. Arrives at Linden Academy with her sisters Wanda, Karma, and Vita and is introduced to the life of a swing kid by her elder sisters. Normally shy, she opens up during activities she is interested in.

Barbara die Fürstin – one of the four middle members of the die Fürstin sisterhood. Arrives at Linden Academy with her sisters Asta, Marianne, and Maud and is introduced to the life of a swing kid by her eldest sisters. Has a slight talent for being able to tell when something is wrong, but does not always act on it.

Asta die Fürstin – one of the four middle members of the die Fürstin sisterhood. Arrives at Linden Academy with her sisters Barbara, Marianne, and Maud and is introduced to the life of a swing kid by her eldest sisters. One of the most dependable sisters, she does her best to support her sisters and stay out of interfamily squabbles, if possible.

Marianne die Fürstin – one of the four middle members of the die Fürstin sisterhood. Arrives at Linden Academy with her sisters Barbara, Asta, and Maud and is introduced to the life of a swing kid by her eldest sisters. Always up for fun, she gets excited over the idea of different kinds of swing parties.

Maud die Fürstin – one of the four middle members of the die Fürstin sisterhood and the eldest of the four middle sisters. Arrives at Linden Academy with her sisters Barbara, Asta, and Maud and is introduced to the life of a swing kid by her eldest sisters. A tomboy and fighter at heart, she often get into fights while in swing girl attire with her elder sister, Willhelmine.

Margret die Fürstin – one of the four eldest members of the die Fürstin sisterhood. Arrives at Linden Academy with her sisters Willhelmine, Rita, and Freya and is among the first to discover the life of a swing girl. She is skilled at handicrafts, and was the first to introduce the youngest sisters to the world and rules of the Lake Constance Swing Club.

Willhelmine "Will" die Fürstin – one of the four eldest members of the die Fürstin sisterhood. Arrives at Linden Academy with her sisters Margret, Rita, and Freya and is among the first to discover the life of a swing girl. A tomboy and fighter at heart, she often gets into fights while in swing girl attire with her younger sister, Maud.

Rita die Fürstin – one of the four eldest members of the die Fürstin sisterhood. Arrives at Linden Academy with her sisters Margret, Willhelmine, and Freya and is among the first to discover the life of a swing girl. After a particular event, she was the first to learn the madness behind both the Nazis' and her parents' actions.

Freya die Fürstin – one of the four eldest members of the die Fürstin sisterhood. Arrives at Linden Academy with her sisters Margret, Willhelmine, and Rita and is among the first to discover the life of a swing girl. Currently in a relationship with a swing boy named Frankie, and she is planning to run away to Switzerland with all her sisters.

The Lake Constance Swing Club

-

Frankie – a swing boy and member of the Lake Constance Swing Club who supports Swing 12's activities. His real name is Alvis and is currently in a relationship with Freya.

Silent Night – a mysterious swing boy who never talks and is a member of the Lake Constance Swing Club who supports Swing 12's activities. His real name is Wor Boswell.

Old Kludge – a swing boy and member of the Lake Constance Swing Club who acts as a bouncer with a high-pitched voice who supports Swing 12's activities. His real name is Klaus Klingemann.

J.B. – a swing boy and member of the Lake Constance Swing Club who supports Swing 12's activities. His real name is Johan Becker.

Old George – a swing boy and member of the Lake Constance Swing Club who supports Swing 12's activities until he is arrested by the Nazis.

Old Sport – a swing boy and member of the Lake Constance Swing Club who supports Swing 12's activities until he is arrested by the Nazis.

Linden Academy Staff

-

Mrs. Kahn – a dim-witted Nazi teacher and disciplinarian at Linden Academy. She often punishes the die Fürstin sisters with chores meant to separate them.

Sister Crispin – a nun who worked at Linden Academy until she was forced out after the chapel was desecrated. She possesses great knowledge of Linden Academy and later becomes vital to Swing 12's plans.

Miscellaneous Characters

-

Mrs. Rita Cohen – the die Fürstin sisters' nanny until her husband and brother-in-law were abducted by the Sturmabteilung (SA).

Mr. Jacob Cohen – Mrs. Cohen's husband who was abducted by the SA; a Great War veteran.

Mr. Abraham Cohen – Mrs. Cohen's brother-in-law and Jacob's brother who was abducted by the SA; Great War veteran.

Mr. Tyr von Bron – a high-ranking member of the local Nazi party and member of the Nazi Thule Men's Club (TS)

Swing 12: Sisters Dancing the Nazis Insane

P.J. Fenton

| 1 |

"Open up!"

Wanda die Fürstin did not know what was scaring her more: the thundering sound of men running through the Cohen's apartment building, screaming and banging on the doors; or the Cohen's reaction to the men. Rita Cohen, Wanda's nanny, was watching her and her eleven other sisters while her parents were out working and was the calmest person the sisters knew. But the moment the noise started, Mrs. Cohen panicked, forcing everyone into small groups, and trying to hide them under beds, and in closets, or anywhere else she could find. It was a challenging job because it involved twelve active opinionated girls.

"What is going on out there!" Freya, one of the eldest of the twelve, asked as she demanded the answer from Mrs. Cohen.

"The Devil has been set loose tonight," Mrs. Cohen replied, anger and fear marking her voice.

"If the Devil's been loosed, let us help you fight him," Willhelmine challenged. Willhelmine, or Will as she liked to be called, was born at the same time as Freya and one of the two tomboys of the twelve. If a fight was coming to the Cohen's apartment building, she wanted to be part of it.

"Agreed. Will, if a fight's coming, I want to meet it head-on." Will looked over her shoulder to see her fellow tomboy sister, Maud, look as eager for a fight as she was. Maud, the first-born of the middle daughters, the fourth born after Freya and Will, bonded to Will—and she to her—from the time they were learning how to crawl. Karma, the second youngest daughter before Wanda, often joked that the two of them must have been friends—at least—in a past life.

"This is not a fight you can win!" Mrs. Cohen cried. It was then Wanda noticed the tears forming in her eyes.

Mrs. Cohen's crying, Wanda realized, shock gripping her at having never seen a grown-up cry before. *Mrs. Cohen never cries, my parents never cry, what is going on out there?*

"Don't bother trying to hide them."

Wanda and her sisters, along with Mrs. Cohen, looked behind them. Mrs. Cohen's husband, Jacob, and his brother, Abraham, the apartment's owner, were dressed in their old military uniforms. Both Jacob and Abraham were decorated veterans of the Great War. Tonight was the anniversary of their return from the Great War, and they were having a small party to celebrate it. Wanda and her sisters had seen some of their medals before and heard the stories behind them. Still, she had never seen them all at once, nor when they were all in their old military uniforms as they were now. The sight of the two of them, usually so friendly and approachable, now dressed in full military regalia, made both of them seem fierce and intimidating.

"Jacob," Mrs. Cohen began before her husband cut her off.

"It will only look worse if we hide them, just protect them while Abraham and I deal with these thugs."

"But Jacob, they'll..."

"No matter what happens, *never* stop protecting your family." Jacob turned his gaze from his wife to Freya, Will, and all of Wanda's sisters eventually stopping on Wanda. She quickly realized Jacob's intentions. *Mr. Cohen is trying to teach us something important, he wants us to make sure we never forget this.*

Finishing his point, and joining his brother, Mr. Cohen turned to face the pounding and shouts coming from the door.

"Are you ready, Jacob?" Abraham asked.

"As ready as I was in the trenches," Jacob answered with a smile, reaching for the doorknob. Yet before he could turn it, the door around the nob fractured. An ax-wielding man in a brown shirt, the first of a mob of men wearing similar brown shirts, smashed their way into the Cohen's apartment.

"Are you a Cohen?" The leader of the mob demanded, as his flunkies grabbed the two of them and started ransacking the apartment. The one with the ax ran straight past Wanda and her sisters, into the bedroom where he and a few other brown-shirted men started hacking the bed and mattress to pieces, ripping apart books, and tearing dresses to shreds. Elsewhere in the apartment, similar sounds of destruction could be heard as the brown-shirted men continued destroying furniture and everything else.

Wanda did not know what to think, neither did any of her sisters. Glancing back at Will and Maud, both eager to fight a few moments ago, Wanda saw they were now shocked at the sight before them. She did not blame them, the men looked like they could turn their attention, and the devastation they were causing, onto them at any second. From where she huddled with her sisters and Mrs. Cohen, Wanda could see the leader of the brown shirts. He was a young and dumb-looking man, wearing a swastika on his arm, and still facing the Cohens. However, Wanda quickly realized that Abraham and Jacob were not as easily intimidated as the rest of them.

"Stop this and leave my family and me alone!" Abraham ordered the leader of the brown shirts, who did not even acknowledge him. "My brother and I are soldiers of Germany," Jacob continued. "We fought in the Great War for the Kaiser, earning these awards, before you and your leader's thugs had even left their mother's side. You have no right to treat any of us like this."

The leader of the brown shirts did not listen, or simply did not care. Ripping each medal off the Cohens' chests, he tossed them onto the floor and then began pulling their beards off their faces.

Their beards, Wanda whiffed, unable to keep the shock off her face as she saw both Abraham's and Jacob's faces bleed from where the hair and skin were plucked off. *My God, he is pulling off their beards!*

Both brothers had short, thick, beards, yet the brown shirt plucked at them happily, with the others soon joining in. Wanda, her sisters, and Mrs. Cohen watched grimly as hair and skin were pulled from their faces, and blood flowed down their necks. Finally, Mrs. Cohen snapped. Having enough, she left Wanda and her sisters, where they huddled together, and charged the brown shirts holding her husband and brother-in-law.

"Enough, stop this, you devils!" She raged, charging at the brown shirts holding Jacob and Abraham. "Don't any of you *dare* lay another finger on my husband, brother-in-law, anyone, or anything in this home! I am a Christian woman, and you devils will leave now!"

Wanda, and all of her sisters, knew Mrs. Cohen since they were infants, and none of them had ever seen her this enraged before. She usually was very gentle, the kindest person Wanda and her sisters knew. But now, she was engaging the men fiercely. The leader of the brown shirts responded by pushing Mrs. Cohen to the floor, her gaze—filled with venom—never leaving their leader.

"Out!" Mrs. Cohen screamed again. The brown shirts, possibly listening, or now satisfied with their destruction, quickly made their way out of the Cohen's apartment, taking Abraham and Jacob with them. Wanda did not know what to think about the destruction, none of them did. The invasion of the Cohen's home, and Mrs. Cohen's sudden transformation, left all of them scared and confused.

"One of us needs to do something," Vita, another of Wanda's sisters, whispered. "Say something."

"I'll try," answered Rita, slipping out from the group to approach Mrs. Cohen. "Mrs. Cohen, can you hear me?"

Mrs. Cohen did not respond, only staring at the broken door.

"Mrs. Cohen," Rita asked again, reaching out for her. "It's Rita die Fürstin, can you..."

Rita never got the chance to finish her question. Just before she could touch Mrs. Cohen, she batted her hand away, turning that same venomous stare onto Rita, Wanda, and all the sisters.

"Out! All you Nazi devils, OUT!" She screamed in a mad frenzy. She saw the sisters now as the same invaders who had abducted Abraham and Jacob and wanted them gone.

None of the sisters hesitated, they were all scared, and nobody knew what was happening, but they did know Mrs. Cohen wanted them gone, and they were not going to argue with her. Thankfully, the Cohen's home was on a ground-level apartment. A back door led to both a garden and alleyway access that the sisters were running for the moment Mrs. Cohen screamed "out." By the time Wanda stopped running, she had realized she was not only missing most of her sisters but that the assault on the Cohen's home was only the beginning.

| 2 |

"Where is everyone?" Wanda gasped, catching her breath, and looking around to see only Karma, Christine, and Asta, standing by her side.

"We must have been separated in the alleyway," Asta huffed, as tired from running as Wanda. "You know what that alleyway is like."

Wanda did, all the sisters knew that the alleyway behind the Cohen's apartment opened up into various other pathways. If one was not careful, which no one was at the time, it was easy to get lost and end up somewhere not intended to be.

"Do you think the Cohens are going to be okay?" Christine asked.

Nobody dared to try to answer. The entire experience had left all of them extremely scared.

"I think we should go home," Asta finally said. "It's night, we shouldn't be out, and I don't think we should even try to go back to the Cohen's, we might just get more lost. Everyone else is probably making their way there now."

Asta's right, Wanda thought, falling in next to her older sister as they walked down the alley. *There's also the fact that if we tried to go back to the Cohen's, we might not be welcomed there, or run into those brown-shirted men again.*

Wanda did not want to think about the brown-shirted men or anything else that happened in the Cohen's apartment. But the invasion, the destruction, the pulling out of the Cohens' beards—skin and all—followed by their abduction and Mrs. Cohen's transformation kept playing itself back in her head. It was not until they neared the end of the alley that a cracking sound under Wanda's shoes drew their attention to the ground.

"Glass?" Wanda wondered, the other sisters also noticing the massive amounts of glass shards under their shoes as they walked out of the alley and onto the street. "Did someone break a window just..." Wanda paused, unable to breathe, realizing now that the attack on the Cohen's apartment was only the beginning.

The entire street was being destroyed. People in brown shirts, like the ones who attacked the Cohens, and others were smashing their way into every store and building. Some of the men walked out of the buildings carrying safes or jewelry. Others with paint cans and knives were marking the building with words Wanda had never seen before. Some dragged out *people,* tossing them into trucks like cattle, but mostly they were simply destroying because they could. It was a horrific scene, as if it were a fiction novel describing the collapse of civilization, only this was really happening. Scanning the street, Wanda spotted a group of policemen, casually standing amidst the destruction like they were watching a play. Forgetting her shock and fear, Wanda ran screaming to the policemen.

"Mr. Policemen, you have to stop this!" Wanda cried. The policemen, ignoring her, simply continued to watch the riot unfold before them. "Why aren't you doing anything, people are being abducted, their homes destroyed, don't you care? Why are you just standing around doing nothing?"

"Now, little miss," one policeman said, turning to Wanda, who was being joined by her sisters. "Proper little misses like yourselves need not concern yourself with this. Just be good and proper little girls and run on home. We're here to make sure things don't get out of hand."

"What do you mean, 'make sure things don't get out of hand!'" Wanda screamed, unable to contain the shock in her voice. "It's completely out of hand. This has to be stopped!"

"Just *go home,*" the policeman said again, this time more threateningly, causing Wanda and her sisters to step away from them. "Children like you are the future of this great country, we wouldn't want to *lose* any of you."

Wanda and her sisters ran, even though they were tired and winded. The pure fear at the realization of what they just witnessed drove them onwards.

The police are on their side! Wanda thought.

The thought spurred the four of them down side streets, alleys, and back roads in order to keep them off the main roads and as far away from both the police and the men in the brown shirts. Yet the sound of breaking glass continued to follow them as they ran through more and more wreckage, their shoes quickly wearing out from overuse. The four sisters would have kept running if they had not run into a cloud of foul-smelling smoke, forcing them all to stop as the burning sting teared their eyes, and coughing fits overtook them.

"What is that?" Karma asked.

"Smoke, obviously," Asta replied. "Something must be on fire. There's a breeze blowing through this alley. Let's just get out of here before we suffocate."

The sisters ducked low, almost crawling onto the glass covering the ground. Moving through the alley, they could soon hear the sounds of the fire burning, but it was not until they were out of the alley that they could see the smoke's source. Standing upright again, they were greeted by the most horrific spectacle yet.

"Dear God," Wanda choked. "The Temple, it's burning, they're burning it."

The "Temple," as the sisters always described it, was the city's synagogue. It was one of the oldest buildings in the city, a place the Cohens called both a house of worship and a cultural heritage site, and it was being *burned down.* In front of the Temple, a large pile of garments, prayer books, scrolls, and pieces of instruments were gathered together and also burning in another bonfire. Nothing was being spared.

"What do you *mean* you're only here to keep the other houses from burning!" Wanda would have recognized that brutish voice anywhere, it was Maud. To the right of the Temple, two fire trucks were stopped, the firemen were outside, their hoses at the ready, and doing nothing but watch the Temple burn to the ground. Hammering in a rage at one of the firemen, Will and Maud were attempting to force the firemen to stop the fire.

"Miss," one of the firemen replied, taking to Will and Maud, "like I told you before, we're here to make sure the fire doesn't spread to the Christian homes. Now be a good little girl, go home, and let us do our job."

"Your job!" Will screamed, both shocked and appalled. "Your job is to *put out fires*! If you don't want the fire to spread, then *put that fire out*!"

"Then talk to them," the fireman said to Will and Maud, shoving them away and pointing to the Temple where a band of boys, barely older than Will, each wearing shorts and a swastika, formed a barricade around the Temple. Behind them, several brown-shirted men, like the ones who had attacked the Cohens, entered and exited the Temple. They carried out mutilated books, clothing, and wreckage that they heaped onto the smaller fire gleefully.

How can they do this? Wanda asked herself, terrified, not only by the night's violence: the attack on the Cohens, the abductions, the vandalism, and now the destruction of the Temple; but most of all by how easily the attackers were getting away with it. The police, the fire departments, the *rest of the people*, all seemed to be complacent about what was happening all around them.

How can they just let *this happen and not* do anything*!* Wanda asked herself again, before another voice, piercing the noise from the fire caught her, and all the sisters' attention.

"Hey, we found another one!" a man in a brown shirt screamed. He was flanked by two more of his teenage supporters. The brown shirt was dragging an old man, bruised, bleeding, and barely conscious, from the Temple.

"Let's throw him in the fire too!" One of the boys screamed to the cheers of the others.

"Throw *him* into the fire," Wanda gasped, standing at the alleyway entrance with her sisters. "They can't..."

Wanda trembled as the execution began unfolding before her. Will, tired of watching and shouting at people who were not going to do anything, attempted to stop the brown-shirted men herself. Maud was right behind her, but they soon found themselves stopped by the barricade of teenage boys.

"Let us through!" Will screamed. "We have to stop this."

The boys only laughed wickedly in reply, like they had simply watched something amusing and could not help laughing at it. All the while, the old man was dragged closer to the fire.

"No..." Wanda squealed, her voice trembling as the brown shirt and two of the boys took hold of the man and began swinging him like a sack.

"NO!" Wanda screamed again, just as the old man was thrown onto the fire, her own screams joining the dying man's cries as they echoed into the night.

"Wanda," Karma's voice, equally disturbed, reached out to Wanda. "Wanda, can you hear me, we have to move, we need to get out of here."

Wanda only responded by screaming more, gaining the attention of Will and Maud, who quickly joined them.

"Wanda, can you hear me? We have to get up and leave. Wanda, GET UP!"

| 3 |

"Wanda, get up, wake up!"

Wanda woke up, startled, shivering, and covered in sweat. She was no longer in front of the burning Temple. She was at an inn in a small town overlooking Lake Constance in a room with three of her sisters: Karma—who woke her, Christine, and Vita. The looks on their faces told Wanda that they were all thinking the same thing.

"The nightmare?" Karma asked, her voice trembling, knowing precisely what the nightmare was about. All of the sisters suffered from nightmares about what they witnessed on *that night.*

"The nightmare," Wanda replied, crawling out of bed, her feet cold on the floor, as she walked over to stare out of the window as her sisters went back to sleep.

It's been two years since it happened, Wanda thought, shivering from the cold. Yet Wanda did not care how cold it was, she liked it. Heat always made her think of *that night,* the horrible things she witnessed, and the things she learned afterward.

I was only twelve at the time, Wanda—now fourteen—remembered, unable to stop thinking about it. *But from the way I was clinging to Asta, after that gruesome spectacle in front of the Temple, anyone would have thought I was only two.*

Asta and Maud, both thirteen at the time, were now fifteen, along with their sisters Barbara and Marianne. As for Freya, Will, and their sisters, Rita and Margret, they were fifteen on *that night* and were seventeen now. The twelve of them finally reunited outside of their house, their shoes worn out from all the running, and the other six sisters witnessing horrors similar to Wanda's group. When their parents came out to meet them, they almost ran away from them in fright at the sight of the swastikas pinned on their collars.

And they wanted us to forget about it, for the good of the Folk and Fatherland, Wanda disgustingly remembered, thinking about what happened after their parents finally calmed them down and talked to them inside of their house. After she and her sisters told their own stories about the night's madness, both of their parents, disturbed themselves, told them to forget the whole event. That everything that had happened was, "For the good of the Folk and Fatherland."

***

"How is thievery, destruction, kidnapping, and murder good for ANYONE!" Freya snapped back, a sentiment all the sisters equally shared. Unfortunately, their parents' opinions on the matter remained adamant. The next day, Wanda's mother sent Freya back to Mrs. Cohen to tell her that she did not want Mrs. Cohen as their nanny anymore. Will and Maud went with her, not only to deliver their mother's message but also to tell her how embarrassed and ashamed they were of their parents and countrymen. And of themselves for not doing anything to help her, her husband, or brother-in-law—neither of whom had returned. Mrs. Cohen broke down, crying at their gesture, hugging each of them, and assuring them that they could not do anything even if they tried, a notion Wanda and her sisters only half-believed. Mrs. Cohen also apologized if her own actions scared them in any way, claiming, "I should have known you were not like them."

Mrs. Cohen was my mother's oldest friend, Wanda thought to herself, staring out of the window, and asking herself the same questions that haunted her mind since *that night. They had known each other since they were five. Our mother was Mrs. Cohen's maid of honor at her wedding, and the Cohens had been a part of our lives ever since Freya, Will, Rita, and Margret were born. What would make our parents just turn on them?*

"Money and party standings," was the answer Rita gave Wanda not long after *that night.*

Wanda, nor any of her sisters, ever paid much attention to politics. They considered it part of their parents' realm. But after *that night*, the four eldest sisters decided to find out just what had made their parents so eager to join the Nazi party almost seven years ago. One of the first things discovered by Rita was money.

"The Nazi government has been paying our parents thirty marks for each of us and receiving another twenty from the city for child support. That's fifty marks for each of us, six hundred marks in total each month. That was more than *double* what both our parents make combined."

"And are you saying that money was all it took to make our parents turn on the Cohens?" Marianne asked bitterly.

Wanda did not remember the Stock Market Crash in America in 1929 that plunged the world into a global depression. She and her youngest sisters were only three at the time, with Marianne's group only a year older. But the oldest sisters remembered it and how their family survived through it.

The sisters' father was a jeweler. Margret often spoke about how her parents thanked God that before the crash, they were not only debt-free, but had also put the bulk of their money, on the Cohens' advice, into pearls her father had access to instead of cash. After the German mark became practically worthless, and their father lost his job, those pearls helped maintain them until Jacob Cohen helped their father get another job, this time at a private bank as a gem appraiser. Meanwhile, the eight eldest sisters remembered what life was like for other people in their community. It was not easy, but because of the Cohens' help, it was certainly better than most.

"Thanks to the Cohens, father and mother didn't become one of the jobless men and women we've seen from the streetcars with the signs asking for work—begging for work. None of us were ever so hungry that we collapsed in the middle of the street for everyone to see. Nor did we ever have to rent out any of our rooms to factory workers just to make a little extra money. We were doing all right, our family didn't need the Nazis or their money."

"But the Nazis wanted our family," Rita countered. "Or to be exact, they wanted the family name."

"The die Fürstin name," Barbara pondered. "What's so important about that?"

"What's important is our family's lineage," Freya answered with a note of disgust in her voice. "You all know how our family is descended from Prussian military and nobility."

"More like *loosely*-descended," Christine interrupted. "Our great-grandfather married one of the Kaiser's daughters over one hundred years ago. Even if the monarchy didn't fall, I doubt that would make us princesses. No one in the family has even carried a title since our grand-parents' time, is that *really* important to the Nazis?"

"It is, Christine," Freya replied. "Remember that family tree project we had to do last month. Both our parents and teacher seemed adamant to have us describe how the twelve of us were linked to our great-grandfather, his achievements, and the nobility. At the time, I didn't think anything of it, but now I think the Nazis wanted proof of our bloodline."

"I also think there has been more money coming into the family *because* of our bloodline," Rita added with a look of disgust on her face. "I've heard our parents sometimes thanking our ancestors privately for their windfalls, almost in prayer."

"But that's ridiculous," Christine almost screamed.

"I agree," Rita spit. "The whole thing is ridiculous, communities are being ravaged, and police, firefighters, and countrymen just look on passively. Meanwhile, our family is given money and status because our mother happened to give birth to three sets of quadruplets, and we have a distant military and royal ancestor. Not only that, but our mother leaves her oldest friend, right when she needs her the most as if she were nothing. And I think it is still just the beginning."

***

It was just the beginning, Wanda thought, staring out of the inn's window over the darkened landscape before her. The crescent moon shining on Lake Constance barely illuminated Insel, the island city near it, and her new school perched on the shore above it. In the weak moonlight, Wanda could see her reflection in the window, a scowl creeping onto her face as she looked at her blue eyes and blonde hair, traits each sister shared.

It was because of these eyes and this hair that no one touched us on that night. Just because my sisters and I fit the cookie-cutter mold that these warmongering fools are making everyone believe is some kind of chosen people. *Nobody even tried to hurt us on that night. We were just* 'proper little misses,' 'good little girls,' *that nobody wanted to lose. None of us understood it then, but all those men cared about were girls who looked like us, like we were some kind of prize-breeding horses. Humph, I still remember Will's and Maud's reaction.*

Wanda's scowl turned into a crazed smile at the memory. Shocked, disgusted, and ashamed that it was their hair and eye color alone that kept them from being hurt, while a man burned to death before their eyes for merely being a little different. Will and Maud set out to rebel by changing their hair color, but the fantastic thing was that they turned it *blue*, using berries and flowers to make their own dye.

"We're not going to have *any* hair color anyone has ever had before," Wanda whispered, repeating the words Will told her when she first looked at Will's and Maud's amazingly new look. Their mother, however, was not so impressed. She looked so scared that she would faint, like she had just found two of her children dead and knew the murderer was still in the room with her. After forcibly rinsing the dye out of Will's and Maud's hair, Will, along with Freya, Margret, and Rita, were shipped to boarding school. Maud and her group of sisters were sent there last year. Now it was Wanda and her group's turn, and they were arriving tomorrow.

"At least we'll finally be together again," Wanda muttered, wanting to feel more excited, but could not. "And at least it's keeping us away from the war. Rita was right, *that night* was just the beginning."

Wanda remembered when Germany's leader, Adolph Hitler, began what was now being hailed as the Second World War. Hitler seemed to be the only man Wanda could think of that was happy about it, no one in her family was. The look of dread on her parents' faces was second only to Will's and Maud's hair-dying attempt. She later wondered if her parents' choice of boarding schools was not only based on the desire to hide Will's and Maud's rebellious tendencies but also to keep them away from the war in general.

Lake Constance borders Switzerland, a neutral nation, Wanda mused, looking out over Lake Constance and Insel, blacked out for an air raid drill and barely visible in the moonlight. *The boarding school is privately owned, it's all girls, and I'll bet mother and father don't expect anything can happen here.*

Wanda did not believe it.

"If the war can't reach here," Wanda definitely whispered, challenging both the stillness and quiet of the night, "then why is the city blacked out, expecting to be bombed?"

The night answered Wanda's question as soft puttering sounds echoed across Lake Constance; several small boats were moving through the water.

"A border patrol," Wanda sighed, turning from the window and returning to the bed she shared with Karma—who was already asleep. "I wonder if they're trying to keep the Swiss from Germany, or us from Switzerland."

"This school, this Germany, it's all just one big prison, isn't it? A prison based on what you look like, what you do, and who you believe in. A prison you can't escape from, no matter how hard you try. Regardless if you fit the 'cookie-cutter mold' or not, you are not even given the freedom to leave. Instead, you're either forced to conform through schools, groups, or projects, or—if conformity doesn't work—you're burned outright."

Tears ran from Wanda's face as the memory of *that night* resurfaced, a painful reminder of *precisely* what Germany was becoming. It was what Hitler was *trying* to create throughout the whole world, and how many people seemed to be following his madness blindly—without even seeing it for what it really is.

Please, Wanda prayed before falling back to sleep, *please, someone, show me the way, any way, even if it's just a small way, to escape from this prison so we can be free!*

| 4 |

"Welcome to the Linden Academy for Young Women. I am Mrs. Kahn, your hall instructor. Excuse me, but where are your Bund Deutscher Maedel (BdM) uniforms?"

"I'm afraid we don't have any uniforms," Vita lied, a pained and sorrowful expression crossing her face. Long before arriving at the Linden Academy, Vita—the best actress of all the sisters—practiced this speech and manners to go with it to perfection.

"We volunteered them for the war effort," Vita continued, false pride now entering her voice and features. "We decided it would be better if they are given to young girls who might have lost their uniforms from Allied bombings. The folks need to do all they can to help each other and provide what they need until the war is over and the Reich stands victorious. I hope that what we're wearing will be enough to allow us to learn here and complete our studies."

"More than enough," Mrs. Kahn beamed, wholly taken in by Vita's performance. "And let me personally say that the Reich thanks you and your sisters. Not only for your sacrifice for other proper young girls like yourself but also for your belief in our eventual victory. I'll just forget about the uniforms for now in light of your sacrifice, you don't seem that noticeable in what you're wearing. Now, please follow me to your dorm room. Your other sisters are waiting there for you."

"Thank you, Mrs. Kahn," Vita replied, genuinely relieved Mrs. Kahn bought her story. Falling behind Mrs. Kahn, Vita, Christine, Karma, and Wanda kept pace as they made their way into Linden Academy.

Vita should get an American Academy Award for that performance, Wanda marveled, genuinely shocked, and impressed by both Vita's performance and Mrs. Kahn's acceptance of it.

In truth, all twelve sisters burned their BdM uniforms secretly, swearing never to wear them again after *that night.* None of the sisters wanted to be a part of any Nazi organization. Unfortunately, the powers that be wouldn't allow it. BdM membership was mandatory for all girls, and necessary just to progress in school. But that did not mean any of the sisters had to go *entirely* along with it. So, instead of wearing the BdM uniforms, the twelve of them dressed in black shirts and white blouses, a style similar to the uniforms. And after Vita's performance, it was a style Mrs. Kahn had no problem accepting as she led them through Linden Academy.

Walking through the school, Wanda noticed other girls in BdM uniforms, none of them paying attention to the new arrivals. In fact, none of them seemed to be paying attention to anything at all. All of the girls looked tired and haggard, moving about in a daze, almost like they were sleepwalking.

"What is this place?" Wanda whispered.

"What was that, Miss die Fürstin?" Mrs. Kahn inquired, overhearing Wanda's remark.

"The school," Wanda answered, trying to conceal her remark. "This school doesn't look like any school I've ever seen before, it looks more like a palace."

"And for a good reason," Mrs. Kahn smiled. "The school originally was a palace, its owners were part of the Prussian, and later German, royal family. Yet after the start of the Depression, and the removal of the monarchy, the palace was repossessed to pay debts. Later, it was converted into this school. Now, please hurry and follow me. Since you are starting the term late, we need to get you settled as soon as possible."

Wanda's parents originally planned to have Wanda and her group enter Linden Academy at the start of the year. But the war, and the civilian transportation problems it was causing throughout Germany, delayed their entry into the school for two months. It was now October, almost the anniversary of *that night.* Yet walking through the school's hallways toward the dormitory section, Wanda and her sisters only seemed to notice how the students looked more dead than alive.

How can schooling do this to anyone? Wanda thought to herself, not daring to let herself be overheard again by Mrs. Kahn. *A school, a palace, this place feels more like just another prison.*

"And here is your room." Mrs. Kahn beamed, stopping to knock on a door. "Your other sisters should be finished adding your bedding by now. Please go on in."

Wanda, the first at the door, noticed a slight eagerness in Mrs. Kahn's invitation. After growing up with Vita, she knew when someone was purposely acting. Opening the door, Wanda and her sisters found twelve beds, in two rows of six, with trunks and an envelope set at the foot of each bed. At the back of the room, a series of dressers lined the walls. Lastly, Wanda saw her remaining eight sisters in the center of the room, dressed identically to the four of them. It was a sight that overjoyed Wanda in itself, standing in two rows of four.

"Ladies, attention!" Mrs. Kahn ordered, blowing a whistle. "Present our school anthem."

Led by Freya, the eight older sisters launched themselves into a monotone Latin recital, at the end of which Mrs. Kahn beamed with pride as she looked over the eight older sisters and the four sisters now joining them.

"Well done, ladies, well done," Mrs. Kahn applauded. "Excellent use of your Latin skills to recite our school's anthem, although I *thought* you were going to recite it with more *energy* and *passion.* No matter, now that your sisters have finally joined us, the twelve die Fürstin sisters are reunited. Ready to begin working together for the Folk and Fatherland. Look at your sisters, they're speechless at both your performance and what Linden Academy has done to you."

It definitely says something about what Linden Academy has done to them, Wanda gasped.

All eight of the older sisters performed the anthem without any pride or enthusiasm. They simply spoke the words more for Mrs.

Kahn's benefit than for anyone else's. They were also visibly more tired than any of the other students Wanda and her group had encountered so far. All of them were trembling on their feet, looking like they were going to pass out any second. Their eyes—barely open—were ringed with dark circles, misting with tears as a few stifled a yawn. None of them looked like they had not slept decently in a long time.

"Well, I'll take my leave now," Mrs. Kahn announced. "Once the four of you are settled, I expect the rest of you to use the remainder of your free day to properly instruct your sisters on how we do things here at Linden Academy."

"Yes, Mrs. Kahn," Freya answered, fatigue clearly visible in her voice as Mrs. Kahn turned on her heels and walked out the door. Once it was closed, Freya and the eight other elder sisters dropped to the floor, Wanda and her group quickly rushing to their aid.

"What have you done to yourself?" Wanda asked, puzzled at her sisters' state.

"And what was the point of that performance," Vita added, helping her sister Barbara to a bed. "I know performing, and that wasn't it. What you were doing was more like going through the motions from the moment we walked in until Mrs. Kahn left."

"You always could tell when something was strange," Barbara confirmed. "You're right, that show just now was more for Mrs. Kahn's benefit so she would get out of here quicker, and we could be sure to see you as soon as you arrived."

"Why wouldn't you think we would be able to see you once we arrived?" Wanda asked.

"It would be easier to show you." Freya yawned, staggering back to her own bed. "Open those envelopes on your beds, you'll see your new class schedules inside."

Wanda rushed to one of the unoccupied beds, ripped open an envelope, and found the class schedule, her mouth dropping open from the absurdity of it.

"They can't be serious about this?" Wanda asked, reciting the schedule. "4:45 AM get up, 4:50 gymnastics, 5:15 wash & make beds, 5:30 coffee break, 5:50 parade, 6:00 breakfast, 6:30-14:30 Class, Work, Home economics, house cleaning, and child-raising studies, 15:00 lunch, 15:30-18:00 marching drills, 18:10-18:45 instruction, 18:45-19:15 cleaning and mending, 19:15 evening parade, 19:30 announcements, 19:45 supper, 20:00-21:30 singsong or other leisure activities, and 22:00 Light's Out.

"Where's the math, science, history, and religion, is it all supposed to be under 'Class?' Where's the *education?* And who are we marching for; the school's headmaster, the mayor, leaders of local Nazi groups? What do the Nazis in charge of this school think we're here for, to be turned into drones with no thoughts of our own except to be someone's housekeeper or wife?"

"That is *exactly* what they think we are here for," Will grumbled angrily from her bed. "Or did you not notice the looks on the other students' faces when you walked in here."

"We did notice," Karma added. "They all looked half-dead. I'm guessing it's the result of this insane schedule, it's like it was designed to break minds. But the lot of you look even worse. What have you been doing to yourself? You must be doing something else besides all this to look this beat. So, what have you been up to?"

A collective murmur of laughter spread among the eight older sisters, now resting in their beds.

"*That,*" Freya teased, "is also something you need to see to believe, but it's going to have to wait until tomorrow. Another reason we agreed to give this little 'welcome show' was that we would get the rest of the day off, and as you can see, we need sleep. I hope you can understand."

"Completely," Wanda, Karma, Vita, and Christine agreed in unison. After seeing the poor state of the students, their sisters in an even worse state, and hearing the insane schedule, none of the sisters could argue that giving a "welcome show" in exchange for a day's rest was not a bad deal.

"I would also recommend that you try to get some sleep yourselves," Freya warned. "The first day is always the hardest, that is when the schoolmasters are keeping an eye out for you. But they're not as watchful as they make themselves out to be. After the first day, it becomes easier to blend in with the other students, even more so since there are so many of us, you'll see. We'll tell you all about it tomorrow night, but right now, we need to sleep."

"Tomorrow night?" Wanda asked. "What do you mean tomorrow night?"

Unfortunately, Freya and the rest of the elder sisters were already sound asleep, not even bothering to undress or climb under their bed covers.

"Wow," Wanda marveled, "they were even more tired than they let on. I guess we should at least take their shoes off."

The other sisters nodded in agreement and started removing their sisters' shoes to make them more comfortable, quickly realizing something strange.

"Freya's shoes," Wanda puzzled. "They're almost worn out."

"So are Barbara's," Vita added.

"And Margret's," Christine said.

"Everyone's shoes are almost worn out," Karma noted, quickly looking at all of her sisters' feet.

"What have you been doing?" Wanda wondered, unable to figure out why each of her sisters' shoes would be worn out. "The schedule is crazy, but not crazy enough to wear out a pair of shoes, is it? None of us have done that since *that night,* and on *that night,* we were running for our lives. What could you have been doing that would make you run just as hard?"

Wanda knew she would have to wait until tomorrow night to find out.

| 5 |

"At least now I understand why everyone looks so tired," Wanda mumbled to herself, gulping down a cup of hot coffee. She hoped the caffeine and bitter taste would help her stay alert until the end of the day. The morning wake-up call seemed to come too soon. Mrs. Kahn, along with several of the school's teachers, was banging on doors, marching into bedrooms, and waking up students. Neither Wanda nor her sisters were given time to stretch out and wipe the sleep from their eyes. Walking down the hallway to gymnastics, Wanda noticed a few overturned beds in some of the open rooms. She guessed what must have happened to some of the more stubborn students who refused to get up.

"Agreed," Vita whispered from the seat next to her. It was lunchtime, and the four youngest sisters had sneaked out of the cafeteria and were sitting together in the school's small chapel. The only other occupant was a lone nun who was acting as its caretaker and regarded the sisters with a friendly smile. They were glad to have found at least one sanctuary in this school, but after the last ten hours, each sister felt like she needed more than a sanctuary. They needed a vacation. Christine and Karma looked like they were already taking one—to dreamland.

Earlier that morning, the twelve sisters were led outside to where the gymnastic equipment was set up. They were then herded into different groups based on their ages and found themselves running, jumping, and bouncing, over a dozen various obstacles as the teachers and coaches merely checked off each student's progress with an expressionless look on each of their faces.

"Gymnastics is how the teachers perform roll call," Will explained after they returned to their bedroom to make their beds before coffee break. "It's the one event we all have to make certain we attend. After that, the teachers become far less attentive to us until the work studies part of the day begins at 6:30, especially considering our refusal to follow BdM dress codes. Just watch the teachers, you'll see what I mean."

Wanda did. Throughout coffee break and breakfast, the teachers hardly spared a glance at them in either the lounge or cafeteria. They were not any better during the parade. If anything, they seemed worse.

During the parade, the school's headmistress invited a squad of Hitler Youth (HY) cadets from the boy's school in Insel to serve as guards and guests. The teachers, who did not seem to notice who was in their group and who was not, marched the school's entire student body into the courtyard. No one else was there except the headmistress, a few Nazi officials Freya explained were part of a local organization, and the HY cadets who eyed them lustfully.

Is that all we are for you, Wanda thought bitterly. She noticed how the HY boys were eying each of them. She found it difficult to concentrate on anything when they were making her feel *very* uncomfortable and self-aware. *Just a spectacle for you to watch and imagine doing who knows what with. I'm surprised Will or Maud hasn't stepped out of this stupid parade and told a few of you off, or just slapped those looks clean off your faces.*

Will and Maud later told Wanda during breakfast that there were more than a few occasions when they wanted to do just that. The biggest reason why they didn't needed to be seen to be believed. Which was why they needed to keep going until the end of the day. But after breakfast, the following eight hours of schooling felt like it could have been eight days.

***

"Ouch," Wanda chirped, splashing herself with the soup she was making in home economics. After breakfast, Wanda and her sisters were separated; first by age, then into groups meant to function in and out of school. Wanda was at first relieved when she found out that there were regular school classes mixed in with part of her unit's schedule. But that relief quickly faded when she noticed they only lasted a short while and were twisted by Nazi logic. Also, it was unlike the class she was in now. The other ones, like adult and child first aid, seam stressing, stenograph basics, scheduled air raid drills, marches, and care package preparation, were clearly war-based.

This place really is just a school in name, Wanda thought to herself, looking at her classmates dressed in their uniforms, almost forcing themselves to smile while they cooked under the watchful eyes of their teacher.

"You need to work harder, Miss die Fürstin," Wanda's teacher grumbled, sampling Vita's soup and then quickly spitting it out. Their teacher had made it a point to single the two of them out whenever he wanted to make a point because they were the only ones not in uniform. But compared to the embarrassment, it was still better than turning into one of their classmates who had decided to conform to the regime.

"Learning how to prepare good food is an essential skill for proper young women like yourselves. In these warring times, our proud German people, both here and on the front lines, will need the food you prepare. Now, and later in life, the food will be needed to see them through to their one true destiny, which will come from their noble struggle. A single drop of wasted effort means *the enemy* will have one more push against us."

***

Blah, blah, proper young women this, proud German people, and the enemy *that. Save us the Nazi speech,* Wanda disgustingly thought. Ever since the war started, Wanda lost count of the number of pro-war propagandist speeches promoting Germany on a noble mission, achieving its hard-fought destiny, and valiantly fighting against "the enemy" that stood in its way.

"School, hah, this *school* is really just a Nazi training center," Wanda whispered to Vita, Christine, and Karma in the chapel. "All it's really doing is training us to fight in the war as soon as we can. And against who, a faceless enemy that some hate-filled beast is pointing us toward?"

"No argument from me," Karma yawned, coming out of her daze. After breakfast, both Karma and Christine were made to march around town and collect donations. It was an easier job than either one thought it would be since they found they could hide and nap for a while. "And who is all of this for, the 'proud German people,' they sold that pride years ago, *that night* proved it."

A shiver ran down all of their backs at the memory of *that night*, the sights, smells, and the total reluctance of the people around them to even try to stop it.

"A people that allows terrorism and hate—sponsored by its own government—to happen on its own soil doesn't have the right to talk about being great and proud."

"Shush, Karma," Freya whispered, walking into the chapel and joining the four of them where they were huddling together on the floor. "Be *extremely* careful about what you say when school is in session. There are ears everywhere."

Wanda noticed Freya's eyes darting left and right as she spoke. Following her gaze, Wanda saw the nun, who also looked at them suspiciously. Wanda doubted that a nun would be a Nazi spy. But she *did* notice teachers with notepads around the cafeteria before they snuck out; teachers that, if Freya's fears were correct, were more interested in what the other students were *saying* instead of what they were doing.

And Freya's probably right, Wanda guessed, having seen many people disappear in the two years since *that night* after openly protesting against the Nazi regime.

"Just try and keep it together until the end of the day," Freya encouraged. "The worst is over now, but once the school day is over, that's when the *real fun* starts."

What do you mean by real fun*?* Wanda wondered, not missing the sly way Freya asked them to trust her, stating that the real fun would be starting after the school day was finished. But first, they had to make it to the end of the first day.

| 6 |

Thankfully, Freya was right about the rest of the school day, it was not as bad as the first part. After lunchtime, Wanda, her sisters, and the rest of the student body were led back out onto the school's parade grounds for marching drills.

At least there's no one staring at us, Wanda thought self-consciously. Marching to different beats and formations, her instructors watched and pointed out when someone was out of formation or out of step. She knew that there was still going to be one more parade at the end of the day, and the thought of marching again for the amusement of more Nazi officials and HY boys made her sick.

"Halt!" screamed the instructor, bringing Wanda's squad to a sudden stop. "Next squadron, march up and perform maneuver A-113!"

With the way they're drilling us, the evening parade must be an even bigger deal than the morning one, Wanda assumed, watching the next group march forward to conduct their maneuvers.

The evening parade *was* a bigger deal. Wanda was actually a little surprised at how big it was. She saw that besides the same guests from the morning parade, there was now a large group from Insel.

I wonder how many people are actually here because they want to be, Wanda thought to herself, looking out at the mixed faces—young and old, male and female—scattered throughout the crowd. *Do they think that because they are watching the parade, ordered to or not, they are demonstrating their allegiance to the regime? Or, like the HY boys, are they just here to watch a bunch of girls marching around?*

Wanda would not have been surprised if a number of the men in attendance *were* watching them march purely for the intention of choosing a prospective one to court. Just before the parade, in the thirty minutes designated for cleaning and mending, the instructors pushed to make sure everyone's clothes were not only clean but also free of damage.

"Make sure your uniforms are spotless. I don't want to see a single stain, cord, or tear," Mrs. Kahn had preached, checking in on each group before the parade. "And for those of you *without* uniforms, make sure you give just as much attention to whatever clothes you are wearing. I don't want to see any worn-out shoes, ripped skirts, or dirty faces. You are all to look your best for the parade."

And yet you don't want any of us looking different from anyone else, Wanda mulled, thinking how almost everyone in the parade marched the same, did their hair the same, was not allowed to wear makeup, and was clothed in the BdM uniform. She did not notice at first during the morning parade, but now she realized that except for her sisters, almost *everyone* wore a BdM uniform.

The bigwigs here really want each one of us to match their own ideal image of what a woman should look like. Anything else...

Wanda let that thought trail in her head, shivering slightly from knowing precisely what the Nazis thought about anyone who seemed different from their ideal image.

Is everyone in this school really okay doing this? Wanda asked herself, stealing glances at some of the other girls in her unit. *Waking up before sunrise, spending the whole day marching, forcing ourselves to smile and look pretty for the amusement of a crowd. All the while preparing for a war we don't even want to fight. Just so we can be safe from our own people. How could Freya, Will, Maud, or any of them last as long as they have without losing their minds or try to run away to Switzerland—especially when we're this close to the border?*

Wanda already knew her sisters promised the real fun would start once the school day was over. She also knew that whatever that fun was, it would have to be something amazing to keep them here for this long already.

The rest of the schedule after the evening parade was thankfully the easiest part of the day. The fifteen minutes for announcements was merely an assembly to praise excelling students, tell the school about upcoming trips awarded to honor class women and excelling gymnasts, and remind everyone that they could all go if they met the minimum academic and physical requirements. It was followed by a mandatory listening of the daily broadcast from the propaganda ministry.

The Snout is really laying it on thick tonight, Wanda thought, trying to block out Propaganda Minister Goebbels's ravings, none of which Wanda and her sisters believed. After that, there was a quick dinner, followed by an hour and a half for leisure activities. Not in the mood to join the other students for campfires or sing-alongs being set up across the school's grounds, Wanda retired to her room. Her other sisters were there waiting for her.

"Okay," Wanda yawned, dragging herself into their room and collapsing onto her bed. "You said that once the school day's over that the real fun would start. So, when is this *fun* going to start, or does it only exist in our dreams, because right now that's the only fun thing I can think of."

"I'll second that," Christine agreed, equally as tired. Vita and Karma also moaned approvals. The others merely giggled, handing each of them a cup of coffee that smelled like chocolate.

"How did you get this?" Wanda demanded; her fatigue quickly replaced by curiosity. Vita, Christine, and Karma were equally curious. They knew chocolate was a luxury that was hard to come by, especially in a form that could be mixed with coffee.

"We have ways," Freya answered ruefully. "Now drink up, you'll need the energy. Like we said, the first day is always the toughest. But once you get into the swing of it..."

Freya stopped mid-sentence as the other older sisters started snorting and laughing, leaving Wanda and the other youngest sisters to wonder what was so funny.

"Let me rephrase that, get the hang of it, your bodies will adapt to the schedule. Just wait a little bit more until Light's Out, then we'll introduce you to the real fun at this school."

| 7 |

"Light's out! Light's out!" Mrs. Kahn, alongside other teachers, called up and down the hallways as the power was turned off. The school quickly became enveloped in darkness, broken only by the moonlight and a few flashlights.

"It's so still," Wanda whispered, sitting awake with the rest of her sisters. The way the sudden darkness and quiet descended all around them was eerie.

"I thought the same thing," Will agreed, getting herself out of bed. "The first few nights we were here, we didn't notice it. We just fell asleep quickly. But once our bodies got used to the work cycle, and we were able to keep ourselves up past lights out, I started thinking to myself, 'It's so still, it's *begging* for something to happen.'"

"So, what did you do?" Vita asked, also getting out of bed. "I'm guessing it has something to do with the real fun you were talking about."

Instead of answering, Will simply walked to a corner of the room where Freya and Margret were moving a dresser. The four youngest sisters watched with a curiosity that suddenly turned to shock as the wall began to open slightly into the room. Freya quickly hushed them before they could say anything about what they were witnessing. Will, Maud, and Asta walked into the wall, returning with a couple of straw dummies that they quickly hid in their beds. More of them were soon taken out of the wall and hidden in the other beds. Afterward, Will called them into the wall with the rest of the elder sisters. Wanda walked into the wall last, a light appearing inside the wall as she approached it. As Freya closed the wall behind her, she finally expressed her surprise.

"It's a secret passage!" Wanda exclaimed, Freya quickly muffling her mouth.

"Quiet!" Freya hushed. "Do you want the whole school to know about it?"

"But Freya, it's a secret passage, a *secret passage.* Do you understand what we could do with this?"

"As a matter of fact, I do. Now, follow Rita, and all of you, keep your voices down."

Rita, holding a lit candle at the head of the procession, led everyone down a path inside the walls of the school. Wanda and the other youngest sisters were all mystified and curious about the strange passageway.

"What is this?" Wanda asked again, much more quietly this time.

"An old servants' passage," Barbara explained.

"A what?"

"Do you remember hearing that the school was once a palace that royals used?"

"Yes, then during the depression, it was repossessed by the government to pay for war debts," Karma chimed in, remembering Mrs. Kahn's brief explanation about the history of the school.

"That's right, Karma. Well, this is an old forgotten passageway the servants would use. I did some research, and I found that passageways like this used to run throughout all the palaces and castles across Europe. The idea was that servants would use them to deliver food and perform household and other duties so they wouldn't be a constant sight to the nobility. They could enter and leave through doors that were parts of the walls, and no one would notice their comings and goings. After the monarchies started to fall apart, or when the palaces were sold off, the passageways were sealed off. Obviously, someone—thankfully—forgot about the entrance in our room."

"So, you can use this passage to get to *anywhere* in the school?" Wanda asked.

"Wanda, we can use it to get *out* of the school," Freya answered, a mischievous smile stretching across her face. "And outside, in town, that's where the real fun begins. Just be patient for a little longer."

Wanda did not know how much more patient she could possibly be, especially now. Following her elder sisters through the servants' passages, knowing that they have used them to sneak out of the school, was setting her imagination ablaze with questions and fantasies. And she knew she was not the only one.

Vita's probably more excited about this than I am. Wanda mused, gazing at her sister, who was practically bouncing with each step she took down the passageway. *Karma and Christine look equally excited, their eyes are sparkling in the candlelight in a way that I haven't seen since* that night.

The sisters continued down the passageway, Asta continuing to lead the way down a flight of stone stairs that ended in a small grotto. In the water, a series of boats were tied up near an exit opening out into Lake Constance. On the shore, a couple of boxes filled with clothes and mirrors were set up, creating a makeshift dressing room.

"Okay, everyone," Maud announced, standing by the boxes, "time to change."

"Change?" Christine asked.

"Of course, we can't go out on the town looking like a bunch of schoolgirls in uniforms. We've already found plenty of clothes in each of your sizes, the only thing you'll have to keep are your shoes. Just pick out anything that you like, be creative. The crowd we're going to be hanging out with doesn't care much for 'proper dress.'"

Maud grabbed an armful of clothing and accessories and walked over to Will, who was also undressing and changing into a new outfit while leaving the youngest sisters to decide for themselves what they wanted to wear. Looking into the boxes, Wanda and the others were amazed by what they found.

"Where did you get these clothes?" Vita asked, digging through them. "America?"

Wanda thought the same thing. The boxes were full of dresses, skirts, blouses, and pullovers. Alongside the dresses were dark glasses, hats, long cigarette-holders, face powder, and lipstick and nail polish of every outlandish shade imaginable. It looked like the things that might have been found on an American movie set.

"We wish these came from America," Freya laughed. "But the bulk of these clothes we tailored ourselves. Sneaking out of the school, we found a thrown away hat here, a discarded dress there. We put all those sewing and mending skills the teachers hammered into us to *good* use, turning them into what you see now. As for anything we couldn't get, we know some people outside of school who were able to get them for us."

What do you mean by "get them for us?" Wanda wondered, noticing the mischievous look on Freya's face again, but deciding not to push the issue. Right now, the allure of the dresses and makeup in the box, and the possibilities it could produce, were all too enticing, especially after Will and Maud stepped out from behind a rock in matching blue dresses, blue lipstick, their hair unbraided and dyed blue—with silver face powder over their faces, hair, and dresses.

"Oh my goodness," Wanda exclaimed. "You two look like the starfield on the American flag come to life. How have you *not* been caught."

"The hair dye, our own invention I might add, washes out clean without a trace," Will explained. "We also learned, when we first started doing this, that the only kind of night inspection that the school performs is a peek through a slot in the door. So, the dummies we leave are more than enough to fool them, and once the rest of you get dressed and we all get in town, you'll see you won't have to worry about being spotted as much as you think."

Wanda could not understand how anyone could *not* be worried about being spotted when they were dressed up like that. But she decided that if her elder sisters managed to pull it off, there was no reason why she could not too. Rummaging through the box, Wanda eventually chose a purple outfit to wear. The rest of her sisters chose similarly different colored outfits with Margret wearing the only white outfit, decorated with a multicolored jacket, hat, and makeup.

"We look like a rainbow come to life, with Margret as the prism," Wanda snickered.

"We're never going to get away with this," Karma injected sarcastically, ready to get in trouble anyway.

"Yes, we will," Freya replied. "Now, take one of these and keep it in your mouths or with you at all times." Freya handed each of her sisters a long cigarette holder.

"But none of us smokes," Wanda protested.

"I know, the point is to make us look as 'American' and 'Hollywood-like' as possible. Trust me, you have no idea how much this is going to help you."

Wanda did not understand how a cigarette holder would help her, but trusted Freya and took one, realizing that the rest of her sisters were doing the same. Wanda noticed her elder sisters were already twirling them around in their hands and letting them dangle from their mouths like they had used them their entire life, even though she knew none of them had ever touched a cigarette before, nor were they planning to.

"Okay, everyone, into the boats!"

Wanda and the others followed Will to where four small boats were docked. Climbing in, the older sisters took an oar and began rowing out of the grotto and into Lake Constance, heading toward the town on the island.

"Won't the grotto fill with water at some point?" Wanda asked, staring back at the grotto's entrance.

"Nope," Rita answered, sitting at the head of Wanda's boat. "We were afraid of that happening when we first found it. We did some tests by taking old clothes we found, weighing them down—so they wouldn't float away, and leaving them in the grotto to see if they would get soaked if the grotto flooded, and it never happened. We think the grotto was also used by the servants when the school was still a palace.

Probably to bring in food and supplies, or as an escape route in case of danger."

"Regardless, it's ours now," Marianne chimed. "And just wait until you see the town. It's going to make you forget that first day ever happened."

I still don't see how, Wanda wondered, as her sisters rowed closer toward the city. *Or how these outfits are going to keep us from getting caught. If anything, they're just going to make everyone want to stare at us more. I guess I'll find out soon enough.*

| 8 |

Wanda was surprised to find out just *how right* Freya was. Soon after they walked into town, the first few men and women they passed by snorted at them in disgust. Turning their eyes away from them like they were some oddity best left ignored, they did not pay them any more attention. In fact, the more Freya and the eldest sisters made themselves stand out, swinging around their cigarette-holders, striking poses for people on the street, the more everyone ignored them. Turning down a side street, after hearing a couple spit the words "swing girls" at them, Barbara walked up to Wanda and began whispering in her ear.

"You see, no one wants to bother or even be associated with us at all."

"But why?" Wanda asked, still curious about why no one seemed to notice them.

"The Nazis have the entire country drugged up on standardization. What they believe is the 'proper attire' for women. That any form of 'fashion excess': individual choice of clothing, even cosmetics, is dangerous. That said, we've found that most people, when confronted with fashion as excessive as our own, do their best to ignore it and avoid being associated with us. They won't even report it because it would mean they have to admit being associated with us."

Wanda understood the idea, but still found it incredible to see that it actually worked. Here she was, walking around town with the rest of her sisters, dressed as flamboyantly as a Hollywood star, and yet everyone was ignoring them because of it.

"What about the brown shirts?" Wanda whispered, remembering the thugs in the brown shirts during *that night.*

"The SA—those brown-shirted men—along with the Schutzstaffel (SS), and the police are really the only people we have to keep a lookout for. That said, don't think we've been striking poses just to show off our dresses, we've been making sure no one is following us."

"Following us where?"

"Listen, we're about to get there."

Wanda did listen, and did not hear anything at first, but it changed as the sisters neared an old house.

"Music?"

The older sisters smiled at Wanda's comment, picking up the pace, and practically skipping to the old house's front door with the younger sisters behind her. After Rita quickly knocked on it, the door opened, and a tall dark-suited man stepped out, looking like an undertaker and examining the sisters warily.

"Hey, Old Kluge, tell Bobby and the boys that Sweetie and her sisters, *all* of her sisters, have finally made it to the club."

Old Kluge did not answer, he merely stepped out of the way and allowed the sisters to walk into the house. Once inside, Wanda noticed all the windows were drawn shut, and the music was now much louder and more identifiable.

"The music, it's *American*!" Wanda whispered surprised, excited, and scared all at once. She knew if American music was being played, someone had a radio tuned to a foreign station, or access to recorded music from either England or America—and was playing that music loudly. Regardless, she knew that both cases were punishable offenses as far as the Nazis were concerned. Karma, Christine, and Vita also knew it, each of them twisting their heads back toward the door and windows to scan for any signs of a raid. The older sisters only seemed excited and entirely at ease with both the music and their surroundings.

"Relax," Margret assured them. "I was jittery the first time I came here, too, but trust me, everything's kosher."

Why doesn't that reassure me? Wanda asked herself, instantly noticing the change in both Margret's mood and speech. *And when did you even start using the word "kosher"? The only time we've ever heard that word before was a few times at the Cohens, and none of us even asked what it meant.*

"We have lookouts on the roof and in the attic to tell us if the Nazis or the HY are closing in on us and we have to run for it. For now, it's time to dance your cares away, enjoy yourselves, and welcome to the Lake Constance Swing Club."

Margret and the other eldest sisters took Wanda, Vita, Karma, and Christine's hands and led them into what would have been the house's ballroom. But instead of a ball, or some other fancy party, with men and women in elegant dresses waltzing slowly to classical music, there were groups of boys and girls—mostly boys—about their age, all dressed as extravagantly as they were. They swirled and danced to music playing on a turntable honorably positioned by the fireplace where a band was tuning its instruments. Freya, breaking off from her sisters, ran toward the band and into the arms of its trombone player.

"That's Frankie, Freddie's boyfriend," Margret explained to the youngest sisters, all of whose mouths gaped open in shock and surprise.

"Wait, Frankie, Freddie, boyfriend," Wanda stuttered, trying to make sense out of what was happening.

"Okay, ladies, rule number one, no one uses their real names. Your sister over there is Freddie, I'm Sweetie, and as for the four of you, you're Winnie, Vicki, Kristy, and Karli." Margret pointed to Wanda, Vita, Christine, and Karma, respectively, as she told them their nicknames. "Rule number two, have fun!"

"Listen up, swing boys and swing girls!" Wanda turned her attention to the stage where Freya's boyfriend, Frankie, was standing alongside Freya and the rest of the band. "Freddie just told me that tonight is a special night, tonight is the first time she gets to swing the night away with *all* her sisters, so let's hear it for them."

Wanda, and the rest of her group, immediately felt self-conscious as they were suddenly mobbed by applauding boys and girls who pulled them all out onto the dance floor.

"Now, let's really get swinging!" Frankie cheered, blowing into his trombone, and starting a new piece. The rest of the band joined in soon afterward as the whole ballroom came to life with music and dancing.

Wanda, like all of her sisters, knew how to dance; it was a skill their mother insisted they learn at an early age. But this style of dancing was like nothing she had ever experienced before. First of all, the tempo was much faster. Everything about the dancing was fast and energetic. She found herself dancing with a random boy one moment, only to soon become part of a jitterbug circle of boys and girls the next. She then danced with a different boy or girl immediately afterward. Wanda knew that she should be getting tired from the dancing, especially after the first day at Linden Academy. But instead, she had never felt more awake. The air in the dance hall was alive and infectious. The more everyone danced and cheered, the more they wanted to keep on doing it. From the stage, Wanda could hear Freya belting out an improvised song to the melody the band played.

Is this even real? Wanda asked herself, stepping off the dance floor momentarily for a brief rest. Her entire body tingled with excitement; she had never felt this alive. Seeing a punch bowl where Will, Maud, and a few boys were sharing a few drinks, Wanda started over to join them until a hand touched her shoulder. Turning around, she found herself facing another boy about her height with black hair and blue eyes dressed as a porter wearing a pair of dark sunglasses. In his hand was a tray with a cup filled with water, which he offered to Wanda.

"Thank you," Wanda replied, taking the cup, and drinking its contents, before placing it back on the tray. Afterward, the boy smiled and bowed his head gracefully before pointing his finger toward the bowl Will and Maud were drinking out of, wagging his finger against it cautiously.

"What, what's wrong with what my sisters are drinking?" Wanda asked. The boy, however, did not answer, just wagged his finger again before walking away toward a water jug in the corner of the ballroom, leaving her more confused. Thankfully, it did not last long, because a cheer from Will brought her attention back to the punch table.

"Oh yeah," Will screamed. "That HY troop, so dressed up in uniform, were looking at us on the way to the swing club one night like they didn't know what to make of us. One of them called us, 'savages disgracing the natural German setting.' I said, 'you want to see savage, I'll show you savage!'"

"That was when the two of us let them have it, right, Will. That troop never knew what hit them. I'll bet they never even thought a couple of swing girls would know how to fight."

They're drunk, Wanda realized, looking at her two sisters, standing on top of the table, and being praised by the boys and girls around it before looking back at the water jug. The boy in the porter's outfit was sitting quietly by himself.

"That's Silent Night." Wanda quickly turned around, looking into her sister Asta's face.

"Silent Night?"

"Well, that's just what everyone calls him. He started showing up at the swing club not long after me and my group started coming, and since walking in here, he's not said a single word to anyone. So, we just started calling him Silent Night, he hasn't objected."

"Do W...," Wanda caught herself, remembering how Margret told them no one uses their real names at the swing club. "Do those two always get drunk?"

Wanda pointed to Will and Maud, retelling their story about the fistfight with the HY.

"Wick and Mickey, not really, and they're going to be feeling that in the morning. Truth is they should know better than to drink out of the punch bowl, it has a tendency of being spiked. The water jug where Silent Night is sitting is actually the safest drink of choice in the whole club."

That's why he gave me the water, Wanda realized, looking at the cup Silent Night gave her.

"But enough talk, the band's starting a new number, and that means it's time for more dancing."

Asta took Wanda's hand and pulled her back onto the dance floor into a big group dance with Maud, Will, Barbara, and Marianne. All six of them were swinging, twirling, and dancing frantically to the beat. The party continued on until about three in the morning, at which point Wanda and the rest of her sisters started to make their way back to Linden Academy's grotto entrance—Will and Maud vomiting the entire boat ride back.

"It's your own fault for drinking from the punch bowl," Rita chastised, as both Will and Maud—each in a different boat—vomited again. Wanda still could not get the excitement of the night out of her system. She wanted it to continue, to keep dancing and forget about Linden Academy, the war, everything. The night also made Wanda aware of something else as she gazed across Lake Constance.

If my sisters have access to a secret way out of the school, and to boats, they could have tried to make it across the lake and into Switzerland. Then they would be free of all of this. "Why have you stayed?"

"We've stayed because we knew that if we escaped to Switzerland, no one could tell the rest of you how to follow us," Freya whispered, answering Wanda's question. "We've planned to eventually run away to Switzerland along with the boys from the swing club before we could be drafted into the Nazi's war. But we wanted to wait until we were all united again. That way, we could all go and start new lives together. Now comes the hard part, waiting until the security boats are just right so we can slip by them."

You're not kidding, Wanda mused, too excited to put her thoughts into words. She remembered how hard it was to wait for the first school day to end so she could discover the swing club. Now she was going to have to wait again, this time for an unknown amount, until they could all slip into Switzerland. Wanda did not know how she was going to do it, and yet her older sisters have already been waiting for *two years.*

"You're excited?" Freya asked Wanda and the other youngest sisters, as they rowed their boats back into Linden Academy's grotto. "Good, keep that excitement, you'll need it to get you through tomorrow. Once we get back upstairs, we'll only get a little over an hour of sleep before the 4:45 AM, wake-up, and then gymnastics. Don't try to do anything there that makes you stand out, just do the routines, so you get through it as quickly as possible. Afterward, you'll get plenty of opportunities to sleep throughout the day—especially if you're put on collection duty."

"What's collection duty?" Wanda asked, just as their boats reached the grotto's dock, the older sisters jumping out and fastening them in place. Freya merely smiled in reply and said, "You'll find out soon enough."

| 9 |

Wanda did find out. The cold morning wind stung Wanda's face as she rattled a donation jar in the town's center.

Collection duty, Wanda thought to herself, holding the jar for collections as people passed her by. *On the other hand, this isn't so bad of a job assignment. I'm not stuck inside the school, I don't have to cheer if I don't want to—unlike some of the other collectors, and I can cover for Rita, Karma, and Christine while they catch up on sleep.*

Wanda turned her head slightly towards an alley where her sisters had found a secluded spot to rest. It was almost time to wake Rita up so she could take over. Wanda was in no mood to stay around longer than she had to, especially with other collectors chanting "help the war fund" and "defeat the enemy," none of which she dared to repeat. The only reason why she did not leave sooner was to avoid being missed by a teacher hanging around the chanting students, a teacher Wanda convinced that Rita and the others were finding more donations in a different location instead of sleeping.

I'll bet it helps that none of us are wearing that BdM uniform, Wanda mused, hiding her disgust at watching the other collectors, and the teacher, all in uniform with the Nazi's symbol on their arms. *Once I get rid of this can, I'm washing my hands.*

A church bell chimed, marking the hour, and Wanda slipped down the alley toward the place where her sisters were sleeping in order to wake up Rita. Yet on the way, she heard something she did not expect.

"Music..."

The word whispered from her mouth before she realized she had said it. But she knew what she was hearing, music, being played softly.

And it's not just any music, Wanda realized, following the music down another part of the alley, almost like she was in a trance. *It's the same type of music we were listening to last night, swing music.*

Wanda continued to follow the sound of the music in the alley. She eventually came to a dead end where her sisters were sheltered together behind some crates—Karma quickly beckoning her to join them, each one called by the music's melody. Looking up from their hiding place, Wanda could now see the source of the music, an old gramophone playing a swing melody. None of the sisters knew how long they were sitting under that window, all they were aware of was the music. It was taking them back to last night's festivities at the swing club. Suddenly, the music died.

"Haul this enemy away!" A hateful voice bellowed, following a sudden crashing noise that each of the sisters remembered from *that night.* It was the sound of a door being broken down. "Destroy this degenerative music, and any other sources of state corruption you can find!"

The noise that followed froze the sisters in their hiding place, not one of them daring to move and risk being discovered. Each felt as if she were reliving *that night* again but on a smaller scale. Smashing, tearing, and other sounds of destruction echoed from the window and the alley. The last destructive act was the gramophone the sisters were listening to being tossed clean out the window and landing with a smash right behind them, leaving everything quiet. Eventually, a voice pierced the silence.

"Is that all of it?"

"Yes, sir, we've destroyed all the degenerative music on the premise. And have collected a recompense for the state."

"Good, the orders from headquarters are to silence this degeneration before it can corrupt any more of our young. Clear out!"

Wanda and her sisters listened as the men in the room marched out loudly. Only after a few minutes did any of the sisters try moving from their hiding place, the episode a grisly reminder of the world that they actually lived in. Wanda timidly walked over to inspect the gramophone that landed near them. It had been destroyed, but miraculously the record in it survived. Picking up the record, she found herself feeling angry.

"How could this happen?" she asked herself. Her hands trembled as they held the record like it was a victim of the war. *"How could we let this happen, again?"*

Ever since *that night,* they had asked themselves: "How could the people of Germany do this to one another?" "How could everyone just stand by and do nothing?" And: "Why did we hide and run instead of trying to do something?" Most importantly—and for some of them personally, they asked: "What would I do if given another chance?" Wanda now had the answer to that last question, and she did not like it.

"This was nothing like *that night,* and yet all I did, all any of us did, was just hide in a corner and let those thugs in uniforms do whatever they wanted."

Wanda was sobbing now, and none of her sisters knew what to say or do. They all felt the same way she did, as they fought to keep back their own tears.

"A man's life was just destroyed, and for what? Because he wanted to listen to a different kind of music that some bigwig decided was *degenerative.* What kind of world is this that this government is trying to create? There are already forbidden radio stations, now forbidden music. Do the Nazis want to control *everything* that we can say and listen to?"

Wanda's question hung in the air, an uneasy silence passing among the four sisters. Rita, one of the eldest, knew the answer to the question even better than the others. Controlling everything that was said and heard, music or otherwise, was *precisely* what the Nazis wanted. It was the reason why the Swing Club met at night instead of during the day or early evening. Every member knew they were doing something that annoyed the Nazis. But there was also a line between being an annoyance and a threat. Once that line was crossed, things became a lot more dangerous. It was a boundary that many in the club were hesitant to cross including the eldest sisters, preferring instead to enjoy the small amount of freedom they could find until the time they were reunited and ran away to Switzerland together.

"Well, somebody say something," Wanda snapped, hoping that one of her sisters would answer her. Instead, one by one, they started to walk out of the alley and silently resume their collection work, eventually leaving Wanda alone with the record. She looked at the record again, thinking of its owner, someone she never saw, who was assaulted in their home, which was then destroyed. And all because he or she dared to play the music that a bunch of hate-filled maniacs declared "degenerative."

"Those animals and their policies are more 'degenerative' to the people of this country than *any* music," Wanda whispered to herself, tucking the record into her sweater before rejoining her sisters.

Wanda spent the next few hours focusing on the way she walked, positioning herself so that no one would notice the record hidden in her sweater until she managed to slip into her room and hide it. Afterward, the day felt hollow. The event from the alley gave her a lot to think about. She thought about *that night* and the questions she had asked herself since then. How much had she *actually* changed? And how the raid—unlike *that night*—was carried out using far less exuberant measures. During and after *that night,* everyone knew what was going on and what had happened. But after this raid, Wanda never saw a sign that it took place. She did not hear a whisper about it from anyone in the city on collection duty, or from anyone else after she returned to Linden Academy. It was like it never happened.

I don't know what's worse? Wanda asked herself again, ducking away from the assembly hall before evening announcements and making her way to the chapel. After the events of this morning, she had no desire to listen to more propagandist snout, or praise for students meeting the school's—the Nazi's—expectations. She wanted to be alone to think.

The fact that it happened, that I let it happen and didn't try to stop it, that no one seems to notice or care that things like this are still going on right in front of them. I just don't know what's worse?

Wanda had talked about the incident with the rest of her sisters whenever she had the chance. Unfortunately, they advised her to keep quiet for her own protection. Even Will and Maud, the most outspoken of the twelve, refused to give her advice. All she did was wander toward the older part of the school, heading toward the chapel, and think. Then she bumped into the nun who acted as the chapel's caretaker, snapping her out of her musing.

"Excuse me, Sister," Wanda hastily apologized.

"Worry not, my child," the nun replied, her face expressing the same sadness and doubt that she was also feeling, only far worse.

"I'm just leaving, it's all leaving, soon nothing will be left." The nun's words were coming out between sobs now as she shuffled past Wanda. The nun, a haversack over her shoulder, slowly walked back the way she came, leaving Wanda more confused. Walking past her and into the chapel, Wanda immediately understood the reason behind the nun's sadness.

"What *is* this?" Wanda gasped, even though she knew what it was supposed to be. The room was the chapel, but it had been completely desecrated. The tabernacle holding the hosts, as well as the cross on the altar, and the Bible, had all been removed. Instead, on the altar was a raised copy of Adolph Hitler's *Mein Kampf*, quotes from it covering the chapel walls over the Stations of the Cross. Above the altar, where the cross usually hung, was a picture of Hitler looking like he was a savior of humanity.

Wanda stepped back in both shock and revulsion. She could not even fathom what the nun—a woman of God—must have felt after seeing the chapel transformed into this monstrosity. It only served one real purpose, to make the leader of the Nazis into a god. Taking another step back, Wanda felt her foot step on a piece of paper. Picking it up, Wanda saw that it was a letter to the nun from the school's headmistress. The letter was polite enough, but what it basically said was that she was fired. That she, Christianity, and its teachings, were *no longer needed,* both in Linden Academy and in the new world being created. Wanda's mind instantly flew back to *that night.*

First, they physically attack Judaism, now they are attacking Christianity and making gods out of themselves. Is there no end to this?

She did not even wait until she could come up with an answer. She ran back to her room, not caring about dinner, leisure time, or anything else. All she wanted was to get away from Linden Academy and do something.

Thankfully, Light's Out would give Wanda the chance she needed.

| 10 |

"Watch yourself, Wanda," Barbara whispered, catching Wanda as she almost tumbled down to the grotto. "And stop shoving, you don't want to knock us all down the passageway, do you?"

Wanda was not listening. She was determined to get out of the school, and nothing was going to stop her. The events of the day had left her feeling on edge and were straining her relationships with her sisters. In fact, Barbara's warning was the most any of them had said all day since the incident in the alley. The rest of them were carrying on as if nothing had happened. Arriving at the grotto, the eleven of them giggled and talked to each other happily as they put on makeup, and changed into their swing clothes. It was only when Wanda entered the group that the conversation became noticeably quieter.

They're uncomfortable around me, Wanda realized, seeing how conversation resumed once she left. *They know I want to talk about what happened, and more importantly, that they* don't *want to talk about it.*

Climbing into a boat with Will, Maud, and Christine, Wanda resolved to focus on rowing to the city rather than talking with her sisters about it. Her sisters also seemed more focused on rowing rather than talking, quickly pulling in front of the other two boats.

I wonder if they're just eager to get to the swing club, away from me, or both, Wanda thought, seeing how hard her sisters rowed the boat and how fast they jumped out once they reached the city.

Like the previous night, all the sisters stuck to the back roads to avoid most of the pedestrian traffic. The few people they did encounter turned their heads away, attempting to ignore them. However, unlike the previous night, the sisters were greeted by a strange signal before they reached the swing club.

"Swing Heil!"

"Swing Heil," Wanda whispered.

"It's a salute for Swing kids, Swing Heil!" Will explained, replying to the three approaching swing boys. Wanda recognized them from the night before as they rounded a corner to join the group. But unlike their previous encounter, two of them were sporting fresh bruises, and one was limping slightly.

"Old Sport, Old George, J. B., what happened to you? Did the club get raided?" Maud asked.

"Ha!" Old George laughed. "The three of us just got into a tussle with a HY squad. They came up to us, thinking they looked all fancy and self-important in their matching uniforms, and started reciting the same spiel. 'Victory over the enemy,' blah blah blah. Of course, when they started calling us a bunch of wild men listening to degenerative music, that's when we decided to show them what we could do."

"Not that they needed to say anything," J. B. added. "The HY hates us swing boys and would pick a fight for nothing, plus the feeling's mutual. I can personally guarantee that those uniforms they were wearing don't look so spiffy now."

"Shame, we weren't there for the fight," Maud said, stepping over to help support J. B. and punching Old Sport in the arm.

"I was thinking the same thing, Mickey," Old Sport groaned, rubbing his arm.

Maud can probably hit harder than all of them, Wanda thought, seeing Old Sport tending his arm, and guessing that Maud *did not* hit one of his burses just now. Yet the three swing boys' tussle was also inspiring.

At least someone is willing to do something about the Nazis. Maybe someone else at the swing club can give me an idea about what to do about the incident, Wanda thought.

"All right, everyone, we're wasting moonlight, and Frankie probably has the band playing right now. I don't know about the rest of you, but I'm ready to swing," Freya proclaimed, taking the lead and heading down the lane toward the swing club. Will, Maud, and Asta hung back to help Old Sport, Old George, and J. B.

"Why do I suspect 'Freddie' is looking to do more than just dance?" Wanda whispered to herself, not realizing she was now at the back of the pack, or that she had spoken aloud.

"It's because you're right," Rita whispered back, also now at Wanda's side, immediately making her feel self-conscious for talking. "Freddie and Frankie have been a couple ever since the first four of us walked into the Lake Constance Swing Club. Frankie's older brother was one of the founders of the club. He was quite the guy until he was drafted and sent to the eastern front." Wanda noticed the longing and regretful look on Rita's face. She wondered how close the two of them might have been, or if any of her older sisters were involved in similar relationships.

The music and dance at the swing club were just as infectious as it had been the previous night. Yet Wanda still could not forget the events of the day. The incident in the back alley, followed by her sisters' reluctance to talk about it, and the desecration of the school's chapel were bothersome. The fact that her sisters *could* enjoy themselves, including Rita, who only a few minutes ago had been on the verge of lamenting over a fellow Wanda never met, left her with mixed feelings about the swing club.

There's no denying it, I do love this place, Wanda thought to herself, dancing in a circle with Vita and two other men. *The music, the dance, the energy, it's all so* free, *so vibrant, nothing like Linden Academy with its insane war-related course schedule. And it's* definitely *not like the world the Nazis are trying to create, a world where everyone and everything fits into the same predetermined mold, and if they don't...*

Wanda let the thought hang in her head as she realized what was bothering her about the swing club. *Yeah, that is the problem, no one is* thinking *at all.*

She looked around the hall at all the members of the swing club and watched what they were doing. Will and Maud joked with a bunch of fellows by the punch bowl—not drinking from it tonight. Silent Night sat next to the water jug. The rest of them were dancing crazily except for Freya, who was slipping back into the hall from a side door with her boyfriend, Frankie. Freya's slightly disheveled look made Wanda blush when she pictured what they might have been up to.

"Are you okay, Winnie?" Vita asked, noticing Wanda's reddening face.

"I'm okay, it's just, this place..."

"I know, it's like a dream. We can completely forget our troubles here."

"But can we really just do that."

"Do what?"

"Forget, I mean, can we really just *forget* what's happening right outside our door while we dance the night away like it doesn't concern us *at all*!"

Wanda did not notice that her voice was becoming steadily louder, and she was drawing everyone's attention.

"Winnie..."

"No, listen to me. The chapel in our school has been desecrated, turned from a House of God into a house of Hitler. They want us to worship him now. Someone was assaulted and abducted right out of their home because he was listening to swing music. Both times, nobody tried to stop it or even talk about it afterward. It's just like *that night two years ago!*'

At the mention of "*that night two years ago,*" the music stopped. Members of the swing club turned pale as each one faced Wanda.

"Haha, you have to excuse my sister," Vita laughed, trying to downplay Wanda's outburst. "She had a sip from the punch bowl earlier and..."

"I am *not* drunk," Wanda snapped back, angry that her sister would try to cover for her. "I can't just ignore it. It's still happening now only with less publicity. You can't tell me you think the Nazis are just going to leave us alone, that they're not going to come for us because of the music we listen to."

"They've ignored us so far," a voice shot back from the hall.

"Yeah, there's no reason for us to make ourselves 'enemies.' Let's leave the political stuff to the grown-ups and the politicians," another voice replied, soon followed by similar sentiments heard around the hall.

"I don't believe this," Wanda said in exasperation. "Do none of you care about what's happening around us?"

"Then what do you think we should do?" Frankie asked accusingly from the stage. "You want to get upset and preach? That we should make a stand because the Nazis are going to come after us anyway. What do you want us to do?"

Wanda paused for a moment, realizing that every set of eyes in the hall was watching her, especially her sisters, but more out of fear than encouragement. They knew the moment she started talking about *that night* she had singled herself out from all of them. There would not be a single club member who would not know who she was, and that was extremely dangerous.

"We could take the swing club out of this hall and dance publicly, show the Nazis we aren't afraid of them, and if they do come, we could stand up to them, for a change. I noticed you two don't seem to have any trouble boasting about the HY boys you've beaten up." Wanda turned her attention toward Will and Maud, hoping for support, remembering how they had bragged about the fight they were in last night. Instead, they both acted like they had something more important to do, turning to take a quick drink from the punch bowl.

"Fine," Wanda puffed, understanding now that whatever she said was going to be without the support from any of her sisters.

"We could rip down propagandist posters, graffiti, anything to make people actually recognize and acknowledge what's going on around them. Doing *something* has to be better than simply *ignoring* it.

How is ignoring it, doing nothing at all, any different from passively helping the Nazis win?"

Wanda hoped someone would respond. No one did, until she heard soft clapping in the back of the room. Turning her head toward the source, the club parted—also curious as to who was clapping, revealing Silent Night applauding for Wanda's proposal.

"Thank you, Silent Night," Wanda replied, nodding in his direction. "But if the rest of you just want to dance your cares away, you're free to do that. I'm going to act."

Wanda marched out of the club, not knowing what she would do, only that it would be anti-Nazi. She did not notice Silent Night also leaving the club, but through another door.

| 11 |

So, what am I going to do? Wanda mumbled to herself, walking down the town's side streets. *It was easy to tell my sisters and the other members of the swing club that we should be doing something, but now, what am I going to do? At least, no one is bothering me.*

Maintaining her swing girl walk, gestures, and mannerisms, served as useful deterrents for the few people on the street. Wanda continued to think. She knew she did not have much to work with, only her hands, head, body, and whatever else she was carrying besides her cigarette-holder, which was only a small tube of lipstick.

Well, whatever I'm going to do, I certainly can't do it on a side or back street, Wanda realized. *If I want to make a statement, I need to make it where everyone will see it. But again, what can I do? What have I got to work with?*

Dancing a little to hide her nervousness, she swung her way out onto the main street and was slightly surprised by how deserted it was.

"Whoa, a street this vacant would make you think the whole city was empty," Wanda whispered, amazed at the emptiness and quiet of the city. "Compared to this, the back roads look more like Berlin, or some other major city. I know it's late, but there should still be *some* activity. Are people just so frightened by the Nazis that they are refusing to even try and live?"

Wanda's answer came in the form of a motorboat engine that echoed across Lake Constance and through the city, reminding her that the people living here did have *one other* thing to be afraid of besides the Nazis.

"The war, of course," Wanda sighed. She realized that besides the Nazis, the people living here were probably just as afraid of being bombed and had taken to staying and sleeping in their basements and bomb shelters. It was easier than having to run down to them in the event of an air raid—drill or otherwise. The few people she did encounter on the back streets, and in the swing club, were probably the most daring ones she would find in the whole town.

"Well, if anything, this just makes what I want to do all the more easier, important, and vital," she continued.

She walked around, looking for anything that might give her some inspiration. She found it staring her right in the face. Before the city's main square, she was confronted with a horde of pro-Nazi and pro-war posters splattered across a building wall. Some were pictures of boys dressed in Nazi uniforms, smiling like fools. Others were of girls like herself in BdM uniforms. And others showed mothers holding children up to Hitler's likeness like he was a savior. The whole scene made her sick to her stomach, and she realized what she was going to do. Working with a dexterity she did not know she had, Wanda started tearing the posters off the wall. It was slow work, especially since they would tear while she pulled at them, but she did not mind the time or pain it caused her fingers. She wanted to get as many of the posters removed from the walls as possible. She was so engrossed in her work that she did not notice footsteps approaching until a flashlight was shone into her face, startling her.

"Out past curfew tonight, madam?" a male voice asked.

Who are you calling madam? Wanda wondered, peering past the flashlight to see who was talking to her. She used her arm to cover most of her face so that her assailants could not identify her, but she could tell they were a trio of HY boys.

"A woman of your *distinction* shouldn't be out this late, especially in such outlandish clothing," the boy with the flashlight said.

Okay, they think I'm older than I really am, Wanda realized, quickly noticing how she was being addressed. *I'm probably younger than all three of you. But you think I'm an older woman because of my clothes. You HY boys really are brainless.*

"And committing such criminal actions," another one of the boys added. "It looks like the tip we were given was correct. Miss, you are just going to have to come with us."

"Now, let's not be too hasty, gentlemen. A fine woman like this must simply be under the effects of some *built-up* stress to make her act this way. I'm sure she could provide the three of us a means to help her *release it,* or provide us with some *compensation,* monetary or *physical.*"

No way! Wanda mentally screamed to herself, doubling back the way she came and into the back streets, the HY boys following right behind her.

I can't lead them back to the swing club, Wanda thought, racing down unfamiliar backstreets looking for someplace she could hide from her pursuers. *Nor can I try any of the houses. Even if someone* was *awake, judging from the reactions we get, I doubt anyone would help, and if I told them I was being chased by the HY, I would* definitely *be shut out.*

Wanda kept running, making quick corners, attempting to throw the HY boys off her trail, instead only trapping herself in a junk-filled dead end road. The HY boys followed soon after, winded, but with a sadistic smile on their faces. They were enjoying the entire event.

"Well, that was a fine chase, madam," the HY boy with the flashlight mocked. "But the hunt is over. It's time for you to present us with our prize."

Prize indeed, Wanda fumed. She knew *exactly* what they wanted from her before she started running, and it was not just to report her or turn her in. The lust was as clear on their faces as it was from the moment they set their eyes on her.

"You want a prize?" Wanda spit, picking up a broken armrest. "Try and take it." But before she, or the HY boys, could do anything, they were interrupted by more newcomers rounding the corner and attacking the HY boys. It took Wanda a second to recognize them: Vita, Barbara, Maud, Will, and a few boys from the swing club. Tossing the HY boys from one to another, and lobbing punches into their faces, they were knocked unconscious and thrown past Wanda and into the garbage heap behind them. Looking at her sisters, she could not help passing them a smug expression.

"Sorry for the delay," Vita responded. Wanda clearly read her sister's expression as she walked past them and back the way she came. Her sisters and the swing boys followed, leaving the HY boys in the garbage-filled alley.

"We didn't say anything, but you gave us a lot to think about after you left," Vita explained. Wanda walked silently through the back-streets toward her work. She still had one last finishing touch for it. "When we noticed that other members of the club had left besides you, Freya and Frankie took a bunch of us into town in case you ran into trouble."

"You mean in case your drunk sister did something anti-Nazi and got picked up because of it?" Wanda sneered, still not having forgiven Vita for claiming that she was drunk, or for the rest of her sisters for not speaking up at the club.

"Okay, we deserved that and more. Me more than anyone," Vita winced, clearly feeling the sting from her sister's remark. "Trying to claim you were drunk and not standing with you was a dumb thing to do, an extremely dumb thing to do, a monumentally dumb thing to do."

"Keep going," Wanda laughed, enjoying the moment.

"How much dumber could we have been?"

"If *all of you* say you were dumber than our parents and their peers were for letting the Nazis take control of this country, then all is forgiven."

Everyone's mouths dropped open for a second. They were all thinking that they could not have been that dumb until they quickly realized that Wanda was right.

"We were dumber than our parents, and their peers were for letting the Nazis take control of this country," the group said to Wanda's smiling face as she led them back to the wall where she was tearing down posters; Freya, Frankie, and the rest of her sisters waited for them there.

"There you are!" Freya exclaimed, wrapping Wanda up in a hug. Her other sisters crowded around her. Wanda, however, merely pushed them aside. She still had a few final touches to make to her night's work.

"I just hope this shows up," Wanda mumbled to herself. She took the tube of lipstick out and used it to write on the side of the wall where the posters were.

"Try this instead," Frankie suggested, handing Wanda a piece of chalk. "I grabbed it from my school. Chalk will show up on the side of a wall a lot better than lipstick and will be a lot less attachable to a girl."

"Thanks!" Wanda said, taking the chalk and scribbling "Allies Victory," and "Swing Heil" over where the posters used to be. "Looks good, doesn't it?"

"Brilliant," Freya beamed.

"Haha, this is going to really tick someone off," Will laughed.

"I think you should sign it," Frankie added, quickly getting the attention of everyone. "But not using your real name, swing name, or any other name you currently use. That way, anyone who sees this knows there really *is* someone willing to stand up to the Nazis."

"Good idea," Wanda agreed. She looked at her sisters, thinking about a signature for her graffiti, before finally moving to a corner of the wall, tearing off some more posters, and writing "Swing 12" in their spot.

"Swing 12? What made you choose that for a signature?" Karma asked.

"Well, I thought about the swing kid salute, 'Swing Heil,' and how I'm one of twelve swing sisters, so I decided to combine it into 'Swing 12.'"

"An interesting choice, but I suggest we start making our way back," Marianne encouraged. "We've already been out longer than usual; we need to go *now*."

No one argued. The older sisters knew that their ability to lead double lives as swing girls depended on the hidden passageway in Linden Academy and the timing of their comings and goings. They ran a higher risk of being discovered if they left too soon or came back too late. Hurrying back to the boats, Wanda could not wait to see what her work looked like in the daylight.

I wonder if I can volunteer for collection duty? Wanda thought to herself, climbing back into the boat with her sisters as they made their way to Linden Academy. *But if I did volunteer, would that make me look suspicious? Wait, those HY boys who chased me said they received a tip that someone was going to be "out committing criminal actions." I doubt those idiots were lying, anyone dumb enough to think me an old "Madam" couldn't tell a decent lie if they tried, so then who gave them the tip?*

Wanda looked back toward the island. She already knew none of her sisters would have said anything. They might argue and get mad at each other, but they would *never* betray one another. That meant the tipster had to be someone from the club.

Old Sport, Old George, and J. B. had a run-in with the HY before meeting up with us. Freya also mentioned other members of the club left after I did. Wanda furiously shook her head, realizing the complete craziness of her thinking.

"Are you okay?" Christine asked, noticing her head shaking.

"I'm all right. Just trying to stay awake, keep my head clear," Wanda assured her. *I definitely need to keep my head clear.* She added to herself, *I mean, seriously, thinking one of the members could be a tipper for the HY, that's how the Nazis* want *us to think. Even if there is a "tipper." It could have been any of the people we passed by on the backstreets tonight, or last night. Anyone who might have seen my sisters on a previous night and have been giving constants calls to the Gestapo or HY chapters to try and make nice with them. Besides, if I want to keep doing things like what I just did tonight, and perhaps even bigger things in the future, I can't be afraid that someone is going to turn us in. If anything, I need to be ready for whatever happens if or when someone actually does.*

Unfortunately, she had no idea what that something was yet. All she could really imagine was what her work would look like in the daylight.

| 12 |

"Here is a coin, young miss, now please move along."

The coin plunked into the collection jar. Wanda watched, half-awake. The workman returned behind the barricade and down the alley to where she had ripped off the posters and scribbled on the wall. She did not need to volunteer for collection duty. After everything that happened the previous night, she and her sisters practically sleep-walked through gymnastics, causing all twelve of them to be given collection duty for poor performance. As soon as Wanda slipped away, she headed for where she had made her mark the previous night. She found construction crews cleaning and painting over it.

They work fast, Wanda thought, slightly surprised at how quickly the Nazis had responded to her actions. *Not that I should be too shocked about it.* Glancing at the front of the building, she noticed the door decorated with a variant of the Nazi emblem, one in which the swastika looked to be in the center of a circle with a dagger set in front of it.

That symbol, Wanda thought, trying to remember what it stood for. *This place is some kind of exclusive Nazi men's club. If I had realized that sooner, I would have messed up the front too. I remember back home, both before and after* that night, *there was another building with the same symbol on it. Father used to get pamphlets from them and always fuss over whether he would be accepted into it. If he was good enough for their society. The whole thing seemed ridiculous to the rest of us. After* that night, *we realized he and our mother betrayed their past friendships to join up with a bunch of elitists. We thought stressing to become more elite among the elite was crazy. At least I know others saw my work.*

Wanda glanced at people walking by the building as she made her way back to her group. The crews were trying to keep the site roped off, but they could not stop the occasional glance or whisper passing from one person to another. "Allied Victory," and "Swing Heil" passed between a few of the townsfolk. Wanda heard a few defiant giggles too.

I'm going to have to do this again, Wanda realized, a mischievous smile appearing on her face. *Only bigger and better, with less chance for a cleanup, and maybe more "sticking it to the Nazis," than writing graffiti on a men's club. Thankfully, I've got the best job in the world to use for reconnaissance.*

Wanda did not feel tired anymore, now she felt awake and energized. As soon as she saw any of her sisters, she planned to tell them what happened. But first, she wanted to get a good look around town now that the sun was up and its daytime activities were underway. So far, all she knew of the town was the little she saw at night going to and from the swing club and what she saw in the morning collecting donations. It was time to see more.

If we're going to make a statement, it's got to be someplace public enough so everyone will see it quickly before the Nazis have a chance to clean it up, but where? It would help if I knew what places in town were pro-Nazi.

Wanda did not have to look far. Just a short walk from her first act of resistance, she entered the city's business district. Food, clothing, convenience shops, as well as the town's bank and police station were all lined up in a row. Each one was decorated with the Nazi flag, posters, and pro-war slogans. The local population moved silently from one building to another, a look of muted acceptance on each of their faces, resigned to the idea that *this* was what life was going to be like from now on.

This would be a good spot to plan something, Wanda realized, slipping her collection jar into a pocket so she would not stand out too much. *Just look at these people, they need something to put the spark back into their lives. If everyone who lives and works here is asleep in their bomb shelters when we act, it will make anything we do less likely to be noticed. Knowing where the police are will also help. We'll know where they are coming from if they chase us.*

Wanda decided to search more, wandering into the backstreets on the other side of town, finding it louder than she would have expected.

What's going on back here, construction?

She soon found out it was construction, but its sight almost made her break down and cry. Crews of men and teenage boys, looking utterly wretched and starved to the point of death, were digging up the street for new sewage systems. Wanda had only seen a sight like this once before, on a building project near her old school back home the year before she came to Linden Academy. When she asked her parents and teacher about why they looked so poorly, and if they should be given more food to eat, they told her those people were "enemies." And that "feeding the enemy" was a punishable offense, warning her not to speak of it again.

We have *to do something,* Wanda realized, turning around sharply to make her way back to her sisters. She did not need to see any more of the city, she had an idea about what she, her sisters, and the other members of the swing club could do. *But I'm going to have to talk to them about my idea, especially the regular members of the swing club since they lived here the longest.* Wanda was thinking so much she did not notice the person in front of her until she ran into him, stumbling to the ground, her collection jar falling out of pocket.

"Excuse me, sir," she scrambled, reaching for the jar—not wanting to be identified as a school student looking for donations, and picking herself off the ground. "I wasn't…" Wanda stopped mid-sentence as she looked at the man she ran into, now helping her up and putting a coin in her jar. It was a face she recognized from the swing club, sunglasses and all, Silent Night.

"Silent," Wanda started until he quickly hushed her with a motion of his fingers before turning around and walking away, leaving her more confused. He did not dress like a school student; he looked like a bomb survivor, or a runaway, and considering the construction camp she just saw, maybe he was.

Who are you? She wondered, heading back toward the spot where she was initially stationed with her sisters. *And what are you doing here?*

| 13 |

"Will, have any of you ever seen any of the members of the swing club during the day?"

Will faced her sister, a look of fear and dread flashed across her eyes. Wanda decided to keep quiet about her encounter with Silent Night while she was still in school. She did not want to mention the swing club where she could be overheard by a teacher. Now that it was night, and they were making their way by boat back to town, she felt she could speak easier about the events of the day.

"Who did you see, and where did you see him?" Will asked.

"I saw Silent Night. It was near a Nazi labor camp on the other side of the island, like the one that was near our school. I almost called him by his club name, but he hushed me before I could. I was scouting the town when I bumped into him. Soon after I spotted the camp, I decided that we should do something for the people. The Nazis are forcing people to work to death and branding them as enemies."

"First, *never* go anywhere on the island alone, especially during the day. Don't you remember what happened last night?" Will continued.

Wanda did not forget, remembering both the chase with the HY boys and the cleanup scene this morning. She also noticed Will's tone not only sounded chastising but also precautionary.

I guess we all need to be more cautious now, Wanda realized. She knew they were all now crossing the line that would start getting them into *real* trouble with the Nazi authorities.

"Second, if you ever see *anyone* from the swing club out during the day, tell us about it as soon as possible. All the other club members should be in school, like us, during the day. To help protect each other, we not only use false names, but we also don't talk about our daily lives.

Nor do we recognize each other if we do see each other during the day—you owe Silent Night a thank you for hushing you. As far as any of us are concerned, we leave our day lives behind at sunset."

Are you serious? Wanda wondered. She thought about Will's words and wondered if she, her sisters, or any of the other club members believed that they could divide their night lives at the swing club with their daily lives. *Considering some of our own past actions, and possible future ones, we've already decided to let those two lives interact with one another.*

"And third, that sounds like a *good* idea. We'll talk more about it at the club, I'm sure some of the members know a few people around town who could 'donate' some food to people who desperately need it," Will concluded.

Wanda giggled slightly over the way Will said, "Donate." She knew her sister meant "steal," and that stealing was wrong. But compared to the Nazis and what they have stolen from other people already, and the stupid reasons behind it, what they were talking about doing did not even compare. Wanda could not wait to hear what the others would say.

***

"I know just the place we can hit," Frankie beamed, a big goofy smile appearing on his face as Wanda explained what she wanted to do. "And best of all, it will be empty. It's the vacation home of a prominent Nazi, and it's stockpiled with food. I have it on good information that the bastard living there is going to be at a men's club tonight while the rest of his family is at social events. We'll be able to just let ourselves in, take whatever we want, and get going."

"But we're going to need a distraction," Freya added, liking the idea as much as Frankie. "Something flashy that can attract everyone's attention, so they don't notice us."

"How about a public swing party?" Vita suggested, bouncing up and down, getting ready to dance there on the spot. "A few of us could take some of the instruments and start playing and dancing in front of the stores," Winnie mentioned. "We can also tear off those pro-war and pro-Nazi posters while we're at it and leave our own marks instead."

"Great idea, Vicki!" Freya and Frankie said in unison. "Any volunteers?"

Finding volunteers was not a problem, almost everyone wanted to be part of the distraction. Eventually, they put their names into a hat and randomly drew names for the distraction party. From among Wanda's sisters, Vita, Will, Maud, and Barbara were chosen alongside several other local swing boys and girls.

I hope they'll be alright, Wanda thought to herself, watching them leave. She knew that although the whole thing was her idea, she still could not shake off her nerves about the potential dangers they would run into.

"Don't worry about them," Rita whispered, having picked up on Wanda's fears and deciding to offer her some encouragement. "Your sisters are more than capable of taking care of themselves than you realize. As for the rest of them, they might be all a little rough around the edges, but they know better than to get caught. In fact, I think they've been looking for a chance like this for some time."

Wanda smiled, her mind slightly calmer.

Rita's right. Barbara, Will, Maud, and Vita can *take care of themselves. Probably better than any of the others with them. I should be focusing on my own task.*

"All right, members of the Lake Constance Swing Club, let's get this movable party started." Everyone cheered Frankie's announcement as both groups began to leave the hall. "We'll keep in touch with the hand radios we use for surveillance. Let's go!"

The two groups raced out into the night, Vita's group leaving slightly earlier so they could begin their distraction sooner. Wanda, traveling with the other members of the swing club, followed Freya and Frankie to another corner of the island, one far more elegant. Soon they forced their way into the back door of an ancient-looking house.

"Let's find the food and swing the night away!" Frankie cheered, turning on the record player, singing and wrapping Freya into a rapid dance. Meanwhile, Wanda and a few others, including her sisters

Karma, Christine, Marianne, and Margret, made their way to the storeroom.

"Wow!" Wanda gasped, opening the pantry and seeing that it was indeed "stockpiled with food," just like Frankie had said. Dried meats, bread, fruits, nuts, even an icebox filled with milk and butter lined the inside of a huge pantry. Since the war started, everyone that Wanda knew lived by ration cards, and was told to sacrifice and live on the bare essentials until the war was over. But looking at all this food in the home of a Nazi, who was probably telling people to "live sparingly," only made her want to take it all away even more. Grabbing a handful of apples, she ran back up to where she had left Freya and the others.

"Hey, thanks!" one of the swings boys laughed, taking the apples from Wanda and passing them around to the other members of the club before she could argue. Wanda stared dumbstruck as the other members of the swing club occupied themselves more with dancing and eating than collecting food for the laborers.

"Don't mind him," Frankie said, walking up to Wanda with Freya at his side. "They're all just a little awestruck at what we're doing, and we *are* supposed to be having a swing party here as part of the distraction. I mean, think about it, we're actually having a swing dance in a Nazi's home. You can't tell me that this isn't a little bit exciting."

"Maybe a little bit," Wanda admitted. She gazed at the ballroom the others were dancing in—painted white and decked in gold cords and curtains. It did present a much bigger stage than the old hall they were used to. "But that doesn't mean we should forget the *real* why we are here in the first place."

"Winnie's right," Freya agreed, leaving Frankie's side to join her sister. "I love a good swing dance as much as the next girl, but we do have a job to do."

"Then you can let me help you," Frankie smiled, walking with Freya toward the food pantry. "And make sure that none of our hungrier swingers decide to help themselves to the laborers' food."

Wanda was glad that some of the other swingers had not forgotten why they were there. But even if they gathered up all the food in the pantry, there was still the problem of getting it to the site of the labor camp.

"I better start looking for a cart or wagon," Wanda said to herself, walking out of the house to look for one. Instead, she found Silent Night wheeling several carts with tarps in them right up to the house's door.

"Perfect, just what we needed. Thanks, Silent Night."

Silent Night merely nodded in affirmation as Wanda took the carts and passed them to Christine, who walked out of the house behind her, arms loaded with food.

"These will be perfect for us." Christine cheered, gratefully putting the food from her arms into one of the carts. "How did you find them this fast?"

"I didn't, Silent Night found the carts, and he had them ready for us when I walked out of the house."

"Well, where did he go? I would like to thank him too."

"What, he's right there." Except Silent Night was not behind Wanda, nor was he anywhere in sight. He had vanished.

"He must have ducked past us while we were filling the cart and went inside," Wanda guessed. But personally, she wondered if that was really what he did, also realizing another mistake she had just made. *I didn't even thank Silent Night for earlier today.*

However, with the steady stream of food now starting to come from the house, she soon found herself with more than enough to keep her busy. Worrying about Silent Night soon became the least of her concerns.

Well, that's all the food, Wanda thought to herself, examining the now empty pantry and listening to the swing music still playing upstairs. *All that's left now is our signature.* Wanda took the chalk out of her small purse and started scribbling "Swing 12 was here" and "Allied Victory" on the pantry walls. *I don't want some Nazi using this as justification to crack down on any of their so-called "enemies." I better make sure this is written in the ballroom, too.*

Returning to the ballroom, she found that there were still a few dancers eating and swinging passionately. In one corner of the room, she found Silent Night pulling the gold curtains off the wall. Smiling, she walked over to him.

"Silent Night," Wanda called, startling him as he jerked, the pockets of his suit glittering with silver cups stolen from the estate.

Well, we're stealing food, I can't hold it against anyone if they want to take a few valuables, Wanda realized. She could not chastise anyone for stealing when that was precisely what they were doing.

"I wanted to thank you for earlier today. I don't know why we saw each other where we did, and I think it's safer that neither of us knows, but I just want to thank you for keeping quiet about it."

Silent Night smiled and looked relieved, breathing out a puff of air he had been holding in since Wanda started talking to him. Wanda was also glad that she managed to thank Silent Night for earlier. Turning her attention now to the dance floor, she began to write "Swing 12" in big letters across the floor. Wanda finished up her third one when Frankie and Freya broke onto the dance hall holding a radio. Their faces looked panicked.

"Wrap it up, everyone!" Frankie hollered. "We just received word from our diversionary party. The police are getting close, and we have to cut and run. According to our scouts, they are making their way toward us right now. We have to get out of here!"

The party broke up at Frankie's declaration so quickly that Wanda thought he was an air-raid siren. The other swingers scattered. The record player silenced. They packed up and carried it out with the rest of the instruments like they were more valuable than the stolen food and goods. Everyone raced out of the house faster than Wanda thought anyone could run.

"We have to get these carts moving!" Wanda shouted, moving to the front of one of them, grabbing the handlebar on it, and pushing with all her might. Her sisters pushed from behind and worked the other carts. Silent Night—tossing his stolen curtains onto the carts—along with Frankie also helped to pull and push the carts, which soon started moving, and did not stop.

"Stay off the main roads!" Frankie yelled from another cart that he was pushing with Freya, the radio glued to his ear. "The police are coming on them. Winnie, do you remember where that labor camp was?"

"Of course, I do," she shot back, barely maneuvering the carts through the back roads and towards where she found the labor camp. In the distance, she could hear the sounds of the police rushing to the house they had vacated.

"I wish I could see the look on that Nazi's face when he realizes that *he's* going to have to 'live by ration cards,' 'sacrifice,' and 'live off the bare essentials' until this war comes to an end," Wanda laughed, thinking about what that house's owner must be thinking right now.

"Serves him, and all the Nazis, right if you ask me," Karma added. "After everything the Nazis have done, including what they did on *that night*, a little payback is long overdue."

"You're both right," Frankie agreed. "I can just see him now. All dressed up like a proper Nazi, with decorations and everything. He is coming home with his wife—or some other mistress—to gorge himself on all that food he had stockpiled in that pantry. Instead, he finds it gone, his 'proper' home the site of a swing party, and signed Swing 12 all over the place. He's probably turning so red right now you would think he is having a heart attack."

They all shared in a collective burst of laughter over the remarks. They agreed with all of them. Also, picturing a fully dressed Nazi turning red in the face with anger, like something out of an American comic, was beyond funny. Only Silent Night maintained his muted stance throughout the joyous moment, focusing more on getting the food to the labor camp.

"Come on, everyone, we can't be getting overconfident now," Freya reminded them, calming herself down as she pulled her cart even harder. "If we're not careful, we could still get caught, and we still have to get all of these supplies delivered. Which way do we go next,

Winne?"

"This way!" Wanda shouted, pulling her cart in the direction where she saw the labor camp. At her side, Silent Night pulled the cart alongside her.

He knows the way to the labor camp better than I do, Wanda mused, thinking about how she ran into him near the camp. *I wonder what connection he has to the laborers? Unfortunately, now isn't the time to find out.*

The group continued making its way through the backstreets, encountering no one as they arrived at the part of the island where the labor camp was. For the first time, Wanda was actually *thankful* that the bulk of the population either slept in their bomb shelters or were too nervous about leaving the house at night. The camp was left in much the same way that she had first encountered it, but without the workers. Ditches for sewage systems were still dug up, tools were scattered about and left in the trenches, and a general feeling of death and misery hung in the air. The entire scene made the worksite look like a massive open grave. And considering the last labor camp the sisters witnessed back in their hometown, none of them would have been surprised if bodies *were* buried in it.

"Well, now that we're here, what are we going to do with all the food?" Maud asked, dropping the handlebar of her own cart. "I doubt we should just leave the carts here with a note saying, 'For the laborers.' They would be confiscated by the guards the second they showed up."

"Let's leave it in the trenches with the workmen's tools," Wanda decided, ripping off a piece of the tarp, taking a few dried pieces of meat and some fruit, bundling them up, and dropping it next to a shovel in the trench. The others quickly followed her example. It soon looked like they were planting massive seeds throughout the trenches until all the food was gone.

"This was a good thing to do, Winnie," Will whispered, congratulating her as they looked over the planted food.

"I agree, but we can't stay and admire our work. We have to leave *right now!*"

Wanda, Will, and the others looked at Freya, who was holding a pocket watch in her hand and checking the time. Her face told them all they needed to know. The night was nearly over, and if they did not return to Linden Academy soon, they would be missed for the morning roll call. And after the night's activities, none of them could afford to raise suspicion.

"We still have the carts. Let's use them!" Vita encouraged, pulling one of them back up.

"Leave pulling the cart to me, Vicki," Frankie assured her, taking Vita's place behind the handlebar. Silent Night also pulled one of the carts forward, motioning for as many of the sisters to climb in as possible. Soon, all twelve sisters, six in each cart, bounced along on top of Silent Night's curtains until they were back at the dock where their boats were waiting for them. Quickly they said their good-byes to both Frankie and Silent Night before making their way back to Linden Academy.

"I wonder if they are going to be talking about us today?" Wanda asked, thinking out loud about what they had done tonight.

"Someone will," Karma answered, an expectational look appearing on her face. "We made a name for ourselves tonight. I don't doubt that Nazis in the news agencies are going to try and keep this quiet, but people are going to talk about this."

"Let them talk," Rita cheered from another boat. "The Nazis have made everyone else in this country so scared of being reported to one government agency or another that no one is willing to talk freely anymore. We need more free talkers."

"And some new clothes," Margret joked, looking at the state of their outfits. "After tonight, these clothes are all but ruined. We're going to need a whole new look before we try this again."

All of them laughed, acknowledging that they were a mess, not that any of them even cared. All any of them cared about was that they had a great time swinging with their fellow swing boys and girls, that they stuck it to some pompous Nazi who was clearly living on far more than the "bare essentials." And that they had left a lot of food for people who desperately needed it. Compared to that, the state of their clothing was not an issue.

"We still have plenty of clothes stored in the grotto." Freya laughed, looking herself over too. "And if we need more, we can always do what we did when we first started out, collect discarded items, and retailor them. We have nothing to worry about there."

Wanda smiled at Freya's confidence. After what they had accomplished, even Linden Academy, who's secret grotto they now approached, did not seem so challenging.

We can beat back this place during the day and find ways of fighting back at night, Wanda mused. *We have each other, and our friends in the city. What can stop us?*

| 14 |

"Miss Wanda die Fürstin, front and center," Mrs. Kahn ordered.

Wanda trudged to the head of the gymnastics hall. The little sleep she managed to capture before the morning wake-up call did nothing to revitalize her after last night's activities. All it did was make her more tired and give her a headache, one that was getting worse from having to answer Mrs. Kahn's summons. She was leading morning gymnastics. And counting Wanda, she had now summoned all twelve of the die Fürstin sisters to the front of the hall after the opening exercises.

"Well, do any of you know why I called the twelve of you up here?"

"No, Mrs. Kahn," they said in unison, biting back several snide and humorous remarks, and trying harder to mask a common fear that their nighttime activities may have been discovered.

They couldn't have found out about us, right? Wanda asked herself, trying extremely hard to hide her fear, and look like an attentive student who genuinely did not know why she was called.

"All of you, about-face," Mrs. Kahn ordered.

Complying to avoid raising suspicion, Wanda and her sisters turned to face the entire Linden Academy student body. All the students were dressed the same. Morning gymnastics was one of the few times when students did not have to wear a BdM uniform. It was something all twelve of the die Fürstin sisters agreed was one of the few good things about it.

"Now class, I want you all to look at the die Fürstin sisters. Can any of you tell me what is wrong with them?"

I don't know what could be wrong with us, Wanda mused, just as perplexed as her classmates in front of her. *Everyone in this hall is dressed exactly the same, doing the same routines and exercises as everyone else. For a*

Nazi like you, this should be an ideal environment. Unfortunately, Wanda was not in a position where she could show her discomfort or confusion at Mrs. Kahn's spectacle.

"Yes, you with your hand slightly raised," Mrs. Kahn pointed to a small and timid looking dark-haired girl about the same age as Wanda standing close to them at the front of the assembly. "Did you notice something?"

"Their shoes are worn out," the girl squeaked, possibly regretting her decision to even speak out in case she was wrong.

"Exactly!" Mrs. Kahn shouted, pointing her finger toward Wanda and her sisters' feet. "Would any of you like to explain why you are here in such disgraceful shoes?"

Because we spent the night dancing and leaving food for starving workers that Nazis like you call "enemies" just so you can torture them any way you want, Wanda screamed to herself, a sentiment she knew her sisters shared, but could not speak publicly. *And why does it matter if our shoes are worn out?*

Wanda remembered when she and the rest of the youngest sisters arrived at Linden Academy. Every elder sister had worn-out shoes, and no one noticed or cared about it. So why care about it now?

"We have all just been working extremely hard," Freya answered. "We apologize if our shoes have become worn, but to conserve for the War Effort, we only have one pair of shoes each. With the added duties that come with our education, they inevitably get worn-out."

"That is the reason why I have never spoken about it before, Miss Freya die Fürstin," Mrs. Kahn sneered, a hint of suspicion entering her voice. "I noticed it happening to you, your group of eldest sisters, and your middle sisters before. But now I see it happening on your youngest sisters, too. That makes all twelve of you. So, now I want to know what is going on?"

"We are all just that diligent," Vita answered, acting as passionately as possible. "We once had to do a report on our ancestor, General Wilhelm die Fürstin. He used to say, 'Everything yields to diligence.' We are just following his example of being diligent in our work, it is just that our shoes are the first thing that is yielding."

Vita's last remark triggered a few snips of laughter from students and nods of agreement from her sisters.

"Then it is a proper example that the twelve of you are setting for the rest of us," Mrs. Kahn cheered, beginning a round of applause that everyone in the gymnastics hall soon did also. "Your work ethic is an inspiration for the rest of us. I'll make sure each of you gets a new pair of shoes before the day is over. Until then, you will be on special work assignments on campus for the remainder of the day so that you can demonstrate that diligence to the rest of the students."

*If Vita went into politics with those acting skills...*Wanda marveled, never getting tired at how Vita could act her way through any problem they faced. *She was able to remember a few notes we found on that distant ancestor of ours, and was able to act out a convincing story that's all but changed Mrs. Kahn's mind about us.*

"Thank you, Mrs. Kahn, we will be sure to do our duty," Freya smiled, seething inside. After being congratulated and applauded by Mrs. Kahn, all of them felt like they needed a bath to clean the dirt off of them. Granted, they knew the real reason they were being celebrated was that they robbed a house of all its food and gave it to laborers. Still, being thanked by a Nazi for any reason felt wrong. Then there was that "special work assignment."

"I wonder what Mrs. Kahn is planning to have us do?" Wanda mumbled.

***

"I had to ask." Wanda puffed, remembering what she asked herself back in gymnastics.

Mrs. Kahn's "special work assignment" was for the twelve of them to clean a large segment of the school. The twelve of them were sent to a different part of the school to clean it before being released for classes or a different assignment. They were left with a teacher watching them from a distance to make sure that they "provided a proper example of diligence for the school and student body."

"We're being made into a 'proper example,' alright," Wanda mumbled, scrubbing the walls before bumping into Vita. "Sorry, Vita, my mind is just not into it."

"It's okay, Wanda," Vita whispered. "I understand, I'm just as tired as you are."

"Do you think this is Mrs. Kahn's idea of punishment or a reward?"

"Both. It just shows how strange a world we live in. I'm just glad she bought my act."

"Have I ever told you that you are a fantastic actress and sister?"

"Yes, but you could always tell me a few more times every day."

Wanda and Vita jointly giggled at the remark, their fatigue forgotten for a few moments.

"It all about confidence, attitude, and clothes, Wanda," Vita added. "You could put on just as convincing a performance yourself. All you need is the right look and to let the other person know you are in charge."

"I doubt that," Wanda sighed before Christine shuffled up next to them.

"Less whispering, more washing, the teacher is starting to notice the two of you."

Wanda and Vita quickly refocused themselves on the walls, neither one of them wanting to bring attention to themselves for any reason. They would not be able to talk to their elder sisters freely until lunch, and by that point, every one of them felt like they had cleaned a third of the entire school.

"Tell me, why *do* we use our school shoes when we go out?" Wanda asked. "Wouldn't using a different pair be smarter?"

"It would and we have tried," Freya explained. "Unfortunately, good shoes are the one thing we *can't* find. Everyone in town wears the ones they own until they are in worse shape than ours. Using our own shoes, and then relying on the school's supplier for replacements, is the only option we have. But enough of that. How are you feeling after your 'special work assignment.'"

"I don't know about you, but if I make it to the end of the day, I think I might sleep clean through the night." Marianne fell into her seat and almost face down into her lunch.

"I know," Freya yawned. "None of us managed to recuperate yet, and the day is already half over. Only a few of us should head out tonight to pick up information before getting back here. We can't do anything if we're falling asleep on our feet."

"If only a few of us are going, then I'm in," Wanda whispered, sticking her head closer to Freya's. "Last night was my idea. I want to know what happened around town because of it."

"We're in, too," Will and Maud added jointly.

"And I'll be the last to go," Freya concluded, recognizing the eagerness building among her sisters. She realized that soon all twelve of them would be going if she did not stop them quickly. "The remainder of you get all the sleep you can tonight. As for the four of us, we'll sleep when we can as soon as we get back. For now, let's just try and make it through the rest of the day without falling flat on our faces."

Trying to stay awake was hard. Between classes, their regular school work duties: stitching, cleaning cloths, and drills, each sister fought bouts of dizziness, exhaustion, and a constant nagging headache that seemed to follow them wherever they went. By the time they were able to sneak back to their room during the leisure period before Light's Out they were so tired that a few of them fell asleep the moment they landed onto their beds.

"I can't blame them for passing out," Vita groaned. She fought back her own fatigue as she and Rita undressed Christine—lying asleep on her bed—and made her look like she had readied herself. "I hope the four of you are up to this."

So do I, Wanda silently added, not wanting to voice her own concerns out loud. Back at lunch, she had been eager to head back to town and talk with the members of the swing club. She wanted to find out if their swing party and food delivery had made even the slightest difference around town. But now, seeing some of her sisters sleeping in their beds—and her own vacant bed, she felt envious of them, and wondered if it would be worth giving up a full night's rest.

"We're about to find out," Freya answered, the lights turning off quickly as the school reached "lights out." With darkness covering the school, Freya and Will opened the passage and filled the empty four beds with their replacement dummies. With snoring coming from the other beds, Wanda, Will, Maud, and Freya silently worked their way back down the passage to the grotto where the boats were waiting.

| 15 |

"Is it just me, or are we moving slower than usual?" Wanda asked.

"It's not you," Freya confirmed. "We are moving slower. After what we just pulled, we're weaker than we normally would be."

Freya was right. The four of them might have been together in one boat rowing toward the city. But all they could feel was the day's fatigue combined with the previous night's escapades eating into them with each pull on the oars. The boat did have a motor, but using it was a choice that they saved in case they ran out of strength entirely, or needed to get back to Linden Academy *immediately.* Looking toward the city, and remembering the previous night's adventures, Wanda wondered if they had any visible impact at all.

The workers in that labor camp must have found the food we left them. Wanda thought. *We left it where they could easily find it. I hope it wasn't taken from them by the Nazis.*

One of the last things Wanda wanted was for all the food they delivered to the camp to have been confiscated before any of the workers could eat it. She hoped that did not happen, and that someone at the swing club might have been able to tell her something about what had happened as they pulled their boat up to a dock and anchored it.

"Remember, we're just here tonight to check in and get news, not dance the night away. Not that any of us could manage to swing without a full night's sleep anyway."

The others chuckled at Freya's remark as they walked down the backstreets toward the swing club. The music echoed toward them before they even reached it. Outside, Freya's boyfriend, Frankie, stood by the entrance and ran to greet them.

"Freddie!" Frankie cheered, scooping Freya up into a big hug. "You're finally here, we've got a lot to tell you, but where are the rest of your sisters?"

"Sleeping off the day and last night," Freya explained. "We're not planning on staying all night either, just long enough to check in and get the news."

"Then come on in, we have news to tell."

Frankie quickly led Freya inside, Wanda and the others close behind them. Soon after they entered the club, the band stopped playing their current number and switched to a swing fanfare. Everyone welcomed the four of them into the club like they were returning heroes, a feeling that was only magnified as the members of the club suddenly rushed them, each intent on shaking their hands and applauding their actions. Only Silent Night, standing by the water jug, refused to greet them and share in the hero's welcome. Instead, he merely smiled and raised a glass in salute to them.

"Whoa, everyone calm down," Wanda cried, excited by the attention, but not thinking it was necessary. "The way you're acting, you think we just ended the war. What happened today?"

"A lot," Frankie cheered, a big goofy grin stretching across his face. "Not even that Nazi bigwig could keep it quiet that his home was broken into by a swing club."

"Yeah," Old Sport added. "If our own music didn't tell everyone we were there, from what I hear, that bigwig's *screaming* at seeing the state of his house did."

"*Officially,*" Frankie continued, "the place was raided by Communists and Jews in hiding, seeking to erode the community's trust in the Nazi regime."

"That's ridiculous!" The four sisters screamed in unison.

"Oh, it gets better. The police are now looking for a group of *men* that are calling themselves 'S12,' suspected of burglary, vandalism, and feeding the enemy."

"Ha!" Wanda laughed, the complete absurdity of the Nazi's claims reaching a new humorous point. "Of course the Nazis are going to think we're men. I'll bet it never once occurred to them that Swing 12, or S12 as they call them, are a bunch of swing girls. Wait, 'feeding the enemy,' does that mean the food made it to the laborers?"

"It did," Frankie confirmed. "By the time the Nazis tried to interfere, all they could get their hands on were the wagons we used and a few empty cans. That's actually where the 'Communist' part of the official story comes from. They think that since you were helping workers, it was symbolic of some kind of 'workers' revolt.'"

"A workers' revolt?" Maud asked, curious if the Nazis were serious. "Is being a complete moron a mandatory requirement to join the Nazi party?"

"You ask me, they're all a bunch of shmucks," J.B. chimed in.

Wanda and her sisters recognized the word "shmuck." It was a word the Cohens sometimes used to describe someone who was a complete fool.

"Shmucks led by a shmendrik," J.B. continued.

"A 'shmendrik'?" Wanda asked, having never heard the word before. "What's that? Sounds like a magician."

"You would think that Hitler was a magician," J.B. laughed. "Or the Pied Piper of Hamelin himself. Especially if you consider the way he's made so many people across Europe magically dance like rats to his tune since he came to power. Convincing them to believe in his delusions. But a 'shmendrik' means 'a small boy acting like he's a full-grown man.' And considering Hitler, one man, who thinks he's some kind of messianic savior that can take on the world, and win. I think the term fits him just right."

Everyone chuckled. Wanda created a humorous picture of Hitler as a little boy in her head, screaming at his friends and parents when he could not get his way, and now screaming the same way again from his podium and always getting his way.

J.B. is right, Wanda realized. *He really is a shmendrik, nothing but a little boy acting like a man, a shmendrik leading shmucks. Shmendriks and shmucks, SS...*

Wanda almost fell over herself with laughter. The humor behind her own private joke, and the idea it was giving her, were almost too much for her.

"Winnie, are you all right?" Freya asked, seeing that Wanda's laughing fit was quickly becoming the center of attention.

"I'm... alright," Wanda answered between laughing fits. "J.B. just helped me come up with this incredibly brilliant and funny idea for our next run through town."

"Well, don't keep us in suspense. What is it?" J.B. asked, curious about what his remarks could have inspired.

"Well, when you were talking about how the Nazis must be shmucks, and Hitler being a shmendrik, I got to thinking 'shmendriks...shmucks...ss,' and then it hit me. We could go out and write, 'Shmendriks & Shmucks' over every SS poster in town. We can put it right over the SS logo, because how can they be a 'protection squad' if they're all shmucks led by a shmendrik."

"That's insane!" J.B. shouted.

"That's brilliant!" Frankie countered.

"It's both! That what it is," Freya remarked. She was also now laughing at her sister's idea. She saw that it would not only be extremely funny, but it would also tick off *a lot* of Nazis; and just like J.B. and Frankie said, it was both insane and brilliant. "But we can't do it tonight, something like that is going to take all twelve of us, and we'll have to find a place to set the band up to distract the locals. How quickly do you think you can find something, Frankie?"

"With all of us looking, we should have a few ideas by tomorrow night, and a definite one a few nights later. Isn't that right, fellas?"

A chorus of approval rose across the hall. The eyes of the other members of the swing club gleamed with anticipation, each looking forward to creating more mischief.

"Then it's settled," Frankie said, looking satisfied. "We'll start looking tonight for places we can stage the event."

"And we'll let our sisters know about Winnie's new plan. I'm getting excited just thinking about it," Freya added.

Freya was not the only one becoming excited. All of them were trembling in anticipation, imagining both what the city would look like with their graffiti over it, and what the Nazis' faces would look like when they saw it themselves. Wanda especially was over-excited, partially because they would be doing something anti-Nazi again, but also because it was her idea.

This is going to be great! Wanda beamed, shaking the other swing club members' hands, and being wished well for a future success. The excitement was almost enough to make her forget about her fatigue and nagging headache. *We can do this, all of us, me, my sisters, the other members of the club, together we can really stick it to the Nazis.* Wanda was so excited that she did not notice she was holding a piece of paper in her hand until after it was there. Confused, she turned to look at the last person she had just shaken hands with. It was Silent Night, turning to go back to the water jug, and unlike the other members of the swing club, wearing a look that was a mixture of caution and concern.

"Come on, Winne, it's time to go," Freya called.

"On the way, Freddie."

Wanda tucked the note into her dress pocket and was soon walking back to the dock with her sisters to take their boat back to Linden Academy, each of them feeling slightly revitalized by the excitement the next few nights were promising. They soon realized they did not even need to use the boat's motor to get them back to the grotto beneath the school, they were able to paddle back on their own. But once they returned, the exhaustion hit them twice as hard.

"I think I'm going to sleep clean through to tomorrow night," Maud yawned, changing out of her dress clothes and into her nightgown.

"I wouldn't try it," Will warned. "We don't want people noticing us any more than they are. Just be thankful for the sleep you can get."

Maud only grumbled at her sister's remark, but she knew she was right, as did Wanda and Freya as they also changed into their nightgowns. While changing, Silent Night's note fell out of Wanda's dress pocket—reminding her of its presence, and drifted down to her feet. Picking the note up and unfolding it, Wanda read what Silent Night was trying to tell her. *A fair-weather friend changes with the wind,* she read, wondering what he was trying to tell her. *Is Silent Night trying to tell me I can't trust the members of the swing club? That's ridiculous.* Wanda might have only known the other swing boys and girls personally for a short time, but she knew her older sisters knew them for far longer. Her sisters would not introduce her to people she could not trust. The other club members have already supported her. They had been there when she was in trouble, and they had no love for the Nazis—how they reacted when she mentioned *that night* told her plenty about their feelings.

"What's that you're holding, Wanda, a love note?"

"It's nothing, Freya," Wanda replied, ignoring Freya's teasing and burning Silent Night's note in one of the candles.

Why would Silent Night, or anyone, call the members of the swing club fair-weather friends. They certainly make better friends than any of the other Linden Academy students that just want to be turned into Nazi drones.

Wanda put Silent Night's note out of her mind as she and her sisters quietly made their way back into their beds. Right now, the only thoughts she wanted to concern herself with were sleep, and finding a place where they could put their next plan into motion.

I'll have to try and make sure I get collection duty again tomorrow, Wanda realized, sneaking back into her room where her other eight sisters were already sound asleep. *That way, I can start looking for posters to write graffiti and places we can plan our dance. I should also look for some paint, brushes, and old cardboard boxes that no one will miss. If we plan to write something like "Shmendriks & Shmucks" across posters, it will help if we can make a few stencils and use paint instead of chalk.*

| 16 |

Just before sunrise, a group of hooded and masked men sat in a circle. They were members of the Lake Constance chapter of the TS, and some of the most prominent party members in the area. They were fuming. The side of the club's building had recently been vandalized, yet cleaned up quickly afterward, by a group calling itself "Swing 12." The group had also ransacked one of its members' homes, stealing and vandalizing it, and using the food from it to feed German enemies. They had made sure the newspapers reported the break-in was the fault of Communist and Jewish insurgence. But the local population was more than aware of the truth, and the truth needed to be dealt with quickly.

"I thought these hooligans and their crazy jungle dances were only in Hamburg?" one of the members asked, his voice muffled by the mask. "Why is it showing up here?"

"This is clearly the result of anti-German insurgents. They must be invading the Fatherland through Switzerland, bringing this decadent American music with them to corrupt our precious German youth. We should make requests to increase patrols on Lake Constance and tighten security on the railroads. Also, provide rewards for information on swing clubs and this group, 'Swing 12.' Swing music must not be allowed to find a foothold anywhere in Germany."

The other members nodded and cheered for their choice of actions. Yet outside of the inner circle, one new member of the society had to fight to keep himself from keeling over with laughter while trying to maintain his silence.

Anti-German insurgents invading through Switzerland, these old men really do live in their own delusional world, the young man thought to himself, listening to the society's leaders talk about the swing club and Swing 12. *Not one of these fools realizes how swing clubs get their music, or why it's appealing.*

No one knew it, but he was also a member of the swing club. He realized why other young men and women were attracted to it. For him, it represented freedom, a freedom he did not want to see jeopardized and would do anything to protect. That was why he tipped off the HY soon after Winnie stormed out of the club. He believed it was better to lose one girl instead of the entire club and the freedom that it offered. But the inner circle's talk of "rewards," gave him new ideas about his position in the TS.

If someone were to tell them that Swing 12 is nothing but a group of teenage girls, they would never believe them. These old fools are so convinced of their own male superiority that the idea of a group of women, especially young women, getting the best of them is beyond their imagination. But this is also the best place to pick up information about what they are going to do about them.

"Son," one of the society's members asked the boy sitting in the back, shocking him out of his reflections.

"Father," the boy replied, trying to hide the bitterness and humor in his voice. His father's home had been the one that had been vandalized. The crime had caused him to lose face with the other members of the Party, the Men's Club, and had left his face red from anger.

"I am going to a camp and pig farm to perform specialized work for the party in a few weeks," the boy's father muttered. "It will help me regain my status after those hooligans attacked our home."

"I don't see how working on a pig farm could help you with that?" the boy said.

"That is why I want you to join me. It will look better if we go together."

"As you wish, father."

But how is working on a farm good for anyone's status? the boy wondered. *Still, if I'm going to maintain my cover, and keep getting information for Swing 12, then it's best to do whatever he wants me to do. It's just a pig farm, after all. I need to keep silent, wait, and get deeper if possible. This could help me to do it. If Winnie and her sisters are as crazy as I think they are, especially if they plan on carrying out this insane "Shmendriks & Shmucks" idea, it won't be long before the Nazis in this town are going to do or offer* anything *for their capture. And if I'm here, I'll be in the best spot to feed them information and get them out of trouble, maybe even out of the country when the time comes. I just need to work and wait.*

***

"I guess finding cardboard on the streets is a lot easier said than done," Wanda said. She had managed to perform badly enough during gymnastics that she was on collection duty again. But after slipping away to look for cardboard for the stencils, she found nothing.

I guess I shouldn't be surprised, she mumbled to herself, looking down another alley and finding plenty of rubbish, but no cardboard. *If anyone actually has cardboard, they're probably holding onto it to burn or use as insulation during winter.*

Before coming to Linden Academy, I remember seeing workers in the labor camp, and other people stuffing their clothes with newspaper and cardboard just to keep themselves warm. No doubt the same thing was happening here, too, especially with winter coming, and the war on. Everyone was collecting and making preparations.

"Wanda, come on, it's time we get back to the school," Vita called, running over to fetch her. "Did you collect anything *special?*" she asked, making sure to accent "special," so Wanda knew she was talking about cardboard. Wanda had told her sisters about the next Swing 12 project once they all woke up. They loved it. Now, all of them were looking for the supplies to pull it off whenever they could find time to sneak away from their duties.

"Just the usual," Wanda sighed, unhappy to have found nothing but donations for the Nazis.

"Likewise, personally though, I wish I could tell the people to take 'the usual' and save it for their own survival," Vita said.

Wanda agreed with Vita, nodding as they trudged back to the truck, waiting to take them and the rest of the students back to school. Wanda's elder sisters had already warned them that if they did not bring back some money, the teachers would make life harder for them afterward.

"It will be worth it if it works against the Nazis," Wanda remembered Karma telling Freya as she handed her collection tin over to the teacher. The teacher shook it to make sure something was inside of it.

That was what we thought, too, Freya had said, the memory of the conversation replaying itself in her head. *Until we found out that the* penalty *for not bringing in a single donation is 'special' after-hours late night work detail on school grounds. You* do not want *to do it. You'll be stuck awake all night doing administration paperwork with a guard watching you. It is* not fun.

"On a brighter note, we started making the headlines."

Vita pulled a folded-up flyer out of her pocket and handed it to Wanda. Unfolding it, she smiled as she read what it said. "The Party is offering rewards for information leading to the capture of the anti-German group S12. Reports are to be made to your local Schutzstaffel (SS), Sturmabteilung (SA), Hitler Youth (HY), Nazi Party (NSDPA), or Nazi Thule Men's Club (TS) office. Details to follow." Wanda snickered, before turning to her sister. "How many different organizations can one government have, half of this flyer looks like alphabet soup."

"I know, but if they're offering rewards for *S12,* then someone must be taking them seriously."

"Not serious enough to offer a real reward for them. 'Details to follow.' No one is going to talk with an offer like that. S12's next operation is going to have to rattle the party a bit more."

Wanda and Vita both giggled mischievously, rounding a corner and coming to the truck that was taking them back to school.

If holding a swing dance was enough to get a vague reward put on us, I wonder what this next operation is going to do, Wanda mused, not wanting to mention it where her teachers, or the other students, could hear her. *Soon, they're going to be offering a* real *bounty for us, not just some vague and imaginary one. I just hope the others are having better luck than we are.*

Wanda's sisters did have better luck finding cardboard for the stencils in Linden Academy and coming up with a few creative ideas for their group, all of which they shared together at lunch, along with a collective laugh over their "wanted" flyer.

"They are not taking us seriously enough," Will mumbled, looking at the flyer before passing it to Maud.

"If they knew we were girls, I bet they wouldn't even take us seriously at all. They would probably make us out into a group of poor little girls that are being used and corrupted by foreign influences. The idea that we would willingly choose to do this on our own must be completely beyond them."

"Agreed," Marianne nodded, checking the hall to make sure no one was listening to them. "I can't wait until tonight when we literally paint the town with both swing and Wanda's SS slogan."

"As long as Frankie and the others have been able to find the places we need," Wanda added, a note of concern in her voice. She knew her elder sisters trusted them, which should have been good enough for her. But it did not change the fact that Frankie and the others were searching the town—with Nazi agents and police everywhere, while the twelve of them were off the streets in Linden Academy.

"I wouldn't worry too much about them," Freya said, patting Wanda on the back. "They're more resilient and craftier than you know. And speaking of crafts, you wanted to show us something, Margret?"

"Right," Margret agreed, reaching into her pocket and pulling out a multicolored crochet broach, made of twelve dancing girls, with the words "Swing 12" written across them.

The girls' eyes were immediately drawn to the broach. It had a sense of fun and festivity to it, standing in stark contrast against what the Nazi regime was trying to enforce.

"That looks beautiful, Margret," Christine giggled, snatching the broach from her hand. "Where did you get the idea, and the time to make this?"

"I've heard from the club members that other swing groups across Germany make their own pins and broaches to identify themselves. So, I thought, why shouldn't we?" Margret explained, taking the broach back from Christine. "As for both the time and the design, I got lucky and was given a crafts class today. They wanted us to make something that could be a gift to 'our proud German soldiers on the front lines.' I originally planned on just aimlessly reading craft books until the class was over, claiming I couldn't find anything fit for the soldiers. But then I stumbled across an old Christmas craft book, and found a pattern for the 'Nine Ladies Dancing' from the song 'The Twelve Days of Christmas.' It gave me the idea of altering it for twelve ladies dancing—signifying us—instead of nine."

"How did the teacher take it?" Karma asked.

"Not too good. The teacher called it a failure since I didn't follow the instructions. She wanted to throw it away. I was able to convince her otherwise when I got into telling her that thinking about Christmas, the 'Festival of the Family,' was making me think of mine. And before I knew it, I recreated me and my sisters."

"And your teacher bought that?"

"Yes, though she did grumble a bit. Afterward, when no one was looking, I added the 'Swing 12' to it to complete it."

"How quickly can you make eleven more of them?" Wanda asked, excited about seeing herself and each of her sisters wearing one of those broaches. "If the Nazis want to shove their symbols into our face, we should be able to do the same."

"I saved the pattern and snatched up plenty of yarn from the crafts room. If we all work on it together during leisure time, a few days, maybe."

"That means we should be finished right about the time Frankie and the others determine where we are going to hold our diversion," Freya concluded. She looked as excited as the other sisters were starting to feel. "I can't wait to see them again and get started."

| 17 |

Frankie and the others were excited when they all met up that night at the club. The boys had already found three places to set up distraction dances. First, a civic center doubling as a meeting place for both the Nazi Party members and the HY, second, a goods distribution office, and finally the club they had graffitied before—which was now covered with SS recruitment posters. The other swing girls in the club were all enchanted by Margret's broach design. She was not the first person to design a broach or pin and bring it to the club, the other members did the same thing—as did every swing club in Germany. Every time a new one was introduced, the girls treated it like it was the latest in American fashion. Wanda and her sisters could feel the overall infectious energy growing with each step as they spent the next few days dancing. They spent their free time working on both their "Swing 12" broaches and "Shmendriks & Shmucks" stencils. Finally, on a cool Friday night, their preparations were complete.

"Are you sure the boys are going to have the paint?" Wanda asked, for the third time, as she and the rest of her sisters dressed in their swing attire.

"Yes, Wanda," Freya replied nonchalantly. "I saw some of it last night, five cans of blue paint waiting for us. Frankie also promised me that there would be more tonight, so try and relax. This was your idea. How is it going to look to the other club members if you are getting nervous in front of them?"

"I'm nervous *because* it was my idea," Wanda rambled. "We're not going to be together like when we raided the house. We'll be a lot more exposed and spread out. If something happens to us..."

"Then at least we can have the dignity to say, 'We stood up to the Nazis,' and that we didn't run away again like we did on *that night*."

The memory of *that night* was all Wanda needed to shake off her nervousness. Climbing into the boat, the sisters rowed out of the grotto and onto Lake Constance. There was no moon, so the entire city looked like a black rock against a star-filled sky. In the distance, the sound of the patrol boats hummed menacingly.

"Air-raid precautions," Wanda whispered, feeling the apprehension in the air the closer she and her sisters rowed toward the island. "With no moon, this would be the perfect night for a raid."

"It's on a night like this that we're planning to eventually leave for Switzerland," Freya added from the front of the boat. "With no moon, and darkness as our ally, we'll cross Lake Constance and into Switzerland. The trick is figuring out the patrol boat patterns so we can slip by them. The Nazis, however, change the boat movements all the time to make it difficult for *anyone* to go to or from Switzerland."

Murmurs of agreement came from the other boats as they pulled into their dock. Wanda already knew that her elder sisters were waiting for all twelve of them to be reunited before they escaped the country. But it still did not stop any of them from watching the boats, trying to figure out their movements. She guessed none of them had been able to figure out their patterns, leaving them all discouraged.

At least with these air-raid precautions in place, it should make what we're going to do a little easier, Wanda imagined as she and her sisters walked toward the swing club. But as she approached it, she noticed something else was missing.

"Music, there's no music playing."

The other sisters were quick to notice the missing music too, breaking into a run and busting into the swing club, their words caught in their throat at the sight before them. The entire hall had been vandalized. The walls and floor were painted with the words: "Heil Hitler," and "Blood and Honor." The Nazi flag hung over the center of the dance floor, almost like it was meant to consecrate the hall. Frankie, Silent

Night, and the other swing boys and girls were staring at the scene before them in shock, before noticing that Wanda and her sisters had entered the hall and were standing next to them.

"Oh, Freddie, you're here," Frankie stuttered, still trying to make sense about the scene in front of him. "As you can see, the Hitler Youth decided to pay us a visit and get even for our own little 'swing party' in that house not too long ago."

"How do you know it was the HY?"

"It was them alright," a new voice squeaked.

Wanda realized that it was Old Kludge who had answered Freya's question. If he looked like an undertaker before, now he looked like the walking dead. His face was scarred by multiple cuts and bruises. It was also the first time she had ever heard him speak, and was surprised that he had a high-pitched voice.

"They made sure we knew it was them," Old Kludge continued. "They made a big show of marching in, dressed in full HY uniform and regalia—shorts, daggers, the works, all before tying up Old Sport and J.B., beating them senseless and dragging them out. Then they went and gave the hall its new decorative look before leaving, making sure I was prepared to tell everyone what happened."

Wanda wondered when she was still nervous about tonight, how she might react if something were to happen to her sisters, or to any member of the swing club that decided to go along with her plan. Now, she knew. She was angry. Her friends had been hurt and taken prisoner. The war was again coming close to home, and she had to do something about it.

"Old Kludge, do you know where they took Old Sport and J.B.?" Wanda asked.

"Yeah, they took them to that civic center we were looking at, they're having a meeting there tonight."

"I think we have our target," Wanda announced, reaching into her pocket and pulling out a final touch for her outfit, a party mask to go over her face. Let's hit that civic center, get our friends back, and paint the town blue."

A chorus of approval rang out from the club members. It was no secret that the regular swing club members hated the HY, and the feeling was mutual. Now that the shock was finally fading, and the regular club members realized the HY decided to come after them, they were ready for a fight.

"Well said, Winne," Frankie agreed. "I can take the twelve of you and a few of the regular swing boys to start painting the town with our SS slogan. The rest of you can hit the civic center, rescue Old Sport and J.B., and set up a swing dance to shock the shorts off the HY."

"Now, hold on a second!" Will screamed, placing her own mask over her face. "What makes you think I'm sitting out any chance to give some HY shmucks a good thrashing."

"Likewise," Maud agreed, stepping next to her sister. "If there is going to be any fighting tonight, I'm going to be a part of it. Don't even *think* about telling us it is going to be too dangerous."

"I'm going with the rescue party, too," Wanda added. "J.B. and Old Sport are in this mess because they decided to go along with *my* idea to begin with. I am going to get them out."

"Wait, Winnie," Frankie argued, "You don't have to go with us. This isn't your fault, J.B. and Old Sport made their decisions on their own, and regardless of your idea, the HY could still have paid us a visit. They have plenty of reason to do so."

"I am going!" Wanda screamed, Will and Maud standing next to her, staring Frankie down, challenging him to continue the fight. He could also feel the eyes of the other club members, especially Wanda, Will, and Maud's nine other sisters, drilling into him and wondering how he would respond to this challenge.

"Fine, you can go with them," Frankie relented, throwing his hands up in a gesture of surrender. "But that's now three fewer painters for the town, we won't get as much..."

Frankie was interrupted by the sound of clanging metal. Silent Night pushed himself to where Frankie, Wanda, Will, and Maud were standing, a dark bag dragging heavy in his hand.

"Silent Night, what do you want?" Frankie asked, confused. Instead of answering, Silent Night ignored Frankie and pushed the bag to Wanda and her sisters.

"Thank you, Silent Night," Wanda replied hesitantly, taking the bag from him. Silent Night's face was unreadable. She had no idea what he was giving her. But once she opened it, there was no way she could keep the shock off her face.

"How did you get these?" Wanda demanded. Silent Night merely shrugged, passing off a look that seemed to say, "How did I get what?" before merging back into the crowd leaving everyone confused about the exchange.

"What did he give you?" Frankie asked, looking into the bag, and becoming as stunned as Wanda. "Paint rollers!" he exclaimed, pulling out the small devices to the shock of the crowd, all of whom suddenly found Silent Night a much more curious figure than they first thought. "Winnie's right. How did you get these?"

Everyone in the room was familiar with paint rollers. They were a new invention from Canada, and the government had sought to import them into the country so that they would be ahead of other nations in one more aspect. But they were not generally available to the public yet. So, the fact that Silent Night could get so many of them, even small ones, and casually hand them off like they were nothing made him a far more mysterious character than anyone had realized.

"Who cares where he got them?" Freya retorted, walking up to Frankie and taking the paint roller out of his hand. "The point is he got them, and now we have them. Between these rollers and our stencils, we'll be able to do twice the work we originally planned. So, what are we waiting for? Let's get this party swinging!"

A chorus of approval rang out from Wanda's sisters and the other swing boys and girls. They grabbed rollers, paint, and started to make their way out into the city. As for Wanda's group, they ceremoniously carried a record player, along with some rope, and a few brushes with a can of paint toward the civic center. Wanda noticed that among the boys in her group, Old Kludge walked at the head—his bruised face twitching in anticipation, and Silent Night brought up the rear—trying *not* to be noticed.

I'm guessing Old Kludge is itching for some payback, Wanda imagined. *As for Silent Night, I can understand if he doesn't want to be asked where he got the paint rollers, but then why is he coming with us?* Gazing back at Silent Night, Wanda could already see a few of the other swing boys pestering him about where he found the paint rollers. Instead of answering, Silent Night maintained his muted stance. *If he wanted to avoid others, it would have been better to work on painting the town. Then he could just work alone. So why join us?* Wanda quickly put those thoughts out of her head as her group turned a corner and came in view of the civic center. Not waiting for an invitation, the group charged in through the front door.

| 18 |

Even if she did not count *that night,* which was extremely hard, Wanda had seen plenty of strange, sad, and sickening things to make her believe that her country was going crazy. But a bunch of brightly clothed swing boys and girls, all dressed in quasi-American and British fashion assaulting a uniformly dressed HY detachment to sounds of swing music, was a new kind of craziness.

"This is almost too easy," Wanda sang as she danced with her sisters to the music, using a rope to whip and trip the HY members. "I thought they would be tougher?"

"It all depends on who you run into," Maud explained. "Sometimes you run into boys who can put up a fight. Other times you get wimps like these who are only here to guard Old Sport and J.B. If there *are* more of them in uniform tonight, they're probably out looking for us."

"I would not be surprised," Wanda responded. She had seen full squads of the HY long before she came to Linden Academy. She knew the moment they burst through the door and into the hall that the number of boys there was less than a quarter of what it should have been. And all they were doing was yawning, dawdling about, and watching Old Sport and J.B. The fight was the only thing that seemed to put any real spark into them. But it did not last long; they were soon knocked unconscious and tied to the same chairs they had once held J.B. and Old Sport in.

"Thanks for coming to get us," J.B. said, stretching himself out after he was untied from the chair. "Now that we're here, we have this place, and we have music playing, what are we going to do?"

"We swing, of course." Almost everyone cheered before breaking out into a wild series of dances. Wanda and her sisters, however, had a few other things they wanted to take care of first.

"Let's *properly* decorate this place first. They decorated our place, it's only fair we decorate theirs, too," Wanda snickered, placing one of their stencils against the wall and onto an SS poster attached to it. Dipping a paint roller in blue paint, and being careful not to get any of it on herself, Wanda painted the words: "SS: for Shmendriks & Shmucks" on the poster right over the SS insignia. Old Sport, J.B., and Silent Night quickly walked over to join them.

"You really didn't think we were going to let the three of you have all the fun, did you?" Old Sport asked. Wanda and her sisters merely tossed them a couple of wry smiles in response. "Come on, you got us out of a jam, so the least we can do is help paint this place blue."

Wanda noticed Silent Night slightly shaking his head over Old Sport's gesture before turning his attention back to the painting. Yet before she could say anything to him about it, a buzzing sound caught her attention.

"What the...?" Wanda turned to see Old Kludge, with an electric shaver, and one of the cans of blue paint, standing over the unconscious HY boys, a vengeful smile on his face.

"It looks like Old Kludge is still itching for more payback," J.B. explained. "He's going to shave the HY boys bald and then paint them blue."

Old Kludge actually started shaving the first HY boy shortly after the words were out of J.B.'s mouth.

"You don't think beating them senseless was enough?" Wanda asked.

"I doubt Old Kludge would agree. Besides, the same thing has happened more than once to a few members of our own club. Old Kludge isn't doing anything to them that hasn't already been done to us."

"J.B. is right, Winnie," Maud chimed in from where she was working. "I've shaved the heads of a few HY boys too. Just keep painting. This was your idea, after all."

Wanda smiled and continued, glancing at the dancing swingers, and the now shaved and painted HY boys. Privately though, she wished a few more people were helping them.

We're trying to leave a message against the Nazis, yet the bulk of the crowd just wants to dance. Not that openly swinging right in a Nazi meeting hall isn't a statement all in itself. But we would still have this place painted a lot faster if more people were working on it.

Wanda, however, kept her complaints to herself. Regardless of what anyone else was doing, Maud was right, this was her idea, and that meant she had to make sure it was completed. By the end of the third swing number, the walls of the civic center and every SS poster had been completely painted blue with the words "SS: for Shmendriks & Shmucks" along with their Swing 12 signature, leaving just enough paint for Old Kludge to dump on the still unconscious HY boys, and time enough for Wanda and her sisters to swing dance one last time.

"Oh, how I've missed this," Wanda laughed, letting herself be swept away in the familiar energy and euphoria of the music as she and her sisters and other members of the swing club danced. Only now, there was a feeling of satisfaction added to the mix. Swinging around the center, her slogan painted on each of the walls, Wanda felt extremely satisfied with herself. She had taken another punch at the Nazi party, and she could not have been prouder with herself. The entire realization put her into so much ecstasy that she did not realize she was dancing with a new partner until she saw his face.

"Silent Night," Wanda beamed, never having danced with, or even seen, him dance before. He danced as vibrantly as everyone else though, and wore a completely different expression than Wanda's. He looked cautious, worried, and intense. The look quickly sobered Wanda from her stupor.

"What's wrong?" Wanda asked, trying to draw a response from Silent Night. His look was making her increasingly uncomfortable. It almost looked like he was trying to tell her something or let her know that he knew something, but still refused to speak himself.

I know that no one has heard a word from Silent Night ever since he first showed up at the Swing Club, but can't he just talk to me? Wanda thought, considering why he would not tell her what was on his mind instead of staring at her so uncomfortably. *Can he even talk at all? Is he mute?*

"Oy, everyone!" Old Kludge whistled, his high-pitched voice interrupting Wanda's thoughts. "We're done here, it's time to go. Tomorrow night's dance is at the 'B' site."

Silent Night broke away from Wanda and rushed out of the center so fast that Wanda—on any other occasion—would have been offended, except that she was following a minute behind. She did not want to be caught by any returning HY patrols any more than the rest of them. But she was also still curious about the meaning behind the look on Silent Night's face.

"Where did you go?" Wanda mumbled to herself, scanning the vicinity for Silent Night outside the center. He was long gone.

"Come on, Winnie," Maud yipped, grabbing Wanda's hand and pulling her down the street. "We got to get back to the boats."

Wanda nodded, deciding—for the moment—to forget about Silent Night and the look on his face. She focused instead on returning to the boats and getting back to Linden Academy with enough time for them to nap before the next hectic school day.

"I wonder how Freddie and the others did?" Will asked. Wanda and Maud wondered that, too, but all three of their questions were soon laid to rest, as they started passing their SS slogan painted on bare walls, and over SS posters. The wall that Wanda first graffitied, now covered in SS posters, all bore their slogan in bright blue paint.

"It looks like they did it," Maud cheered, scanning their work as they made their way through the town. "Some of them even added their own creative designs."

It was true. Besides the SS slogan, some of the others had also painted "Swing Heil," "Allied Victory," and drew little cartoons of the Nazi swastika being chased, or thrown into the garbage. Wanda giggled at the sight of them, but in the back of her mind, a lingering doubt remained.

Did everyone get away safely? Wanda had not seen any of her other sisters yet. In fact, she now realized that shortly after they scattered from the center, she had not seen anyone from the swing club except Will and Maud. *If we're the only ones who make it back to Linden Academy, the teachers will* know *we've been up to something. We can't just say that nine of us have suddenly become sick and can't get out of bed, can we?*

Thankfully, Wanda did not have to worry about that for long, because upon reaching the dock, she saw her sisters waiting for her. Climbing into the boats, they began their return trip to the grotto entrance, a smile stretching across each of their faces.

I can't wait to hear how things went for everyone else, Wanda thought excitedly, yet restrained herself until they made it back to the grotto where they could all talk freely. *But more than that, I wish I could be there to see the looks on those Nazis' faces when they see our slogans splattered around town. I hope it makes them mad and gives the people around town something to smile about. We all need something to put a smile on our faces, especially now.*

| 19 |

"I'll tell you what will put a smile on my face. For the twelve of you to report to the uniform room and get those worn-out shoes replaced, again!"

"Yes, Mrs. Kahn," Wanda and her sisters replied.

"How anyone could wear out shoes that fast is beyond me. There must be inferiors making them."

Or maybe you're just a big dumb Nazi who can't see beyond her own superiority complex, Wanda thought to herself.

It was the next morning after they had painted the town blue with their slogans. They disposed of the clothes they had worn the previous night, which were now speckled with blue paint, but they could not replace their shoes. They had only one pair each, and used them for school in the morning, and swing at night, and after last night's event, they were worn out again. Thankfully, Mrs. Kahn was either too stupid, dense, or full of Nazi philosophy to imagine how their shoes could be getting worn out beyond the story, Vita had fed her.

"Do you think we'll be stuck cleaning the school again?" Karma asked, putting on a new pair of shoes.

"I don't think so," Freya answered, testing out her own new pair. "I don't think the school bigwigs would want us doing anything around the school that could cause us to ruin another pair. They might see it as damaging to their image. *Especially* when we're supposed to be sacrificing for the war effort."

The twelve of them laughed at that comment, each one remembering the Nazi bigwig's home that they raided not long ago.

That place was so extravagant, so stockpiled with hoarded food, that it was practically begging to be burglarized. Wanda remembered, not wanting to talk about their Swing 12 activities in the school in case the wrong person might overhear her.

"So, what do you think we're going to be doing?" Karma asked again.

"Hopefully, just more collection duty in town."

Freya was half right. The twelve of them were back in town, but not for collection duty. It was for cleaning duty.

***

"All right, ladies, it's time for you to demonstrate your cleaning skills in the field."

Standing in front of Wanda, her sisters, and a large group of girls from Linden Academy, Mrs. Kahn extruded a sense of pride, addressing them like they were about to march into battle. Yet she, like the rest of them, was dressed in a long apron, galoshes, a bandana on her head, and a mop in hand. She looked like a weird cross between a farmhand and a sewage worker. Except they were not on a farm, or in a sewer; they were in front of the slogans they painted on the town walls last night.

"As you can see, this 'Swing 12' group, this mad edifice of Jewry and Communism which is infecting our proud community, is now becoming even more destructive in its antisocial behavior. They have vandalized the walls of our city with their defeatist propaganda. So, at the request of the city council, and leading party officials, we have been tasked with painting over, and cleaning up this mess. The Hitler Youth chapters will be patrolling to ensure we're not bothered. Now, let's get to work and show the men of our community what the women of Linden Academy can do."

And what exactly are we supposed to be showing them? Wanda asked herself. Honestly, she did not know what to think about the situation. She felt happy that she could see her work from last night out in the morning sun, and proud to attract attention. But she was also frustrated that the Nazi party was still sticking to the story that they were some kind of Jewish or Communist group. She would have loved to tell them otherwise. She was also angry and embarrassed that they wanted her,

her sisters, and their classmates, to be the ones to clean it off the walls. Then there was the squad from the HY.

Those HY idiots look far more interested in patrolling us *than making sure we're not bothered.* Wanda could feel the stares coming from the boys meant to keep them from being troubled, and it was giving her goosebumps. A quick glance, and she soon realized that not only the twelve of them, but *all* the girls making up the cleaning crew were clearly uncomfortable. They were all being stared at by a bunch of HY boys.

No one wants to be here, Wanda realized. While their reasons might have been different, Wanda knew that as far as the crew was concerned, Mrs. Kahn was the only one who genuinely wanted to be there. *So how can we get out of this mess, and still keep our slogans up for as long as possible? I doubt any of my sisters want to clean them off, or paint them over, any more than I do.*

"All right ladies, now who wants to be the first proud Linden Lady to dip their mop into the paint and start erasing this antinational defeatist propaganda? But be careful, we only have so much, and we have a lot of walls to cover."

"I'll go first!" Wanda yelled, running up to Mrs. Kahn and the bucket, as an insane idea quickly formed in her head. Before reaching the bucket, Wanda tripped herself, knocking the bucket over, and splattering herself, and Mrs. Kahn, with paint.

"Miss die Fürstin!" Mrs. Kahn screamed, laugher suddenly erupting from all the girls in attendance.

"Oops," Wanda whimpered, trying to sound as genuinely sorry and apologetic as possible, remembering what Vita told her about confidence, attitude, and clothes—she definitely had the clothes part down. "Mrs. Kahn, I didn't mean to, I...I just want to be the first to show what I was capable of. I didn't mean to trip and make a mess, I didn't..."

"Just get back into formation," Mrs. Kahn ordered. "And the rest of you, *stop laughing,* you'll never attract a husband if you can't control yourself." Mrs. Kahn's last comment was spoken more quietly as the laughter of the other girls died down, but Wanda heard it clearly.

I'll bet that's *what we're really here for. Us being out here cleaning isn't about erasing graffiti. It's so the Hitler Youth boys can scout out potential marriage candidates. We've* got *to get out of this insane country.*

Wanda wondered how much longer it would be until they could execute their escape plan as she walked back to her sisters. The earlier laughter was still in their eyes. Vita even mouthed the word "Bravo" to her. But even more so, the joy still lingered in the eyes and faces of her other classmates. Some of them even seemed to regard her with a new sense of curiosity and admiration.

I wonder how long it's been since any of them genuinely laughed at anything*?* Wanda asked herself, their formation breaking up into smaller groups and being sent to different parts of the town.

"That was crazy and brilliant," Vita whispered as soon as they were alone. "I'm a little bit jealous I didn't think of it first."

"I'm just glad it actually worked." Wanda giggled. "I literally came up with that the second Mrs. Kahn told us there was only a limited amount of paint. I guess sometimes crazy works."

"In more ways than you think," Karma added, joining the conversation. "I managed to speak with Barbara before they split us up. You made a lot of people happy with your comedy routine, not to mention giving everyone a good idea about how they can get out of this job really fast."

It was not long before several other girls—all in different groups—started falling, dropping, and knocking over paint cans everywhere. Soon, the only place with any visible paint was on the painters and road, instead of on the walls covering the graffiti. Wanda and her sisters suspected that none of the Linden Academy girls really cared about what was written on the walls or about cleaning them up. They only wanted the assignment canceled, so they could get as far away from the HY boys and their lecherous eyes as possible, a sentiment all the die Fürstin sisters shared. Mrs. Kahn, though, did not take the matter so lightly. Every time a can dropped or paint spilled onto the road, Wanda noticed her face twitch into a new expression of both anger and fear.

Mrs. Kahn is being "evaluated" just as much as we are. Wanda realized, happy to see her Nazi teacher nervous for once, and even more so because it was *all* the Linden Academy students putting the pressure on her. *With all of us annoying her, using up paint like this, I wonder how long it's going to be until she cracks and decides that we would be better off back at Linden Academy?*

It did not take long at all. Halfway into the cleaning, Mrs. Kahn canceled the whole outing and hustled them onto a bus back. Every girl's face was brighter than Wanda had ever seen since she first arrived, but Mrs. Kahn's own face was wracked with nerves and fear.

| 20 |

"Bring in the informant," a muffled voice said.

A masked figure silently and nervously walked before the council. He said nothing as he was brought in, and as his body twitched in fear. He had just returned from a trip to a "pig farm" with his father. What he learned on that "farm," the things he had done, had made *that night* into nothing by comparison.

Now's my chance, the boy thought, his mind racing with possibilities. *After what I heard happened at the cleanup, they'll be more likely to believe who "Swing 12" is, but how much information should I give them?*

"You have information that can lead to the arrest of this, 'Swing 12' group?" one of the men asked the informant.

"I do," the informant replied, his voice muffled so that it could not be recognized outside of the meeting hall. "And my information *will* be rewarded?"

"Really?" A councilman mockingly challenged. "Tell me, how old are you?"

"Turning eighteen."

"Then you should soon be going to fight for our proud German People. What other rewards could you ask for?"

I could think of plenty of things, the informant thought as a murmur of laughter passed among the councilmen. *But if I say the wrong thing, they might just send* me *back to that "farm" as a permanent resident. I doubt they're really planning to give* anyone *a reward for information on Swing 12. They'll just claim it was them who caught them. But if they think going to the battlefield is reward enough, then I can play along.*

"I want to choose the battlefield upon which I fight for Germany. I also want the chance, before I go, to leave an heir so that my family line may continue. I think we can all appreciate the fact that Germany needs more children, especially a child of the hero responsible for the capture of Swing 12."

That made the council quiet as they considered his request.

They know how much the regime has been pushing for population increase. Even more so, for the children of old families, athletes, celebrities, and modern-day heroes.

"First, give us your information, and tell us how you plan to capture these Jewish and Communist insurgents. Then, if you can actually do it, we'll speak about your reward," a councilman announced.

"*First,*" the informant countered. "You have to acknowledge, to yourselves more than anyone, that you are not dealing with 'agents of Judaism or Communism,' you are dealing with a gang of swing kids."

"Bah!" another councilman scoffed. "Those hooligans are only in the Hamburg region. The children of our community wouldn't dare stoop to *that* wild level. It's just a clever ploy by corrupting agents."

"And yet every piece of graffiti on the town walls bears a swing kid reference. The name of this group alone should tell you what kind of people they are, it's called *Swing* 12. Not too long ago, Linden Academy sent a group of their students to clean up a massive amount of swing-inspired graffiti. Instead, they made a mess of themselves, leaving the walls almost untouched. If you want to keep lying to yourself about who you're after, then the next place you'll be cleaning graffiti from will be right here. Or you can listen to me, and my plan, and I'll deliver you Swing 12, for the reward promised."

The council rose uniformly before the informant. He could not see their faces through their masks, but he could see their eyes, and they were mad and wild. Their gaze instantly put the informant on edge.

I overplayed myself, the informant trembled, knowing full well what these men could do to him if they wanted to. He had seen firsthand how the Nazis treated their enemies and undesirables. *If they think I'm mock-*

ing them, they could send me to the front lines right now out of spite. My plan's not even complete, and it does carry some risk. I know who the members of Swing 12 are. But I still don't know anything about how the die Fürstin sisters are even getting out of Linden Academy. Until I know that, I can't reveal their identities. But if I can pull this off, I should be able to keep at least some of us safe from the war and Nazis without even needing to go into battle, and that *is worth any price.*

"Tell us about your plan," one of the councilmen announced, removing a large mental load from the informant's head.

"This is how I will deliver you Swing 12," the informant began, as he described his plan to the council.

***

Wanda smiled as she walked from the parade grounds back to Linden Academy. It had been two weeks since Mrs. Kahn had taken her and the rest of the students into town to clean up the graffiti—which they botched beautifully. The effects of that incident were still showing across the school. The daily schedule was still insane, classes were ridiculous, and the pace made it feel more like a military camp than a school. But everywhere Wanda looked, her classmates' eyes looked just a little bit brighter, and their expressions more refreshed.

Messing up that cleanup was probably the first taste of real fun *that anyone has ever experienced since coming to this school,* Wanda thought to herself. She had just completed making an inspection of the parade grounds with the rest of her sisters. None of them had been allowed to march in it because of their "lack" of BdM uniforms and were straightening up the field before announcements. Walking back, the twelve of them were especially giddy for tonight.

"Is it true? He has the latest?" Vita asked.

"I'm sure of it," Freya answered. "*You know who* told me who knows a guy who knows a guy who knows a dealer. It's the latest from the *homeland.*"

All of the sisters giggled over Freya's code. They all knew. "You know who," was Frankie, and "the latest from the *homeland*" meant new swing records from America, purchased from a black-market source. News like that was enough to put them all into high spirits. It was taking all of their self-control to keep themselves from breaking out and experimenting with new dance moves there on the parade field.

"I can't wait to hear them," Vita sang softly, wondering what new music would grace the swing club tonight.

"I can't wait either," Wanda added, in just as good a mood as the rest of her sisters. "It's a shame we have to listen to announcements first."

Wanda glanced back to where, beyond whispering distance, a teacher watched them to make sure they finished the parade grounds and then returned for announcements. If not for the teacher, they would have skipped both announcements and the following supper, and headed right back to their room.

"It's just going to be more of the same pig slop," Will hissed, having listened to announcements for a lot longer than Wanda. "Nothing to worry about at all."

***

All of the die Fürstin sisters soon realized that they *did* have something to worry about, as twelve mouths simultaneously opened at the reading of the announcements.

"Let me repeat myself in case you didn't hear me the first time," Mrs. Kahn stated, a tinge of irritation in her voice. She was giving the evening announcements today, and what she had told the students made not only Wanda and her sisters, but also all of them visibly disturbed. "After the disgraceful behavior during the Academy cleanup project, the city, party, and school officials are concerned that impure foreign elements might have found ways to corrupt the student body. Therefore, local members of the Hitler Youth, and volunteers from other schools, will patrol and inspect the school and dormitory at night, until such time that the insurgents who have been vandalizing the city have been captured. They begin tomorrow. That is all."

It was *not* all. Every girl in the auditorium started whispering to each other and asking questions. The suspicion and fear were becoming so visible Wanda and her sisters could practically see it.

Everyone is suspecting everyone else, Wanda quickly realized, instantly feeling the gaze from several of her classmates coming to rest on her. *And I'm going to be suspected more than the others. I was the one who first made a mess of the cleanup, I'm the* reason *for it in the first place. If anyone starts talking about me, it could lead to my sisters, our activities, it could mean...*

Wanda could feel the panic rising in her, threatening to overtake her. She could also feel a hand being placed gently on her shoulder. Whipping around, she looked into Freya's eyes. From those eyes, Wanda could tell her elder sister was as nervous as she was, but was managing to keep herself slightly more composed, mouthing two words.

"Room, now."

Wanda nodded in understanding.

This isn't the time for supper, Wanda thought to herself, trying to follow her sisters out of the hall. *This is the time to talk and figure out what to do. But aren't people going to be suspicious of us not being at supper? And since I was the one who first made the mess, isn't that going to make us all look guiltier?*

***

"After an announcement like that, no one is going to be suspicious of us for missing supper," Freya reassured Wanda, once they were back in their room. "I can almost promise you that many of the other students are doing the same thing right now—probably to write to their families and complain about the idea of boys watching them at night. *That* is what's really got everyone so troubled."

Wanda could certainly understand that. She remembered the looks the HY boys were giving them at the cleanup and the feelings those looks gave her. The boys had the eyes of animals ready to jump on a piece of prey. It made her shiver with the possibility that they might do just that. The thought that those same boys, patrolling and *watching* them while they were supposed to be sleeping, made her even more nervous.

It's going to be the cleanup, mixed with those boys who tried to assault me when we left our first graffiti mark, all over again, Wanda feared. Worried about the prospect of having strangers close to her, who would probably take as many *rights* as they believed they were entitled to.

"On a different note, I wouldn't worry about your actions at the cleanup bringing any suspicion on us," Vita added, trying to break Wanda out of her fears.

"Vita's right," Karma said. "The first person who did it, namely you, will just be regarded as clumsy. The suspicious students are going to be the first ones who copied you. We can all agree, we saw plenty of other girls repeating your 'accident' without provocation. *They* are the ones who are going to be suspected."

The remaining die Fürstin sisters nodded in agreement. However, it did not completely relieve all of Wanda's worries.

"That still doesn't solve our more immediate problem, what do we do about these boys?"

That was a question none of the die Fürstin sisters could come up with an answer for. Each of them knew that if someone seated right outside their room came in while they were supposed to be sleeping and *physically* checked their beds, instead of just peeking through the door like what had been done before, then the school would know that they were sneaking out at night. From there, it would not take them too long to find, or invent, the connection between them and Swing 12.

"I think we may have to tell the boys at the Swing Club what our daily life is like," Will finally answered, drawing shocked expressions from the rest of her sisters.

"But you are the one who first told me we had to keep our day and night lives separate?" Wanda challenged, remembering how Will reacted when she told her about the run-in she had with Silent Night near the construction work camp.

"I know," Will replied, feeling the weight of her own words in her mouth. "But I think we can all agree that both the school's administration and the Nazis are bringing those two sides of our lives together, whether we like it or not. Remember, they're not just using Hitler Youth boys, but getting regular boys to volunteer as well. How do any of us know if Frankie, Old Sport, Old Kludge, J.B., or even Silent Night, are already agreeing to start walking through those hallways if they haven't already? Wouldn't you rather have someone you can trust on the other side of that door instead of a stranger?"

"Will's right."

Everyone turned to Freya and her sudden agreement with Will's idea.

"We need people that we can trust not only on the street and in the Swing Club, but here in the school, too. Also, we *don't* know if any of them have figured out that this is where we go every day. But I would be surprised if they haven't, or at least suspected it. We've always kept this part of our lives a secret from them, but if we want to keep being Swing 12, if we just want to keep being *swing girls,* we will need their help here. We'll tell them about it tonight."

The rest of the die Fürstin sisters turned to each other, eventually nodding in agreement with both Will and Freya's proposal. Yet in the back of her mind, something unsettled Wanda.

I understand what Will and Freya are saying, and they're right. We are going to need help, so why can't I shake this feeling that there's something wrong about all of this? I hope I'm just being paranoid.

| 21 |

The Lake Constance Swing Club was still meeting in its "B" site. The "B" stood for "bomb shelter," since they were meeting inside a large bomb shelter beneath a crumbling house on the northwest side of the island that had been abandoned for over ten years. When Wanda first saw it, a few days after their successful rescue and graffiti operation, she half-expected a ghost to show up, especially with the way the band's swing music echoed through the house. It was an expectation that a few of her other sisters shared. Now, walking up to that house again, that same eerie feeling was back. Only this time, it was feeding her doubts.

Relax Wanda, she repeated to herself, trying to force her nerves to be quiet, and trying even harder to not let them show on her face. *Freya and Will are right, we have to tell them. They've already been trusting us, been trusting* me, *ever since I came up with the idea for Swing 12. If we can't trust them with something as simple as where we go to school during the day, and ask them for help with keeping Nazis off our backs—figuratively and* literally—*how can we say we've trusted them at all?*

Wanda knew her arguments against her fears were a good one. Yet they still bothered her. Listening to the music as she made her way down into the bomb shelter, she could forget her doubts. The bomb shelter carried sound so well it was easy for her to think that they were in a large dance hall, complete with everyone having a merry time throughout the night. But that night, as they entered the shelter, the music abruptly stopped, as the twelve of them quickly became the center of everyone's attention.

"They're here!" Frankie cried, hurrying to them with the other swing club members behind them.

"I'm trying to volunteer for Linden Academy," J.B. gasped.

"Me, too," Old Sport added.

"We all are," Frankie concluded, sweeping his gaze across the bomb shelter.

Wanda and her sisters, however, were dumbstruck. Despite her own misgivings, Wanda agreed with Freya's and Will's idea to tell the other members of the swing club about their daily lives. But to walk into the club and find that the boys already *knew* what those lives were, even though Freya anticipated that they would have guessed it, none of them were ready for it.

"How..." Wanda squeaked. She could tell by the look on all of her sisters' faces that they were all processing this revelation, and asking themselves the same question. She was simply the first to vocalize it.

"It wasn't that hard to figure out," Frankie explained. "There are only a few schools in the area, and only two of them, the elite ones, are same-sex—one for boys and the other for girls. The rest of us here represent the other schools, and we have already seen each other plenty of times during the day. That means you either had to be living off someone else, or went to the all-girls school of Linden Academy. None of us wanted to ask which because it's a general rule never to bring our daily lives into the swing club before now."

"But after the mess that happened with the cleanup a few days ago, it wasn't hard to guess where you were," Old Kludge continued, his high-pitched voice sounding highly out of place. "Why else do you think the Nazis have taken such a special interest in your school? You're going to need help if you're going to stay hidden."

Wanda could not think, she could not register anything for the next few seconds as the weight of Frankie's and Old Kludge's words sank into her head. It was a feeling all the die Fürstin sisters shared until Karma started giggling. The amusement spread until all twelve sisters were wildly laughing at the confused looks of the other members of the swing club.

"We're all right," Freya assured them, breaking out of the laughter first, the others following soon after. "We just needed to get that out, and you're also right about how easy it was to figure out that part of our daily lives. And if you could, then the Nazis could, too. So, besides volunteering, does anybody else have any ideas that can help us?"

"I already have one for you," Frankie smiled, pulling a small bottle out of his pocket and handing it to Freya.

"What's this?" She asked.

"Sleeping medication," Frankie explained. "And as I understand it, a potent one. My father keeps so much of the stuff in his medicine cabinet that I doubt he'll notice one vial has gone missing. Just slip a few drops into some tea or coffee for whoever happens to be stationed outside your door. They'll be out for the night, giving you the freedom to do whatever you want."

The die Fürstin sisters did not know how to react. Freya handled the bottle of sleeping medication like it was a baby. The other sisters watched it as preciously as one, until Freya gently tucked it into one of her pockets, right before jumping into Frankie's arms and kissing him on the lips.

"Well, what are we waiting for?" Wanda asked, feeling slightly embarrassed at watching Freya's display. "I thought this was a swing club. Get the music playing. Let's *swing*!"

The club members quickly complied. They turned the record player back on and played the latest American swing music, the band accompanying it. As for the remaining die Fürstin sisters, they broke away from Freya and Frankie and began passionately swinging together with the other swing boys and girls.

This is the best! Wanda thought to herself, lost in the music, the dancing, and most importantly, the friends and pure freedom the swing club offered. *I just love these people. It didn't matter to them that we came from an elite school. All that matters to them is that Nazis are closing in on us—on fellow swingers—and their first instinct is to find ways to help us escape. Frankie, more than anyone, we're lucky to have him on our side.*

Wanda glanced back to where Frankie and Freya were. They had broken their embrace, but were now slipping back up the stairs out of the bomb shelter and into the house above. A slight blush and a mischievous smile crossed her face as she imagined what they would be doing.

Once we make it to Switzerland, I wonder how long it will be before Frankie becomes our new brother? Not that I, or any of us, would disagree with Freya's choice. Frankie's been nothing but helpful to us from the moment we started Swing 12. I'll bet he's been helping Freya and her group since they first walked in here. I can't think of anyone who might have been quite as helpful. Well, maybe one person...

Wanda looked over to where the water jug was set up, and sure enough, Silent Night was seated right next to it, watching the swingers. He looked like he was inspecting the club, getting ready for a raid that might happen. In his hands, he held a small pad and a pencil, which he was using to write something down.

Silent Night did help us just as much as Frankie did during the food raid, Wanda remembered, thinking about how he helped load food and was right there, pulling a wagon to make sure the food was taken to the labor camp. *And before that, there was the time he spotted me in town. As far as I know, he's never told anyone about that, and then there was that letter.*

Wanda had not kept it, but she still remembered the note Silent Night had slipped her warning her against fair-weather friends. Of course, she could hardly see how any of the friends surrounding her could be considered "fair-weathered."

If they were "fair-weathered," then the moment trouble started, they would be staying as far away from us as possible, but here they are volunteering to help us out, Wanda considered, thinking about the other swing boys and girls in the club. *I wonder if Silent Night will actually have something to* say *about that? I think I'll go find out.*

Leaving the crowd, Wanda walked over to the water jug with a smug look on her face, daring Silent Night to protest against the swing boys' actions. Silent Night did not disappoint her. Scribbling one more note, he tore it from his pad before rising up to meet Wanda and placing the folded note in her hand. Still smiling, and expecting some kind of protest from him, she opened the note and read it to herself.

"Beware Greeks and the gifts they give."

Wanda almost laughed. She knew what the saying meant. It was a reference to the Trojan Horse, a gift left by Greeks that was actually a trap after a ten-year war with the city of Troy. It allowed Greek troops to enter the city secretly and destroy it. But in this case, Wanda guessed Silent Night was calling them the Trojans. Frankie and the other members of the Swing Club were the Greeks. And the support they're offering—the sleeping medication and volunteering, the "Trojan Horse"—their "gift."

"Seriously, is this all you want to contribute?" Wanda asked, crumpling the note and shoving it into her pocket. "Are you still not going to *say* something?"

For a second, Wanda thought his expression was changing and that he might actually speak. But Silent Night quickly returned to his muted expression, writing one more note which he quickly passed to Wanda.

"I'll talk when I want to," Wanda read, looking back up to find him giving her a smug smile.

Is he enjoying this? Wanda wondered, adding his second note to the first one before rejoining her sisters in dancing.

That night was the best night Wanda had experienced at the Lake Constance Swing Club. The songs sounded better, the dancing was more intense, and the overall energy itself was more alive.

Is it really something different about tonight's music? Wanda asked herself, swinging and dancing frantically among several of her sisters and swing boys. *Or are we all just* really *happy tonight?*

Wanda already knew the answer to her question. She was happy, happier than she had been in a long time. After *that night,* Wanda often felt like the only people she could count on were her sisters, but that had changed. She did not feel like it was only her and her sisters anymore now. Through the swing club, she met others who wanted to run away from the Nazis and their regime, or stand up to them as much as she did. By creating Swing 12, she was able to *do* something to the Nazis with family and friends that despised them as much as she did. Now those friends were taking their commitment to helping them one step further by walking into their school to help guard them against the Nazis' prying eyes. Wanda felt so happy, so full of energy that she had to get it out, and there was only one way to do it, dance.

"I could dance like this all night," she mumbled to herself, not realizing that she and her sisters were doing that too. By the time they left the club, not only were their shoes worn out again, but it was also late—so late it actually could be considered early—than they had ever been out.

"Pick up the pace, everyone!" Vita hollered, leading her sisters as they sprinted through the backstreets to the boats. "We have to get back to school, fast!"

No one argued, especially after realizing that they left the club almost a full hour past their maximum allowable time. They all knew how long it took to get back to the school once they set off in their boats, change, prepare for bed, and get some rest before facing the day. The timing was everything to avoid getting caught. And if they did not return quickly, "getting caught" would be the least of their worries.

"Into the boats!" Freya ordered, jumping into the first boat alongside Vita, pulling a ripcord to start one of the engines.

"You're turning on the engines!" Karma gasped, jumping into another boat. They all knew that the engines were only to be used as a last resort, and also once they were closer to the grotto. The reason was that the sound could alert patrol boats on Lake Constance and tell everyone where they were.

"We've got no choice," Barbara argued, joining Karma in her own boat and pulling the cord to start her own engine. "We need the speed to get back quickly. Otherwise, we won't make it back in time."

Barbara's right, Wanda thought, gazing up to the sky, a slight sense of dread coming over her as Will started the engine of their boat. *At least there's fog on the lake this morning that should help hide us. The only thing we can do now is to get back to Linden Academy as quickly as possible—and pray.*

| 22 |

Thanks to the engines, the die Fürstin sisters' boats glided through the water, but it was a nerve-wracking trip. Wanda was not the only one praying. She could hear Christine and Rita mumbling their own prayers, asking for stealth, swiftness, and safety. It did nothing to calm any of their fears. Every shadow in the fog was a patrol boat that would catch them. Worse was the boats they could not see. They knew their engines were making a lot of noise, and the biggest fear, beyond getting caught, was that someone was following them back to the grotto.

We should hide the boats, Wanda considered, thinking about what they should do if they were being followed, and not wanting to say it out loud in case they were being pursued. *The clothes, and everything else, in the grotto too. If anyone is following us, they can't find any trace of our activities, but we* don't have the time*!*

While the threat of Nazi boats was the immediate problem, time was the far greater adversary, and it was winning. Every second brought the sisters closer to morning gymnastics, and with it, roll call. If all twelve of them missed *that,* causing the teachers to thoroughly inspect their room, their secret *would* be out. Regardless of the risks, none of them could let that happen. Approaching the grotto, a few sisters began letting out sighs of relief.

"I don't think I have ever been so glad to see this grotto as I am now," Rita said, exhaling as they finally docked their boats and began changing clothes.

"Don't get too comfortable, Rita," Freya reminded her, redressing into her sleeping clothes and quickly lighting a candle to lead everyone back up the stairs to their room. "We're not safe yet."

Taking the lead, Freya and the others made their way back up the stairs and into their room through the servants' passage and exchanged the dummies for themselves. Finally, back in their room, Wanda exhaled a long breath of relief.

"We made it. Now we can get some rest before..."

"Rise and shine, ladies!" Mrs. Kahn's voice echoed up and down the hallway as she knocked harshly on every door. "It's time to get up. Gymnastics in five minutes. Do NOT make me go into your rooms and drag you out of bed myself, because I will do it."

Wanda had to fight back the tears, but she knew there was nothing she could do. Rolling out of bed, she and her sisters redressed and made their way down to gymnastics.

***

"What is wrong with you today, Miss die Fürstin?"

Wanda did not answer, she could hardly hear the question. She felt too tired, too dizzy, and her head ached like nothing she had ever felt before. Last night's dance at the swing club, followed by their frantic return to Linden Academy, had completely overtaxed her. Now she was feeling the effects.

"Let me ask you again, *what is wrong with you?* Your moves are sloppy, the worst I've ever seen, you seem dead on your feet, and your shoes are worn out—again! Is there a problem?"

"I just don't feel well," Wanda squeaked, which was not a lie. She did feel terrible, mostly from exhaustion, and wanted nothing more than to curl into a bed somewhere and go to sleep.

"Fine," the teacher surrendered. "Just go get a new pair of shoes from the uniform room, then report to the nurse. Dismissed."

Wanda staggered off the gym floor, grateful for her dismissal. She made her way to the uniform room where she found three of her sisters already there. Each one looked as bad as her—if not worse.

"New shoes first followed by a trip to the nurse?" Vita asked.

"Yes," Wanda yawned, nodding her head, and guessing they were there for the same reason.

"Maud, Will, Asta, and Margret were here not too long ago. Counting us that just leaves Freya, Rita, Marianne, and Karma. Want to place a bet as to when we'll see them, too?"

"Pass," Wanda replied, not in the mood for playful wagering. Instead, she walked to the counter to find the clerk ready with a new pair of shoes in her size.

"I thought I would need another pair for all of you once you started showing up," the clerk stated, handing a pair of shoes to Wanda. "Try not to wear these out so fast."

"Thank you," Wanda answered, before leaving with her sisters for the nurse's office.

The nurse's office looked more like the die Fürstin sisters' room than any doctor's office. The "office" was actually a small hall isolated from the rest of the school. It was probably used as a parlor when the school was still a castle. It was lined with beds, four of them occupied with girls sleeping soundly. The nurse on duty took one look at them before sighing and pointing them to the empty beds.

"If you're not sick, then I don't have time to spend examining cases of exhaustion from this crazy schedule the administration is enforcing. Just pick a bed and get some sleep."

"Thank you," the four of them replied simultaneously, each grabbing a bed and quickly falling into a deep sleep.

***

Wanda awoke feeling better than she had felt in a long time.

I needed *that.* Wanda thought to herself, stretching in her bed to remove the stiffness. *I feel like I must have slept all day.*

"How long are you going to let those girls sleep?" Mrs. Kahn's voice echoed into the office from somewhere else in the school. "They had already missed two full days."

"Two days?" Wanda chirped. "No wonder I felt so stiff and refreshed."

Wanda tried sitting up. She moved slowly, and her body felt heavy, but she managed to sit up. She noticed a few of her other sisters were also sitting up, yawning, and stretching themselves out. Outside, an argument between Mrs. Kahn and the school's nurse continued.

"They can sleep for as long as they need to," the nurse countered. "It is *my job* to make sure that the women in this school can perform their duties, and they *cannot* do that if they are dropping from exhaustion. Now, unless you want to further bother my patients, I respectfully ask that you please leave."

"Humph, I liked it better when Dr. Crouse ran this place."

Wanda listened as Mrs. Kahn marched away from the office as the nurse reentered it. Wanda immediately found herself liking this member of the school's staff.

"Well, if you're all finally starting to wake up, I'm not going to be able to keep you here," the nurse stated, almost melancholy. "You should count yourselves lucky that Dr. Crouse isn't running this place anymore. If he was, you would have been tossed out of here after maybe two hours of sleep at the most. Now once everyone is up and about, I suggest you get back to your school duties quickly and be ready; you are going to find that a few things have changed."

The die Fürstin sisters quickly realized what the nurse met when she said, "a few things have changed," soon after they returned to their regular schoolwork. All around Linden Academy, a new sense of apprehension, suspicion, and even jealousy was in the air. Wanda and the others could see it clearly in the eyes of the girls they spent the rest of the day with as easily as they could see their reflection in a mirror.

"It's from having the HY boys on campus," Freya said, the twelve of them sitting down together at lunch, discussing the change in their classmates' attitude. "As soon as they showed up, everyone began acting as friendly as possible to them to curry favor, which quickly led every girl in the school to become suspicious of everyone else."

"They're worried that someone is going to say something to one of the HY boys the next time they're here," Karma reasoned. "It doesn't even have to be about Swing 12. Anyone with a grudge could use this as a means of revenge. They just have to say something, it doesn't even have to be true, and in return, they see themselves earning points with the HY *and* the Nazis outside of the school."

"Exactly," Freya said.

"At least there's one good thing about all of this."

"What's that, Wanda?" Rita asked, the other die Fürstin sisters wondering the same thing.

"When we try to slip the HY boys on guard tonight the sleeping medication, no one will suspect that we're trying to get something from them. Everyone is already doing it."

All the sisters giggled mischievously over that remark, realizing Wanda was right. Several of them had even heard their classmates mention providing the HY boys with gifts and refreshments once they arrived on campus. What they were planning to do now would not really be that out of place. It was only a matter of making it to the end of the day so they could prepare it for them, a task that was easier than any of them had imagined. After two days of sleep, they had more energy than they had in a long time.

"We should sleep for a couple of days more often," Christine said.

"*That*, Christine, is the first thing I promised myself I would do once we make it to Switzerland," Margret whispered, smiling as she poured both the tea and the sleeping medication, into a kettle before quickly returning to their room.

The two of them had hurried to the student lounge, skipping dinner, to prepare the tea they were going to serve to the HY tonight in case other students planned to do the same thing. They quickly found a lot of students heading to the lounge with tea, coffee, and kettles in their hands as soon as dinner was finished. Both Margret and Christine silently thanked their sisters for promising to save food for them in the room. Not long after they returned, they ate the bread, cheese, and meat, saved for them. Then they heard heavy marching coming down the hallway. It was followed by a loud knock on the door, uncomfortably reminding them of *that night.*

"Good evening, young ladies, may we come in?" a pompous voice asked.

Uneasily, Freya slowly opened the door, and six uniformed HY cadets marched in, all dressed in HY uniform—short pants, insignias, and all.

"Good evening ladies, my name is Otto Vogel, you may call me Sir Vogel. I can personally say, on behalf of myself and my men, that it is our most exalted duty and pleasure to watch over you tonight. Protecting proper young ladies as yourselves from whatever Jewish and Communist agents are at work in this school."

"And it is a pleasure to have you, Sir Vogel," Freya replied, as graciously as she could. She tried extremely hard not to twitch at how every part of this exchange, especially when Vogel called them "proper young ladies," was reminding her of *that night.* It was a sentiment all the sisters were sharing. "Two of my sisters have just prepared tea for you and your men. Would you like some?"

"Of course!" Vogel cheered, pulling a small flask out of his pocket and handing it to Christine to fill with tea. The other members of Vogel's squad followed. It was not long until all of Vogel's men were drinking the tea, and boasting to the die Fürstin sisters about jobs they had done as part of the HY.

"And then there was that teacher at our school, the one who was making the big deal about Christmas, remember Captain Vogel?"

"Yes, I do, Hendrick," Vogel laughed. "She made a big stink about removing the decorations for the Christmas celebration, as if anyone *believes* those myths anymore. Christmas is the 'Festival of the Family.' As a teacher, she should be 'educating' herself on the true ways our people should be celebrating the holiday. Have you read the latest memo on it?"

"We have. I hope you enjoy it, Sir Vogel," Freya trembled, pouring him another cup of tea. The other sisters easily understood Freya's anger and discomfort, both because the HY squad was so close to them and with hearing more about how Christmas—now barely two months away—was being corrupted by the Nazis.

For all of the die Fürstin sisters, Christmas had always been a Christian celebration. And before *that night,* they also enjoyed celebrating Hanukkah with the Cohens. But now the Nazis wanted to convert it into a winter solstice festival worshiping Hitler and the "proud German people," and wanted it to be run with the help of the BdM with no religious ceremonies. The die Fürstin sisters wanted nothing to do with any of it.

"If I may, Sir Vogel, what did you and your *brave men* do with all those Christmas decorations?" Wanda asked.

"They're in a storeroom on the northwest side of the island near an old mansion with a large bomb shelter beneath it." Vogel yawned, his expression suddenly turning droopy. "The Party commissioned it yesterday and put the symbol for the Nazi Thule Men's Club on it. We stored everything there. We collected piles of useless gold, silver, and glass baubles that are going to be recommissioned for the war effort along with some other junk. Nothing of any value."

I wouldn't say that, Wanda thought, a scheme entering her mind.

"Well, my men and I need to be taking up our positions," Vogel continued, his eye blinking from the drug's effects. "I will personally position myself outside your door in case something happens to trouble you proper young ladies. Have a pleasant evening."

"Yes, we will," Freya chimed as Vogel led his HY troop out of the room. A few minutes later, they heard a chair bang up against the wall next to their door as the cry for "Light's Out" was issued across the school.

"How fast do you think it takes that medicine to work on them?" Maud asked. "The lot of them looked like they were getting ready to fall asleep soon after they took it."

"I'll find out," Vita volunteered, creeping to the door and opening it slightly to check on Vogel. She found his eyes shut, and his body slumped in his chair, a soft snore coming from him.

"He's out," Vita proclaimed to the relief of her sisters who wasted no time opening the servants' passage and getting their doubles ready so they could enjoy a night of swing.

| 23 |

"Can you believe how pompous those HY jerks were acting?" Maud asked sarcastically once they reached the grotto. "'You may call me Sir Vogel, I can personally say…that it is our most exalted duty and pleasure to watch over you tonight.' Is it just me, or did any of you also want to punch him in his smug face once he started belching that garbage?"

"Me, too," the other sisters announced simultaneously.

"But enough about those fools," Freya proclaimed as she stepped into a boat. "Let them sleep the night away and then explain to Mrs. Kahn and the other bigwigs why they couldn't keep their eyes open for the night. That's also assuming they'll even admit to it. As for us, the night is young, and we have a lot of swinging to do."

"I've also got an idea for the next place we can raid tonight," Wanda added, climbing into the same boat as Freya.

"And what is it?" Christine asked.

"You heard how Vogel was bosting about a bunch of Christmas decorations 'and other junk' that they were going to scrap for the war effort?"

"The word he used was 'recommissioned,'" Vita sneered, imitating Vogel's pompous voice.

"Exactly," Wanda confirmed. "I was thinking we could raid that warehouse and take the decorations and whatever else they could be stockpiling there. We could use them in our own Christmas Swing Party in a few weeks."

"I like that idea," Marianne chimed as she climbed into another boat. "I would love to see a *real* Christmas party instead of this solstice celebration the Nazis are trying to institute. But personally, I think your idea needs to be bigger."

"How so?" Wanda asked.

"Instead of just doing a Christmas swing party for us, why don't we make it the most extravagant and public swing party yet and invite the whole town."

"That's just begging the Nazis to arrest us," Barbara warned.

"We just have multiple parties then," Will suggested. "I like the idea, and that storehouse they mentioned sounds like it's near our club's 'B' site. If we raid it, I doubt the Nazis would think we would hide their loot only a short walk away from where it was taken. That might actually be the last place they would suspect."

"Well then, let's get to the club and ask everyone else about it," Freya encouraged. "If everyone else likes the idea, then we'll do it tonight. Let's go!"

The sisters were soon onboard the boats and rowing into town with Wanda's plan and Marianne's and Will's suggestions bubbling in their minds. The Swing Club's music was playing loudly as they approached the mansion and the shelter beneath it, with Old Kludge guarding the door as usual. Yet, once he saw them approaching, he abandoned the door and ran inside to the puzzlement of all of them.

What was that all about? Wanda wondered, a sentiment shared by all of her sisters that only grew as the other members of the Swing Club soon rushed out to meet them and bombard them with questions.

"Who was at your school tonight?"

"Did the sleeping medicine work?"

"Are you sure no one saw you leave Linden Academy?"

"Were you followed?"

The same questions came from so many different voices that none of the sisters could tell who they were coming from.

"Everyone be quiet!" Old Kludge screamed, his squeaky voice sounding so bad that it hurt everyone's ears. "Let the girls speak."

"Thank you, Old Kludge," Freya gasped before retelling the events of the evening. Wanda noticed that while Freya told everyone about Vogel, including the success of the sleeping medication, and Wanda's plans for a Christmas swing party—complete with Marianne's and

Will's suggestions—she left out the part about how they snuck out of Linden Academy.

That's the one part of our lives we can't afford to reveal, Wanda realized, listening to Freya. *If anyone knew about the grotto and the servants' passage, it would not only put us at risk but them as well. If the Nazis think they might know how we get in and out of Linden Academy, who knows what they would do to them to force the information out of them?*

"So, are sure you weren't followed?" Frankie asked, a look of worry clearly etched on his face.

"They would need to have been invisible and be able to swim as fast as we can row," Freya reassured him. "Try not to worry so much. But anyway, what do you think of our Christmas swing party idea?"

"I like it," Frankie cheered, a sentiment soon shared by the other members of the Swing Club.

"I also know where that warehouse Vogel mentioned is located," Old Sport added, a mischievous look appearing on his face. "That bastard Vogel and his HY shmucks go to my school and have been a constant pain in my backside from the moment we first crossed paths. Before school let out, he was boasting about how he was not only going to be staying at Linden Academy tonight but that he *personally* helped stock that warehouse. I would love to see his smug face tomorrow after learning that he not only slept through his duty but that the warehouse he was so proud of had been burglarized. Let's do it!"

The sisters and other members of the Swing Club started to make their way toward the warehouse. Since Old Sport knew Vogel from school and where the warehouse was located, he led the group through the night until they reached the northwestern coast of the island. The northwest corner of the island was set slightly apart from the main city with only a few abandoned buildings and a drop down to what could have been a private beach. The whole place felt eerie like something out of a ghost story.

"What was this part of town?" Karma asked.

"Before the monarchy fell, it was the private residences of members of the nobility when they would visit," Old Sport explained. "My grandparents used to tell me stories about how the whole city would fly into an uproar whenever they came to town. After the monarchy fell, the property was seized by the government. Once the depression hit, the men in power decided to let the place rot instead of trying to fix it up since it served no purpose."

"I'm surprised you never used any of these buildings for a swing party," Vita added. "The place is isolated enough."

"We'll show you why we never used it," Frankie explained, leading them up to a point overlooking Lake Constance. He produced a pair of binoculars. "You can't see them that well at night, but look straight along the shoreline with these, and you'll see what we're talking about."

Vita took the binoculars and looked where Frankie indicated and almost shouted at what she spotted.

"Are those zeppelins?" Vita asked before passing the binoculars to each of her sisters.

"They are," Frankie confirmed. "There is a large zeppelin facility on the shore away from the island. Because of its location, you don't see any of them taking off or landing unless you are on this side of the island. But it's *because* the facility is here that everyone in town thinks an air raid might happen. When it was built, the bigwigs claimed that since it was a small facility set on the border of Switzerland that it wouldn't be a target. That Insel was set far enough from the factory that even if it were attacked, the town would be missed. You've noticed by now how much the townspeople have trusted that claim."

"Not at all," Wanda answered, looking through the binoculars herself and seeing the facility. "I also understand why you never had a swing dance here now. There are probably guards watching that facility even now. I imagine any kind of major disturbance would be spotted and reported. That said, how do we know there aren't soldiers over there watching us right now?"

"We don't," Old Sport replied, worry now in his voice. "Like you said, it's why we never did anything on this part of the island before and why I think we shouldn't waste any more time here than we have to. Let's keep moving."

Old Sport quickly led the group away from the beach and back into the abandoned buildings until they eventually came to one with a dagger and swastika painted on it.

"This is it," Old Sport cheered as he hopped down to the storehouse. "That pompous Vogel was *supposed* to set a guard on this storehouse. Instead, he bragged about how 'no one goes to the royal quarter anymore. The junk we collected isn't going anywhere yet.' I would love to see his face when he gets the news tomorrow."

Me, too, Wanda mused. She imagined Vogel and his men panicking because the storehouse was burglarized. It almost made her break out laughing.

"Help me break this door open," Old Sport asked, putting Old Kludge, Frankie, Will, and Maud working on a different part of the door. Old Kludge provided tools they used to break the lock and force their way into the storehouse. Once inside, Old Kludge lit a candle to illuminate its contents to the wonderment of everyone.

"Wow!" Wanda gasped, a sentiment shared equally by everyone.

The storehouse was filled with silver, gold, and glass Christmas decorations that sparkled like diamonds in the candlelight. Old Kludge's candle also revealed candle stands, crucifixes, and nativity sets taken from churches, menorahs stolen from synagogues, and dozens of brass instruments; enough for several swing bands.

"I know," Old Sport whispered, breaking the silence. "And that bastard Vogel called this 'junk' that was going to be 'recommissioned for the war effort.' Let's get it out of here and back to the B site."

Everyone worked quickly, but reverently, to gather everything in the storehouse and take it back to the site, leaving a big "Swing 12 was here" signature over the Nazi emblem before they left. Wanda and her sisters could understand why everyone felt they needed to treat what they were carrying with special care.

These decorations, religious pieces, and instruments are as much a victim of the Nazis as the Cohens, the people they hurt on that night, *and the workers laboring for them,* Wanda thought to herself as she carefully carried two boxes of ornaments away from the storehouse. *The Nazis would just destroy these to fuel their war, all because they don't fit into the world they are trying to create for themselves. If they ever turn that ideology against the people, killing the people they don't want—and if the people they do want go along with it—then God save us if it's right that He should do so.*

| 24 |

By the time everything was moved to the B site, it was almost time for the sisters to start making their way back to Linden Academy. Yet, considering how close they still were to the storehouse, Wanda and a few of her sisters still had doubts about storing everything there.

"Are you sure Vogel, or any other Nazi thug, isn't going to find our B site and everything we stashed in it?" Maud asked, voicing the question not only on her mind, but also on Wanda's mind, too.

"Absolutely," Old Sport reassured them. "Vogel is not the type to think that you would steal something only to hide it right next to where it was taken from. He would be more likely to believe that the crooks would have to be completely stupid to hide something in the most accessible and obvious spot. You'll see what I mean if you get the chance to see how he reacts to the burglary. Just relax and get back to Linden Academy and try and get some sleep before the wake-up call and someone realizes you're gone."

"That sounds like a great idea to me," Karma yawned, bringing a round of laughter to the other sisters as they said their good-byes and left.

The early morning was dark and foggy throughout the town with hardly a soul on the street. But that did not stop the die Fürstin sisters from dancing through the streets to make sure they were not being followed, and every one of them knew they had to be more on guard now than ever before. Thankfully, no one followed them. They arrived at their docked boats and were soon back on Lake Constance heading toward the grotto leading up to school.

The waters of Lake Constance were calm and quiet except for the sound of patrol boats in the distance. Thankfully, the morning fog kept the sisters from being spotted by anyone on the water. The school now seemed to loom over the lake the closer they approached it.

Why do I suddenly feel nervous? Wanda asked herself as a feeling of dread blew through her. *We've snuck out to swing and to stick it to the Nazis through our Swing 12 activities before. Each time we came back to Linden Academy towering over us like it is now. So, why is it that* this *time it's giving me a bad feeling?*

Wanda did not want to admit it to herself, but she knew what was giving her a bad feeling, and it was not the school. It was Vogel and his men. There was no way to tell if the sleeping medication worked for as long as they were hoping. Vogel could have easily woken up partway through the night, found them gone, and be waiting for them right now. The final test of its effectiveness would be when they returned and saw for themselves whether or not he and his men were still sleeping where they left them. Wanda and her sisters docked the boats in the grotto. She noticed the same apprehensive look she was positive was now on her face.

They're worried about the same thing as me, Wanda realized as they changed and made their way back up to their room. None of them was sure about what they would find once they got there. Thankfully, opening the servants' passage, they found the room exactly how they left it. After stashing their replacement dummies, closing the servants' passage, and hiding it again, Freya peered out of their room. She found Vogel and his men still sleeping just like they left them, only now they were slumped over and nearly falling out of their chairs. Closing the door behind her, she let out a long-held breath. The sisters knew now that the medication had worked and that they could now get a few hours of sleep before facing the next grueling day. But as they closed their eyes, a single humorous thought passed through each of their minds, the look on Vogel's and his men's faces when they woke up.

***

"Get up!"

The die Fürstin sisters reacted and started getting dressed before they realized the order was not meant for them.

"You call yourself the future. Is this how the future is supposed to act? Sleeping on duty. Do you need a few lessons in duty?"

"I'm guessing that must be Vogel's superior in the HY," Barbara mumbled as she pointed toward the door.

"You know what your orders are in regards to the proper German girls of this school. Tell me, how do you expect to carry out those orders if you are sleeping on duty!"

"Sir! There is no excuse for our dereliction. However, I can personally assure you that the die Fürstin sisters are exactly the kind of proper girls Germany needs."

"I'll be the judge of that," Vogel's superior said before barging into the sisters' room to find all twelve dressed with their beds made as if they were waiting for an inspection, which they were.

"Good morning, sir. How may we assist you today?" Freya asked, taking the lead.

"Humph, well, at least you look presentable," Vogel's superior scoffed as he walked between them and scrutinized each one of them carefully. "I admit I'm impressed that you are all up and ready to go before the 4:45 AM wake-up."

"It is all to serve the proud Folk and the Fatherland," Freya replied.

And because you woke us up when you started raving at Vogel, Wanda almost wanted to blurt out, fighting hard to not roll her eyes at Freya's over the top performance for the sake of Vogel's superior.

"However, I've noticed that each of you are wearing worn-out shoes. Can you explain to me why your shoes have become so worn out?"

"We just had to move quickly to prepare ourselves for you this morning," Freya answered honestly. "Not only that, but seeing to the needs of Vogel and his men the night before and accomplishing our own duties also required a great deal of movement. It should only be natural that our shoes would become worn out after so much work."

"Really, so the twelve of you were *seeing* to the needs of Vogel and his men, and it took a great deal of *movement.* Perhaps one of you might be able to enlighten me on the meaning of that."

"We wouldn't dare dishonor any of them," Vogel started to protest before another HY member ran into the die Fürstin sisters' room and whispered in his ear. Vogel immediately turned white as his mouth dropped open and his face contorted from shock into an extremely panicked expression.

Vogel must have just found out about our raid. Wanda figured, trying very hard not to snicker and feeling very satisfied with seeing his expression with her own eyes. *First, he gets in trouble with his superior thanks to our sleeping medicine. Now, that superior think they were fooling around with us all night—only worsening their reputation. The only way this could be perfect would be if...*

"Care to tell me what just happened, Vogel?"

His superior tried to find out about what happened last night. Wanda mused, finishing her thought as she watched Vogel fry under his superior's gaze.

"No, sir. It's nothing that you need to concern yourself with."

"Then tell me, Vogel, why do you look like I'm about to shoot you? I will be the judge of what concerns me and what doesn't. Now tell me before I ask your subordinate directly, what happened, that's an order!"

"Yes, sir," Vogel conceded, his face a mix of terror and defeat. "It's just a small matter really. Someone broke into a junk-filled warehouse."

"Someone broke into a junk-filled warehouse?" Vogel's superior repeated, clearly not convinced. Both he and the sisters were thinking the same thing, that Vogel was trying to mitigate the event and not reveal too much about it.

"Which 'junk-filled warehouse' had the misfortune of being broken into?"

"The one on the northwestern corner of the island in the abandoned nobility district."

"The one that was *supposed* to be guarded? Correct?"

"Yes, sir."

"And why wasn't it?"

"Well, sir, no one goes to that district, so my men and I thought..."

"If you and your men were thinking they would have thought that an abandoned district that no one goes to would be the perfect place to steal from and left a guard there!" Vogel's superior barked in outrage. "Because of your stupidity, resources that could have been used to fight the enemy are now in the enemy's hands."

"I'll find them!" Vogel panicked. "If the enemy wanted to get the material away from the warehouse, they would have used boats to move it along the coast of the island; we will find them *right now*. Men, let's go!"

Vogel and his men raced out of the room, leaving the sisters alone with Vogel's superior officer and trying hard to keep the shock and humor from their faces.

"I apologize for that outburst just now," Vogel's superior claimed. He changed personas so quickly it would have surprised the sisters if they had not seen similar shifts since *that night*. "I hope proper young girls like yourself understand that when one is the leader of men, it requires one to be firm with them at times."

"Of course," Freya replied. "It is all for the good of the Folk and the Fatherland."

"Well said, young lady. Excuse me."

Vogel's superior turned and left the sisters alone in their room. A few minutes later, after they were sure he was gone, and that nobody else was around, they all released a collectively held breath, laughing over their recent encounter.

| 25 |

"I have to admit, I'm actually surprised that it worked." Wanda laughed as she changed clothes with her sisters. "And even more surprised that it's *still* working."

It had been three nights since the die Fürstin sisters drugged Vogel and his men, and since then, two more HY patrols had attempted to watch them only to be subdued in the same way.

"We better not push our luck, though," Marianne advised. "After the Christmas party, we might want to lay low for a bit or let the HY boys have a night of watching us before anyone notices a pattern in which boys sleep the nights Swing 12 is active."

"I'd rather face the whole German Army than let those creeps watch me sleep," Will spit in disgust.

"Me, too," Maud agreed.

"I never intended that *we* weren't going to keep watch on them as well," Marianne clarified.

"Anyway," Freya interrupted, trying to change the conversation. "Now that we have all three sights chosen for the Christmas Swing Party, it's time we get to work on getting the word out around town."

The sisters nodded in agreement, making their way back up the stairs and through the passageway to their room. Over the last few nights, they had split up to look for the best places across the island where they could host their Christmas swing party. It was unanimously decided that the Swing Club's B site would already host one party. As for the other two, Freya's group found an abandoned yet enchanting set of gardens in the corner of the island that used to be reserved for the monarchy, which would function as the main party. Wanda's group also found the ruins of an old church that would act as one of the decoy parties along with the B site.

"How many of these flyers do you think the boys will be able to spread around?" Vita asked, a bundle of party flyers in her arms.

"A better question is, how many are *we* going to get the chance to hand out?" Karma replied sarcastically. "And that's assuming we even get to hand them out at all. Personally, I'm just glad we were able to make them. Remind me to send a letter to the Propaganda Department."

The sisters almost broke into laughter at that comment. The "party flyers" were actually propaganda posters they had spent the last few nights tearing down while leaving their "Swing 12" signature. But as they made their way back to their room, the question about spreading the posters across town lingered on all their minds.

Karma's right, Wanda thought to herself. *It's not like Mrs. Kahn is just going to send us all out into town today.*

***

"I'm sending you all out into town today," Mrs. Kahn announced to the gawking stares of the sisters and almost every other girl in Linden Academy's morning assembly. "With Christmas upon us, we, as well as other schools and organizations in the area, have been issued a memo on the 'Organization of the Folk's Christmas Eve Ceremonies.' I want all of you to deliver these instructions to every home and community center in town. You will be working alongside other schools so it will not take the whole day. I expect you to be completed by lunch. Above all else, I want you to be sure that the Folk understands that we do not want a *religious* ceremony. Instead, the Folk should think of this season as the winter solstice, the return of the light, and similarly remember how our people, soldiers, and especially our Führer, are struggling against the dark powers surrounding them to return us to the light. You have your instructions. Refer to your copies of the memo for more detailed instructions. Dismissed."

***

"I don't believe this," Wanda mumbled. It was half an hour since the assembly, and the sisters were on a bus together heading into town. Since then, Wanda had read the memo with a more detailed list of instructions for them three times.

"What part?" Maud asked sarcastically. She already knew Wanda's answer.

"All of it," Wanda replied. "Look at this, specific days and times for 'important guests.' Trees have to be 'especially beautiful' and decorated with candies, cookies, apples, and homemade ornaments made out of straw, garland, pinecones, and runes. Even the gifts have to conform to what the Nazis want with baking goods for families and candy for children with toys only permitted for children under ten."

"Don't forget the 'Silent Night' rewrite they want us to sing," Vita spit out in disgust. "They've turned a beautiful Christmas song into a propagandist speech about how 'Only the Chancellor stays on guard,' and that 'Adolf Hitler is Germany's Star.' I genuinely feel like I'm going to throw up just from reading this."

"Keep your voices down!" Freya murmured before checking the bus's other passengers. They were all engaged in their own conversations, and the supervisors riding with them did not seem to notice their *particular* conversation. "Do you want to get us all in trouble? Keep your complaints to yourselves. Trust me, you're not the only ones who share them. Just be thankful for the opportunity this service is providing us."

Freya's right, Wanda realized, understanding now that she and her sister were complaining a little too loudly for their own good. *We can't let our disagreements become public knowledge. All it would take would be one report from one of the other students or supervisors that there are anti-Nazi supporters in Linden Academy. Then we would all be in trouble. We might as well just shout that we are Swing 12.*

"Sorry, Freya," Wanda whispered, now feeling far more cautious than she was before. "And you're right, we are all thankful for the service we are providing. This errand is going to allow us to distribute lots of *useful information.*"

Freya and the other sisters giggled quietly over Wanda's comment, not only because they considered the information in the memo to be complete drivel, but also because they were using this trip to distribute information about the Christmas swing party. Each stack of memos that they were carrying was also laced with flyers for their party. The plan was to drop or post a flyer wherever they went as inconspicuously as possible. At least three sisters would travel together at any given time so one could plant the swing flyer, and the other two could cover her while she did it so no one would notice her.

I just hope a lot of people will come to the party. Wanda thought to herself, imagining what the party would be like. *Between the War, and the Nazi's policies, we all need this. Not to mention when we do pull it off, it will be the biggest stunt Swing 12 has ever accomplished and will really tick off the Nazi bigwigs.*

Wanda, nor any of her sisters, wanted to admit that the idea of their party being successful and ticking off the Nazis because it was exactly the kind of celebration they *didn't* want to have excited her more than the season itself. She knew what Christmas was supposed to be about. But imagining the Nazi bigwigs' faces when they realized the people were celebrating a *real* Christmas party, instead of the warped ceremony they were trying to create, excited her more than anything.

"I just can't wait to get started," Wanda mumbled as their bus stopped in front of the first stop, the ration office.

"Squad 1, disembark and begin handing out your information. Be sure to obey the orders of your squad leaders. We will be back to pick you up after we have dropped off all the remaining squads. Squad 1, dismissed."

Squad 1 consisted of Wanda, Karma, several other girls, and one of their eldest sisters, Barbara, the Squad Leader. The ration office had a line going out the door and around the corner, twice. The past few days had seen the cold take a turn for the worse. Everyone was exchanging as many ration cards they had managed to store up for the food and clothing needed for the coming winter. Wanda was a little shocked and amazed by the site.

So many people in need of food and basic necessities, Wanda marveled. *Meanwhile, instead of helping, our country fights a world war and wants us to put on this Nazi-oriented celebration. When will it all end?*

Wanda was so lost in her thoughts that she did not notice the man next to her until she bumped into him, spilling both her own and the man's ration forms on the ground.

"I'm sorry!" Wanda hastily apologized, bending down to pick up her own forms—before anyone could see the swing flyers, and the man's forms as well. "I didn't see you there... Silent Night!"

It might have been a while since she had seen him at the Swing Club, but it was definitely Silent Night. But he looked older now, dirtier, more rugged, almost like he had aged several years in the several days since she last saw him. Silent Night, however, did not openly react to her. Instead, he just picked up his forms, pocketing one of the Christmas swing party flyers, and handing the rest back to Wanda.

"Thank you," Wanda replied, taking the flyers and walking away to find Barbara running up to her side.

"Wanda," Barbara whispered. "Is that…"

"It is," Wanda replied. "He took one of our *special* flyers but didn't seem to recognize me beyond that. But he looks a lot older than the last time I saw him."

"It's a disguise," Barbara explained. "Through the club, I've heard of several tricks that families have used since the war started to get more food from the ration office. Disguises, forged reports of bomb damage, breaking in to steal and butcher the meat itself, all things people have done to keep their stomachs full in the wake of this war. The best thing we can do is not spoil his job and hope he doesn't spoil ours. Now, let's get back to spreading these *special* flyers around."

"Okay, Barbara," Wanda agreed. She did not give another look to Silent Night.

| 26 |

"This will be the night I deliver you the members of Swing 12."

The informant, wearing a mask to hide his face and voice from the other Nazi bigwigs present in the room, presented them with a flyer. It detailed the locations of three Christmas swing parties that Swing 12 would be hosting.

"This information is superb," one of the bigwigs gleefully replied. "With this, we will be able to send patrols to all three sites where these hooligans will be gathering and capture them all. Along with whomever else they have desecrated with this 'Jungle Music' of theirs."

"With all due respect, gentlemen," the informant interrupted, "simply sending in a squad of police and HY cadets won't be enough to capture Swing 12."

"You doubt our proud German police and the Hitler Youth?" Another bigwig gasped in shock. "You should know better than anyone how reliable they are."

"I do know how reliable they are," the informant replied.

Especially when dealing with those you determine to be real *enemies,* he added privately to himself, the nightmare of the "pig farm" still as fresh in his mind as it was when he left.

"I also know how good Swing 12 is at avoiding both the police and the HY."

The informant knew he was pressing his luck with his comments. The looks on the bigwigs' faces was proof of that. But if he was going to get what he wanted from them, he knew he needed to take more than a couple of risks.

"If you raid the three events," the informant continued, "you'll capture swing kinds, hooligans, and whatever members of the Folk who are being drawn to their ways. But *the* swing kids that you want, the members of Swing 12, will disappear into the confusion, and you'll never see them again."

"Then Swing 12 must be made up of a bunch of cowards," one of the bigwigs joked, bringing the others to a laugh.

If you only knew, the informant mused.

"So, if you don't think our proud German police or the HY would be able to capture Swing 12, how do you intend to do it? How do you even know so much about them to begin with?"

That was the question the informant did not want to be asked. He knew that if he revealed that he himself was a swing kid and knew Swing 12's identity from the start, he would be subject to the same punishment as them, or worse.

"How I know is part of how I will deliver them to you," the informant answered, choosing to be as vague as possible. "You have trusted in my plan to this point, so I ask that you keep trusting it and grant me the reward that I was promised, the opportunity to choose the battlefield upon which I fight for Germany. And the chance, before I go, to leave an heir so that my family line may continue. I will deliver you Swing 12 on *this night.* If I can't, do with me as you see fit."

The bigwigs looked at him like a meal they were about to devour, and he knew it.

I've just promised them Swing 12, and I've used my life as collateral, the informant fretted. *Unfortunately, these bastards won't take me seriously* unless *I take that big of a risk. If my plan fails, they can do whatever they want to me; they could even send me back to the "pig farm."*

Going back to the "pig farm," either to work there, or worse, chilled him to his core, even more so than fighting on any battlefield.

But if it does work and I deliver Swing 12 to them, then I'll be able to spare all of them that fate. Now, I just have to hope the girls act the way I'm expecting them to act.

| 27 |

"Tonight's the night." Wanda merrily sung to herself as she, Karma, Vita, and Christine, walked back to their room after supper.

"Why don't you sing it a little louder?" Vita poked. "I don't think they can hear you yet in Berlin."

The four sisters laughed at the comment. They knew Wanda was not singing loud enough for anyone to hear them, and they were all excited about tonight. After passing out the flyers announcing their Christmas swing party, the eldest and middle sisters had been going out in shifts every night to prepare the event sites while the rest of them slept. And with their "protector" drugged every night to the point where he was asleep, the sisters knew they would be able to sleep soundly. But tonight was different. Tonight was the night of the Christmas swing party. It was also going to be the first time any of the youngest sisters saw how the main site was decorated.

"What do you think it's going to look like?" Christine asked.

"We're just going to have to wait until we get there to find out," Karma replied. She was also eager but hid it better as the four of them returned to their room. Several of their sisters were waiting for them, looked slightly disturbed.

"What's wrong?" the four of them asked in unison.

"We might have a 'complication' involving tonight," Will answered.

"What kind of complication?" Wanda pressed until the door opened. Mrs. Kahn entered their room with Freya and a very familiar face none of the sisters ever expected to see in Linden Academy.

"Good evening, ladies," Mrs. Kahn announced. "Your sister Freya and I wanted to personally introduce the HY cadet who will be protecting you tonight. This is Alvis von Bron."

"It is my esteemed honor and pleasure. It's my duty to meet and protect proper young ladies like yourself from the foreign influences that are worming their way into the Folk and Fatherland. Especially now during this Festival of the Family when the Folk must be united against the influences that threaten them."

The sisters did not know what was shocking them more. That this Alvis von Bron, who they already knew as the swing boy Frankie and Freya's boyfriend, was standing in their room; that he was a HY cadet, dressed in the exact same uniform they had seen other HY cadets in; that he was spouting the same drivel as Vogel and his troop not too long ago, or the whole bizarre picture it all made together. One thing was for sure, they were going to find out.

"Well, you have an hour and a half for your leisurely activities, so I'll leave you to get acquainted," Mrs. Kahn said as she turned to leave the room. "I trust that you will stay awake for one night, unlike your predecessors."

"I can assure you, Mrs. Kahn, I will do my duty to both the Folk and to the Fatherland. I will properly guard these twelve proper young ladies throughout the night without fail," Alvis replied as Mrs. Kahn left the room, only to soon find himself assaulted by a dozen sisters with a battery of questions.

"What are you doing here?" Freya asked.

"What are you doing in that uniform?" Will gasped.

"Have you been in the Hitler Youth all along?" Maud demanded.

"Are you playing a game with us?" Vita challenged.

"Is this a joke to you?" Barbara wondered.

"How many more of you are in the HY?" Karma demanded.

The questions kept coming, one after another, that Alvis did not know where to start. He was overwhelmed by the entire experience.

"Enough!" Alvis shouted. "If everyone would just be quiet for a few minutes, I'll explain everything."

"Five minutes," Freya said. The sisters may have decided to let him speak, but anyone could tell they were still angry. Alvis, or Frankie as they knew him, was Freya's boyfriend, a swing boy, and a member of the Lake Constance Swing Club before Swing 12 was formed. It was no secret he hated the Hitler Youth. So, to find out that he was a *member* of that organization, something that none of the sisters—including Freya—even knew about, was a shocking surprise.

"First, I did not want to be here tonight. My school's principal sprung it on me at the last minute, so there was no way I could talk my way out of it, trade with someone, or fake an illness without it looking too suspicious. Believe me, I wanted to be at the party tonight with you, too. Second, yes, I'm in the HY, and I've always been in the HY. A lot of the swing boys at the Lake Constance Swing Club were members. Old Sport, Old George, and J. B. were all members of the HY. It's why they hate the HY so much, and its members hate them; because they used to be on the same side. I stayed in the HY so I could keep watch on their movements and tell the other members of the Swing Club when they were up to something. You remember when Winnie was almost assaulted by those HY bastards in the alley. How did you think I knew how to get to her. I knew that patrol was going to be out there. They've bragged before about chasing women into that alley. That's how I knew where to find you. Besides, what do I have to gain by playing you? If I was working against you, I would have already turned you in a long time ago, wouldn't I? Freddie, you know I'm telling the truth."

"Enough, *Alvis*," Freya replied. "You wait outside. The twelve of us need to talk."

Alvis did as he was told. He turned around, dejected, and left the sisters alone to discuss what they were going to do now that they knew *this* detail of his daytime life.

"I'll get the sleeping drops," Will stated, not wanting to listen to anyone else's opinion. "Maud, you brew the tea. *Alvis* needs a double helping."

"On it."

"Now hold on, you two," Freya interjected.

"What!" Will and Maud shouted.

"This revelation is a surprise," Freya explained. "But don't you think it could be useful to us."

The other sisters looked at her confusedly.

"Yes, he's HY, but he's still Frankie. He's still the same boy many of us have known for years now. The same guy who helped us save Wanda from that HY squad in the alley, who helped us raid that Nazi bigwigs' home and give food to the poor, and who has helped us on every Swing 12 job we've pulled. Who better to trust with covering for us? Like he said, if he wanted to turn us in, he could have done it a long time ago. Don't forget, he *gave* us that sleeping medicine to begin with, to use against other HY cadets. Why would he do that if he wasn't on our side? What could he have been waiting for?"

"The opportune moment to catch us here," Will reasoned.

"Agreed," Karma added. "The other swing kids might have figured out we went to Linden Academy, but we never told them our real names or how we got out."

"But both Freya and Frankie make valid points," Asta chimed in. "We've known him for years, and he was the one who gave us the medicine. If I had to pick someone to stand guard outside our bedroom, he would definitely be my first pick. We were also just talking about how after the Christmas Party, we might want to lay off drugging the HY cadets for a while. We can start by not drugging Frankie, maybe even give him a glowing recommendation about how we felt safe with him here. The bigwigs might keep sending him back. It would be great to have someone we can trust outside that door."

"Exactly!" Freya cheered.

"But, he is still HY," Barbara reminded them. "Remember, they were also present during *that night,* and we saw how they treat the people who thought they could trust. Personally, I wouldn't trust him now at all."

"Me, neither," Vita agreed.

And there's still the possibility of a mole in the Swing Club, Wanda wondered, remembering the night she was assaulted by those HY cadets.

Several members of the club left about the same time I did. Old Sport, Old George, and J. B., who had a bad run-in with the HY that night, were also former HY cadets. What if one of them still is? Frankie claims he is a double agent for us, but could he be the only one in the club?

"This is getting us nowhere!" Margret shouted. "There are just too many reasons, both for and against, to make a decision anytime soon. Let's just do the American thing and put it to a vote, and we go with whatever the outcome is."

"What if some of us want to abstain from voting?" Marianne asked.

"You can abstain, just so long as we have a decision," Margret clarified.

"Sounds good to me," Rita added. "I'll get a hat and some paper."

Rita picked up both a hat and some paper from the foot of her bed and tore the paper into smaller pieces for her sisters to vote on whether to trust Alvis or not.

"Write a 'T' for 'Trust' a 'D' for 'Drug' and leave your slip blank if you want to abstain," Rita explained as the sisters went to pick up a pen or pencil to cast their votes. Looking around, Wanda could already guess some of her sister's votes before they cast them.

Freya wants *to trust him,* Wanda realized, gazing at the pained look on her sister's face. *She wants to believe in the swing boy she's known for years and that the HY uniform is merely another costume. Will and Maud, on the other hand, are a different story. Once they saw Frankie in that uniform, they decided on whether or not they could trust him. But the real question is, do I?*

Wanda eventually decided to abstain from voting and left her ballet blank. She had too many reasons in her mind both to trust and doubt him. After all of the votes were collected, Rita counted them and announced the results.

"Five in favor of drugging him, four in favor of trusting him, and three abstaining. That settles it. Will, prepare the tea."

"With pleasure," Will smiled, happy at the outcome.

"I'll take it to him myself," Freya grumbled, equally unhappy with the outcome as she gazed at her sisters with a wondering judgmental look. She wanted to know why her sisters could not have more faith in Frankie and which ones abstained from voting.

If me and one more of the abstaining votes had chosen to trust Frankie, we would have turned the decision completely around. Wanda realized, now sorry she did not vote at all. *Is this what it is like in America when no one votes?*

Wanda did not have much time to think about her decision as Will presented Freya with the drugged tea to give to Frankie.

We might have just sacrificed our most trustworthy ally. Is this really the right thing to do?

Freya did not think so as she walked out to where Frankie was sitting near the window. Curious, and doubting her decision, Wanda peered around the door to watch their exchange.

"They don't trust me, do they?" Frankie asked.

"Not all of them," Freya mourned. "But can you blame them? This is a surprise none of us expected."

"Believe me," Frankie begged, "I did not want you to find out about this. I had hoped we would be in Switzerland long before a situation like this ever happened. Unfortunately, circumstances don't always allow us to make the choices we want to."

"Believe me, I understand *that* all too well," Freya said exasperatedly. "That said, I hope you enjoy this tea my sisters and I made for you. Just know, I still trust you."

"Thank you," Frankie replied, taking the tea. "This tea has the sleeping medicine in it, doesn't it?"

Freya nodded slightly. But even without doing so, the shame on her face was more telling than any word or action could be.

"It's okay, Freddie. I understand. Let me just say this one more time. I'm sorry you found out this way. We don't always get to make our own choices. Just know, I'm always looking out for you and your sisters."

"I do trust you, Frankie," Freya exhaled. "Have a good night."

Freya turned around and started walking away from Frankie. Frankie, spotting Wanda at the door, saluted her slightly with the teacup before drinking it. Walking together back into the room, Freya seemed more at peace now than she had a few minutes ago.

"Are you alright?" Rita asked.

"I am now," Freya replied. "I'm sure now Frankie understands why we drugged him, and even more that he's going to be on our side, no matter what might happen."

"I just hope you're right," Rita replied.

"I just hope he drank the tea," Maud added.

"I saw him drink it," Wanda began before a loud thump from the hallway drew several of them out to check on Frankie. He was slumped in the chair, snoring loudly, with the empty teacup dropped on the floor beside him.

"He's out!" Karma exclaimed, the extra portion of the sleeping drops having done their work.

"Yes, he is," Will noted, sounding more relieved now that he was unconscious. "Now, let's go to the Christmas swing party!"

| 28 |

The die Fürstin sisters hurried into the servants' passage and down into the grotto to prepare for the Christmas party. All of them were excited, especially Wanda and her group of youngest sisters. They had not seen how the main site had been decorated yet. The coming festivities almost erased any concern they had for Frankie and what he would face because of their actions—almost.

"A shame there wasn't a way we could have brought Frankie with us," Wanda pondered aloud, still feeling guilty about abstaining from the vote.

"There is nothing you or any of us have to be ashamed about," Freya assured her. "Frankie *will* understand. I have no doubt that he knew he was going to miss the party the second he got assigned to us."

"And even if he doesn't understand, who cares?" Will interjected. "He can cry all he wants with the rest of his HY buddies."

"Here, here," Maud agreed. "Now, let's not talk about him anymore. Tonight's a night for celebration. I don't think any of us want anything to dampen tonight."

Several of the other sisters also nodded in agreement with Maud's statement. They all wanted to enjoy the Christmas swing party and forget that they had left Frankie behind asleep outside their door. Once they had learned that Frankie was an HY cadet named Alvis, their opinion of him had changed entirely. Now, all they wanted to do was swing and forget that he had arrived at Linden Academy.

"It's going to be a beautiful winter night for dancing," Wanda noted as they rowed their boats out of the grotto and onto Lake Constance. No moon or clouds were in the sky, and the stars were sparkling. The lake was also quiet, eerily quiet as no patrol boats could be heard anywhere on the water. "You know, we are all together now, and the lake doesn't seem to be guarded. You think instead of dancing tonight we should maybe make our escape to Switzerland right now?"

"And leave Frankie and the rest of our friends in the Swing Club behind? Not a chance," Freya chastised harshly. "When we escape, we escape together. Besides, there are people in town waiting for us and this party tonight. Don't you want to see what we spent the last few nights putting together?"

"Yes, I do," Wanda answered, putting more weight into the boat's oars.

But why do I have this itching feeling that we are letting a golden opportunity slip right through our fingers? She privately mused, looking across Lake Constance toward Switzerland and imagining the twelve of them rowing to the Swiss side now. Yet those feelings soon retreated to the back of Wanda's mind as they docked their boats and made their way to the main party's destination in the old royal section of town.

"Whoa!" Wanda and the other youngest sisters collectively gasped as they passed through an entryway into a garden to find the trees covered with silver tinsel and decorations. Some of the decorations were stamped with the words "25th Anniversary" on them. The whole scene made the trees look like they had turned into real silver.

"Not bad, isn't it?" Will asked, admiring the work she and the other elder sisters accomplished as the sound of Christmas swing began echoing in the air. "You remember when we liberated all those ornaments from the warehouse? When we started looking through them and organizing them, we found that a lot of them were made for the town's anniversary celebrations. So, we decided to build up the entry garden as we go to the party. Now come on. It only gets better from here."

Will was right. It did get better. The silver trees soon gave way to ones decorated with golden ornaments.

"Wow!" Vita marveled, gazing at the golden tinsel and ornaments that now decorated the trees, the music from the Christmas swing party becoming louder the closer they got to it. "When this party is over, I'm going to keep some of these decorations to remember this scenery by."

"I'm one step ahead of you, Vita," Christine piped, picking a golden ornament from a tree and placing it in a picket where a silver one twinkled brightly. "This whole scene is breathtaking. It's like you've turned this grove into something out of an American movie or a fairy tale."

"That was the idea," Asta replied, smiling as she played with a "50th Anniversary" ornament hanging in a tree. "For this party, we wanted to transform this neglected garden into something so out of the ordinary, out of place, that it would seem like it came right out of a fairy tale or a fantasy story."

"And go completely against the cookie-cutter mold the Nazis want us all to fall into," Maud added, looking equally proud. "Now come on, the best is yet to come."

"The best," Karma inquired. "You've already given us an entryway filled with silver trees and a passageway of golden trees. What's next?"

"Diamonds!" Maud shouted.

Karma and the other youngest sisters soon discovered that it was not "diamonds" but fancy glass and crystal ornaments. They were hung alongside silver tinsel decorating the trees around the clearing where the band played Christmas swing. Yet those trees sparkled like real diamonds in the moonlight. The music and fun only increased the magical feeling the whole sight invoked.

"Boys and girls, Swing 12 has arrived!" J.B. cheered to the joyous swing music, which stopped briefly so everyone could applaud and welcome them to the party. "The organizers of not only this main party but our two dummy parties which I am happy to say are going on right now without any problems. Let's all give them a warm welcome."

All of them felt both a little overwhelmed at the "warm welcome" and satisfied by it at the same time.

All of these people came to the party. Wanda marveled, seeing not only J.B., but also Old Sport, Old George, and Old Kludge coming to meet them. *Plus, who knows how many more are now at the other two dummy parties. Everyone was here just to dance, swing, and celebrate Christmas.*

"Everyone, thank you for both the welcome and for coming." Freya proclaimed shakily, unsteady about having so many people cheering and thanking her all at once. "And thank the people who wanted to be here but stayed behind to make certain we could be here."

Freya is thinking about Frankie, Wanda realized, seeing the look in her eye and hearing the longing in her voice.

"And I want to also thank the founder of our group. Without her, we wouldn't have become Swing 12 in the first place. My sister, Winnie."

Wanda blinked, suddenly self-conscious. All of the eyes and clapping from the party suddenly turned on her. Her sisters pushed her to the front of the group to receive the applause. Wanda, in return, merely waved a reply with an extremely awkward expression on her face.

"Still, we couldn't do any of this alone," Freya continued. "It was everyone here and at the other two parties who was able to make this happen. Without you, the twelve of us would just be twelve silly girls dancing by ourselves all alone. *You* are the ones who decided to take a stand. You are the ones who decided they wouldn't be fitted into the model the Nazis wanted and decided to come here instead. None of this could have been possible without you, and that should show you, show everyone, what we can all do when we get together. Now, let's get the music restarted and *swing*."

And they did. The music started again, and the sisters, along with every other guest present, began dancing. Freya danced with several boys throughout the night. She almost seemed to forget that Frankie was drugged and sleeping back at the school. Will and Maud danced with each other, and several other boys and girls. Rita and Barbara gave some of the younger swing boys a Christmas miracle by walking up to them and asking them to dance. As for the other die Fürstin sisters, they each found partners and danced through the night. By 3 o'clock in the morning, their shoes had become worn-out *again*. Also, an overcast of clouds had rolled in and covered the night sky. Taking a break from the festivities, Wanda and Rita walked to the lookout where Old Kludge had a spyglass focused on the zeppelin factory across the water.

"See anything over there, Old Kludge?" Wanda asked.

He shook his head. He did not want to use his squeaky voice unless he absolutely needed to.

"You almost sound like you want something to be out there," Rita joked, elbowing her sister playfully.

"Maybe I do," Wanda replied, causing both her sister's face to twitch and Old Kludge to look away and peer at Wanda curiously.

"What?" Rita asked.

"I know," Wanda sighed. "Call me crazy, but I just can't shake this feeling that we missed a golden opportunity to go to Switzerland tonight. One that we *should* have taken."

"Just relax, Winnie," Rita comforted her. "We will get there. Why don't you get back to the party and dance a little more? We've only got so much time left before we have to start making our way back to Linden Academy."

"Maybe you're right," Wanda conceded, turning away until a sound caught her ear. "Wait, do you hear that?"

Rita began listening out over the water. Old Kludge returned to the spyglass checking for any signs of boats. They both knew to never take any strange sounds lightly.

"Yeah, I hear it now," Rita confirmed. "It sounds like a plane."

That was the last word Rita said before an explosion rocked the zeppelin factory and sent shock waves through the party.

| 29 |

"Air raid!" Wanda, Rita, and Old Kludge screamed. The air-raid sirens blared across the island as more bombs began appearing through the clouds, exploding across both the zeppelin factory and the island.

"Why are the Allies bombing the island?" Wanda blurted out, running back to the party.

"The bombs hitting here are probably missing," Rita explained. "Besides, you really think bombs can tell what's a 'target' and what isn't once they're dropped?"

Wanda already knew they could not. She did know that it was time to get undercover or back to Linden Academy, fast. Returning to the party, Karma, Rita, and Old Kludge already found it dissolving into a chaotic mob that scattered through the trees. The bombs exploded across the island and the zeppelin plant, shaking the trees and blasting the ornaments out of them.

"Party's over, everyone back to the boats and back to Linden Academy NOW!" Freya screamed, running from the grove, as a cloud of foul-smelling smoke from the island began rolling through it. The cloud brought back terrifying memories.

This is almost like "that night," Wanda feared, racing through the smoke, losing track of her sisters and heading back to where—she hoped—the boats were docked until an explosion knocked her off her feet and blew away the smoke.

***

"Where *is* everyone!" Freya screamed, panic building as the smoke blew away, leaving only herself, Rita, Karma, Barbara, and Margret at the dock. The other sisters were unaccounted for.

"They know where the dock is. I'm sure they're coming." Margret stuttered, trying to reassure Freya. But she knew it was lip service only. With explosions and fire echoing and raging from the zeppelin plant to the town, they were all scared, scared that one or more of them would be killed in this attack and not make it back to Linden Academy. And even if they survived the attack, they all knew that soon Lake Constance would be swarming with patrol boats and the city equally filled with soldiers. They *could not* waste time looking for everyone. The more time they spent in town, the greater the chance they would be killed or captured.

"I'm going back into town to look for everyone," Barbara decided. "The rest of you get back to Linden Academy."

"Do that, and then everyone will *know* at least one of us is missing," Karma protested.

"Would you rather we all didn't go back?" Barbara challenged.

"We never should have come *here*," Rita countered. "Wanda was right. We had a perfect chance to slip into Switzerland together, and we threw it away because we wanted to party."

"It doesn't matter now," Freya shouted, silencing the argument. "What matters is that we protect as much of our family as we can, and I am not about to risk any more of us in the city that is being bombed. We have three boats, everyone knows where they are, and we can use the engines since the noise will be covered by the attack. The five of us will get back to Linden Academy and work on a cover story with Frankie to explain why, heaven forbid, some of us might not be able to leave our room. We can figure out what to do from there, but we need to leave now!"

The other sisters could tell Freya was not going to be moved from her position as she herded them onto one of the boats. But that did not mean they were happy about the situation. Barbara still wanted to go back and look for the others. Rita lamented not listening to Wanda earlier. And Karma and Margret were both unsure about the whole situation. They had always come to the city together and, even rushing, left together. Leaving one at a time like this did not feel right.

Wherever the others are, I hope they get here soon. Barbara was worried as the boat's engine came to life, and they raced back to Linden Academy's secret grotto. Meanwhile, Wanda found herself in familiar territory.

***

"I was wrong," Wanda mused aloud as she gazed at the sight before her. "This isn't like '*that night,*' this is *justice* for '*that night.*'"

Wanda had been separated from her sisters and had ended up back where she had found the work camp and had left the laborers food. Only now, the camp was a disaster area as a bomb from one of the Allied planes had destroyed the area and set fire to the surrounding building.

"During *that night,* there was mass rioting and chaos in the streets with authorities who could not care less about it. Now the Allies are destroying what the Nazis were forcing their own people to build, and no one is here to do anything to save it, and it doesn't deserve to be saved. At least now, I know where I am. Time to get back to the boats."

Those were Wanda's last words before a building exploded next to her, knocking her into one of the trenches and covering her with mud and dirt.

Ow, Wanda groggily thought to herself. Her head and body now hurting to the point where she could barely open her eyes and her ears rang so she could not hear anything else.

Come on, Wanda, get up! She encouraged herself, struggling to find the strength to pick herself up, open her eyes, and begin moving again to the docks where she knew her sisters were both waiting and worrying about her. Unfortunately, the blast and fall knocked more out of her than she realized, and despite her effort, she could not move.

If you can't move then how will everyone explain your absence at Linden Academy? You have to get up!

But before Wanda could move a muscle, she felt the mud and dirt being cleaned off of her and someone lifting her up into their arms.

"Will, Maud, is that you?" Wanda asked, too tired and hurting now to open her eyes. "Yes, it has to be one of you. You're the only ones strong enough to pick any of us up on your own. Do you think you can do me a favor and just carry me back up the stairs to our room? I just need to get some sleep right now."

If whoever was carrying her answered her, Wanda did not hear the reply, the ringing in her ears was that loud. All she cared about was that someone was carrying her away from the worksite. And as she felt herself being placed in a boat, the water rocking the boat beneath her as it moved away from the dock, she was sure she was heading back to Linden Academy.

Tomorrow I am going to really be holding this over Rita's head. We definitely should have gone to Switzerland tonight.

***

"Where is everyone?" Vita screamed.

Asta, Vita, and Marianne had made it back to the dock to find it deserted except for one boat still tethered to the pier. After being separated from their sisters, it had taken them longer to get back to the dock than they had imagined it would. But they did not expect to find that everyone would be gone.

"They must have already gone back to Linden Academy," Asta figured.

"Without us?" Vita shrieked, already panicking over the entire situation.

"We would do the same," Marianne admitted, climbing into the boat. "Lake Constance and the town are going to be swarming with Nazis now that the air raid is dying down. We *have* to get back to Linden Academy as fast as we can. Unless you think your acting skills are good enough to convince a squad of Nazi soldiers why the three of us are out here instead of asleep in our beds. Or how we managed to get out of the school in the first place undetected, leaving dummies in our place, without having to reveal every secret about us."

Vita knew her acting skills were good, but Marianne was right, they were not *that* good. Climbing into the boat, Asta starting the engine and climbing in herself right behind her, the three sisters began speeding back across Lake Constance to the secret grotto. Racing back, the sisters shivered over how the sky had an eerily red tint to it from the fires raging in town and at the zeppelin plant. It was reminding all of them of *that night.*

On that night, *all we could do was run then, too,* Asta remembered, ashamed that after two years, they had not changed as much as they thought. *I thought that after seeing those horrors, the twelve of us would have grown to the point where we would be able to do something if we ever encountered a night like that again. I know that a lot of us saw Swing 12 and the Lake Constance Swing Club as a way to "do something" instead of just running away into the Nazi machine and hiding there until the Allies destroyed it. But as soon as the fire really came down on us, what do we do, we run away again. Straight back to the* safety *of Linden Academy.*

Asta was disgusted with herself about what she was thinking, and looking at her sisters and the stares they were giving to the scene behind them, she knew they were thinking the same thing. Yet as the three of them pulled into the grotto, they realized their own regrets were going to have to wait. The rest of their sisters were crowding around someone on the ground whom they could barely see.

"What happened?" Asta and Vita asked together. They jumped out and pushed their way into the group where Will and Maud were nursing someone on the ground.

"She got knocked out by an explosion," Maud replied hastily. "I carried her back, and Will got her on the boat. We're lucky she's not hurt. We can tell Mrs. Kahn she had a nightmare and fell out of bed."

Asta and Vita looked down and saw Christine lying on the ground with a large lump on her head and dirt partially covering her.

"At least now with Marianne, Wanda, and the two of you here every one is back now," Freya exhaled, looking relieved to know that all of her sisters were back in the grotto.

"We thought Wanda was with you!" Marianne, Vita, and Asta shouted, a look and sense of terror suddenly appearing on each of their faces, spreading infectiously throughout the sisters.

"You mean she's still out there?" Freya gasped, realizing that they had left one of their sisters in town during the middle of an air raid with no secret boat ride back to school. Worse, with one of their sisters gone, they now had to figure out how to hide her disappearance until they could find her and bring her back. And that was assuming there was even anything *to* bring back.

"Freya, what are we going to do?" Vita pleaded, the other sisters also looking to her for help.

"I don't know," Freya whimpered.

"You can stay where you are!" a cold sounding voice echoed throughout the grotto answering Freya's question. Shocked, all of them moved slowly to face the intruder that was hiding behind them.

| 30 |

A spotlight suddenly flared to life, illuminating the cave, and blinding the remaining die Fürstin sisters who jumped to their feet. It was a man who had spoken. But as they tried to peer past the light and into the cave, they could not see anything. Suddenly, a dozen Nazi soldiers in black uniforms streamed past the light and surrounded them, apprehending each of them while two more men can into view from behind the light, one of whom was very familiar to them.

"Frankie," Freya whimpered, unable to believe her eyes.

"You HY bastard!" Will screamed, her voice filled with rage. "I knew you couldn't be trusted. How are you even here?"

Frankie did not answer Will with words. Instead, he threw a wet sponge down at their feet. The sponge smelled of both tea, and the sleeping drop they used to try to drug him with.

So that was it, Will figured. *Frankie must have hidden the sponge on him, and then when it looked like he drank the tea, he let the sponge absorb it so we would think he was out. Meaning he was planning to betray us the whole time.*

"As I promised my commander, the members of Swing 12," Frankie declared, pointing the sisters out like they were a trophy. "As I explained, after an unsuccessful attempt to drug me, I secretly watched as they used the servants' passage in their room to reach this grotto. It was from here that the twelve of them managed to sneak out of Linden Academy regularly and perform their activities as the anti-establishment group Swing 12. And if you want further proof that these girls are Swing 12..."

Frankie walked over to where Christine was lying on the ground, the spotlight illuminating something in her pocket.

"Ornaments stolen from the warehouse in the old royal district," Frankie continued, "And if you look over here."

Frankie walked over to one of the trunks in the grotto. The sisters quickly realized he must have examined it thoroughly after they left, planting evidence to prove they were Swing 12 before calling his Nazi superiors.

"A cup stolen from my father's vacation home when it was vandalized by Swing 12." Frankie showed the cup off like it was another trophy.

"Your *father!*" The sisters shouted in unison, remembering the house Frankie led them to, a house he claimed belonged to a Nazi bigwig that they raided and took its food to feed members of a work camp.

"Yes, my father, Tyr von Bron. He almost had a heart attack when he saw the state you girls left the house in. My commander, I present this cup and these silver, gold, and crystal ornaments to you as a trophy and as proof that these girls are Swing 12."

"I only count eleven of these girls," Frankie's commander stated, taking the cup and ornaments but clearly unimpressed and unwilling to believe that a group of teenage girls could have accomplished what they had.

"The twelfth member, Wanda die Fürstin, was lost in the recent air raid that hit both the city and the zeppelin factory. By now, I have no doubt she is lying dead in the rubble, which is a tragic loss to the die Fürstin Family, a family descended from Prussian military and nobility, and a personal loss for these sisters having lost one of their own."

"We don't know Wanda is dead, you HY bastard!" Maud spit, before trying to bite the soldier holding her, only to be gagged by the guard holding her. The other sisters were similarly gagged soon afterward.

"These poor girls just need time to adjust," Frankie pityingly remarked. "Now, have I fulfilled the pledge I made to you and the others, sir? Have I delivered you Swing 12?"

Frankie's commander walked forward to inspect the remaining die Fürstin sisters. Each one was dressed in their swing attire, a "Swing 12" badge pinned on their chests, and wearing shoes completely worn out from dancing. Frankie knew that only a complete fool would not be able to tell that they were swing girls at the least, and the members of Swing 12 at the most. But inwardly, he was still nervous.

This is it, Alvis, he thought to himself, using his real name. *It would have been better if Wanda was still here, then all twelve could be present. But even if they were not, the commander could still just say these are not the members of Swing 12 and only a group of swing girls so he will not have to admit Swing 12 was made up of a bunch of schoolgirls, girls that have been running the authorities crazy for a while. It all comes down to this.*

"Congratulations, Cadet Alvis von Bron. You have done what you have promised."

Alvis did not show it, but he was extraordinarily relieved about his commander's praise.

"Now, as part of our agreement, for successfully capturing Swing 12, you wanted to choose the battlefield upon which you fought for Germany. Where do you wish to go?"

"I want to be part of the first invasion of Switzerland," Alvis stated proudly. "When our proud German forces finally crack the Swiss nut on our doorstep, I want to be there to see that history. It will also become an excellent piece of the von Bron family lineage."

"Speaking of lineages," Alvis's commander continued, "you also wanted the chance to leave an heir before you left for the battlefield so your family line may continue. Did you need arrangements made, or did you have someone in mind?"

"I do have someone in mind," Alvis replied, walking over to Freya who's eyes opened wide with shock as he approached her.

"I wish for Freya die Fürstin to become my wife. She is of legal age to marry and comes from an old family of good stock. She will also be the one to eventually bear my heir."

"You want a member of Swing 12!" Alvis's commander barked, an uncomfortable sentiment clearly shared by the other soldiers present and even more so by the die Fürstin sisters themselves who were now struggling against their captors and trying to speak through their gags.

"The die Fürstin family descends from both the Prussian military and nobility. It would be a shame and tragedy to lose more members of such a bloodline to the war our proud German people are fighting now against their enemies."

"You do make a good point," Alvis's commander conceded. "But still…"

"Furthermore," Alvis continued, "Freya warned me of the sleeping drop in the tea before I drank it. She recognized what she was doing to me, a young soldier of the Reich, was wrong and sought to warn *me.* She is not as corrupted by 'Jungle music' and 'foreign influence' as she would lead others to believe. After all, are not a woman's looks one of her most deceiving weapons?"

The guards mumbled in amusement and agreement while the other sisters turned their eyes to Freya, anger, hurt, and betrayal all etched into their stares as they tried in vain to shout at her.

"Finally, in regards to looks, all of the die Fürstin are perfect examples of Aryan beauty. That is something that should not be wasted for future generations of proud German people, the *Master Race.* Besides, after losing one sister, I am sure they would enjoy gaining a brother, a proud and glorious German big brother who will guide them back from foreign influences and help to better become proper young women of the Folk and Fatherland."

Freya was too stunned to think. She could not believe what she heard. Frankie, or *Alvis* rather, had completely sold them out. Now, he wanted her hand in marriage as a reward for his betrayal, acting like she was a trophy that could be handed over and put on the shelf. He claimed that she warned him about the sleeping drops. But he was the one who gave them to her in the first place, and that she was "not as corrupted by 'Jungle music' and 'foreign influence' as she would lead others to believe." He overly flattered his superiors with talk of family lineages, Aryan beauty, how the *proud* German people were a "Master Race." And that he would be a guiding big brother that would help them become "proper young women of the Folk and Fatherland." And she could tell he *meant* every piece of it. Freya wanted to vomit.

The other sisters were not reacting any better. The looks on their faces ranged from anger, betrayal, to disgust, and back again. If it was not for the gags in their mouths, a few might have vomited over Alvis's display. On the other hand, Alvis's commander and the other Nazi guards were basking in every word coming out of his mouth. If a man could glow, Alvis's commander was glowing with hubristic pride. The other guards were similarly basking in Alvis's declaration, hanging on his words and waiting to see who would speak next.

"You speak passionately of our heritage, the proud and glorious German people, and your duty to the Folk and Fatherland," Alvis's commander proclaimed. "Very well, Cadet von Bron, you will have your request."

Alvis beamed over those words. Standing a little taller as he took a breath, it was clear he was nervous making his request but was not ready to relax just yet.

"I will make the arrangements immediately; we will have the ceremony here at Linden Academy. Unfortunately, you do understand that some form of punishment will have to be dealt upon the other ten die Fürstin sisters."

"Then might I humbly request that it be nothing which will leave any permanent scars or markings," Alvis begged. "Remember, all ten of them can still become proud German women and mothers for the Folk and Fatherland."

"Now that can be arranged. Guards, escort the die Fürstin sisters back up to Linden Academy, and request crews to seal up these passages for good, for the good of the Fatherland."

"Heil Hitler!" The guards cheered before dragging the sisters back up the stairs to their room, each one struggling with every step. Casting one last glance to the opening of Lake Constance, several lingering thoughts floated through Freya's mind.

You were right, Wanda; we should have gone to Switzerland instead of our party tonight. I hope you are not lost, captured, or worse out there. Where are you now?

| 31 |

"Where am I?"

Wanda woke from the best night of sleep she had had in years to a sight that was anything but what she expected. Instead of being back in her bed at Linden Academy, she was lying on a cot in a windowless basement, a few candle lamps barely illuminating it. Not that it mattered to her as a frightening realization soon struck her.

It has to be morning by now, past morning, Mrs. Kahn and the rest of the faculty at Linden Academy will have realized we've disappeared by now. And if the others went back, how are they going to explain my disappearance. That said, just where did I disappear to!

Wanda realized now that the person who saved her could not have been Will or Maud like she initially thought. Scouring the room, she tried to determine if her kidnapper/rescuer left any clues to their identity. Thankfully, the room was littered with it.

"Bomb damage certificates," Wanda mused as she rummaged through the paperwork lying in the basement. "This one is for a Frey Bismarck, officially stamped, and ordered by the SWM, whoever they are, to be given provision after his home and family were killed in an air raid."

Wanda never heard of any Nazi organization with the initials SWM. But she needed to know more and kept reading.

"This one is for a Sigmund Brawn, Odin Seig, Roy Brown. Each form is officially stamped, claiming that the owner was the victim of a bombing raid, and provided provisions by some agency whose initials I don't even recognize. How many people live here?"

"Just me and the old nun who lets me use this cellar as an apartment," a strange voice answered Wanda's question, spooking her.

Turning around, she saw a familiar face entering the room, Silent Night.

"Silent Night," Wanda gasped, unsure what was spooking her more: the fact that he was here, or that he had just *spoken*.

"It's Wor actually," Silent Night explained. "Wor Boswell, and since I brought you here, I don't really see any reason to keep up the whole 'mute' act, don't you think?"

Wanda did not know what to think. She had just found out that Silent Night, or Wor Boswell, was not only the one who rescued her, but that he really could talk, something she had doubted for a while now. Not only that, his accent proved he was clearly not from Germany, but could not figure out where he was from. All she could do was watch as he walked into the cellar and reorganized the paperwork Wanda was going through like he was cleaning his own house.

"Those papers," Wanda finally muttered.

"They're real," Wor explained. "I stole them over a year ago during an air raid soon after I came into Germany. As for the names and organizations on them, all fakes. I've used them to take advantage of the Nazi's convoluted bureaucracy. You would be surprised how dumb the Nazis who work at the ration offices can be. All they have to see is 'bomb damage,' some jumble of letters—making them think a new organization has been established, and they'll give me food. I learned a lot of tricks in my travels."

"If you're so good, then why didn't you tell us?" Wanda asked. "Why all the secrecy?"

"Secrecy is what's kept me alive," Wor shot back. "When I escaped from a Gypsy internment camp in Poland, the people gave me one piece of advice, which I had followed very strictly until now; 'Trust no one.' There's a reason I slipped you that note about fair-weather friends. I've seen friends, families, close-knit families, crumble like a house of cards and turn on each other from just a bit of Nazi pressure, or the promise of more food and benefits. Groups like your Swing 12 have ground to a halt from just one real hit from the Nazis. All across Germany, I've only spotted a few groups that I can actually say had the genuine spirit to stand up to the Nazis, but they are few and far between. The rest are just playing the part until they realize they have crossed the line."

"And is that what you think we have been doing?" Wanda asked, now becoming angry. "Just 'playing the part.' If that's what you think, then why did you help us to begin with?"

"I helped you because I realized you and your sisters were going to get yourselves arrested or killed without it," Wor replied. "Raiding the von Bron mansion—which I won't lie, I did enjoy it and it helped a *lot* of people—would have gotten you all caught if me and Frankie, or Alvis I should say, didn't help you get all of that food out of there. And yes, up until now, I do think you have all been 'playing the part.' Otherwise, how do you explain this?"

Wor reached into his jacket and pulled out a newspaper. Handing it to Wanda, she saw it was the morning paper. Although she had only slept through the night, the headline made her forget all about sleep.

"Swing 12 captured!" Wanda read aloud. "The members of Swing 12, revealed to be the twelve die Fürstin sisters attending Linden Academy, have been captured through the efforts of HY Cadet Alvis von Bron!"

Alvis's picture mockingly smiled from the front page of the paper as Wanda continued to read.

"Cadet von Bron attributes the capture to not only his own skills but also the forewarning of the eldest member of the die Fürstin sisters, Freya die Fürstin. In celebration of this victory for the Folk, Fatherland, and German culture over foreign influences seeking to corrode it, Alvis von Bron and Freya die Fürstin are set to wed in two days' times. The die Fürstin family comments that they look forward to having a proud and proper son of Germany entering into their family."

"What is this? Slop!"

Wanda threw the paper down in disgust. She could not believe what she had just read.

"That 'slop' as you put it, is what happens when someone 'playing the part' realizes who they are up against and caves under pressure," Wor replied.

"Alvis *gave* us the sleeping drops." Wanda countered. "He didn't need us to warn him. And there is no way Freya would consent to any kind of marriage like this. She wouldn't sell the rest of us out to get married to a HY Nazi, not after *that night*, not ever!"

"Just because she wouldn't, doesn't mean Alvis would," Wor reminded her. "The Nazis can be *very* persuasive, and Alvis, when I first met him, was about as anti-Nazi as the twelve of you. So, to sell you out to the Nazis means they made him a heck of a good deal, scared him to the point where he didn't want to fight them anymore, or both. Personally, I think both. You have no idea what the Nazis are capable of."

The way Wor talked sent a chill up her back. She wished she could get a good look into his eyes, but he was still wearing his sunglasses.

What else have you seen and are not telling me? Wanda wondered, but she had far more pressing matters she needed to attend to. She needed to get to her sisters and get them out of Linden Academy right now. She knew she would not be able to walk through the front door. Without a boat, she could not get to the grotto—not that she would chance the lake route now after an air raid, but she did have an idea of where she could go for help, and despite what Wor said, she did not think they were "fair-weather friends."

I just hope everyone is okay.

| 32 |

"Freya, it's me, Alvis. I'm coming in."

Alvis had not seen Freya since the previous night when she and her sisters were arrested by the Nazis he led down the servants' passage to the grotto they were using to sneak out of Linden Academy. Since then, Freya had been kept separated from the rest of her sisters so she could "prepare" for her "wedding" to him. Alvis knew he was forcing the wedding on her because of a deal he made with the Nazis; he did not expect this meeting to be a happy or easy one.

"You, Nazi bastard!" Freya screamed the moment she saw him, walking over and punching him in the face.

"Okay, I deserved that," Alvis admitted, taking the punch and preparing himself for any more punches Freya might give him.

"You deserve that and more," Freya countered. "How could you do that to us, to *me*? I defended you. I trusted you. I was in love with you. And you sold us out so you could *marry me*! We were all going to escape together and go to Switzerland. After we found work and got established, then we were going to get married. We *talked* about this, we had a plan. And you just turned Nazi on us. What were you thinking?"

"That I am protecting both you and your sisters," Alvis claimed.

"*Protecting* us!" Freya could not believe it. "How does turning us over to the Nazis, separating me from my sisters—Wanda could still be alive out there. And forcing me to marry you, in any way protect us?"

"Freya, it's time we both grew up," Alvis said in exasperation. "You, me, your sisters, none of us ever *really* believed or wanted to leave Germany and strike out on our own. If we did, we would have left a long time ago. Going to Switzerland, starting new lives there, those were just the delusions of children who didn't know anything about the world. This way, at least, I'll be able to really protect you, your sisters, and ensure that you get the lives you deserve."

"You can't seriously believe what you're saying," Freya gasped. "You sound like the war is already over. That we already decided it was over. Since when did you think the Nazis would win?"

"Since I learned they *will* win," Alvis shouted, panic appearing on his face. "You have no idea of what the Nazis are capable of doing, all like it was just a day on the pig farm for them."

Freya noticed Alvis shiver when he said the words "pig farm." She realized he knew something, something terrible.

"The Nazis are a machine, an animalistic machine that will knock down anyone in their path and destroy anyone they deem an 'enemy' or an 'undesirable.' Switzerland and the Allies might be holding out now, but they *will* eventually fall. They can't hold out against this machine forever. As for Swing 12, none of you wanted to start it in the first place; you were all just going along with Wanda because it seemed like childish fun, and you were getting away with it. And while you and other swing kids across Germany might have been a nuisance before, that will change. Once my superiors decide they are enemies, too, nothing I do will be able to protect you from what's coming. That's why I'm telling you to *grow up*, face the truth, and do what's best for your family and the Fatherland."

"Where are my sisters?" Freya demanded, forcing herself to look Alvis in the eye, and fighting the urge to back away from him.

"Freya..." Alvis begged before she cut him off.

"Where are my sisters, *Cadet von Bron?*" Freya knew now that the swing boy she loved was gone, if he had even existed. The person standing before her was a Nazi sellout through and through. She did not know what he had seen, nor did she care, but she did know that he had given up all hope that the Nazis would lose the war and decided that joining them was his best chance for survival. And she and her sisters were the price of admission.

"Come with me," Alvis conceded. "I'll take you to your sisters."

Alvis led Freya out of her room and down the hall, Freya following cautiously behind him. She did not trust him anymore, but he was the only lead she had to her sisters' whereabouts, so she followed him. Thankfully they did not go far, only down one floor to a different section of the dormitory where two cadets were patrolling another room. The cadets snapped to attention the moment Alvis approached.

"At ease," Alvis ordered. "I'm just showing Miss die Fürstin to her sisters."

"Yes, sir," one of the cadets replied. "Please allow us to accompany you inside. They have just finished receiving their punishment, and it has left them *excitable.*"

"What punishment?" Freya asked. "What have you done to my sisters?"

"Nothing permanent," the cadet assured her. "See for yourself."

The two cadets led Freya and Alvis into the room, and Freya had to force herself to keep from crying out. All ten of her remaining sisters were there, only now their heads were shaved to the point where they were completely bald.

"Well, look who decided to pay us a visit," Will announced sarcastically. "It's the future *Mrs. Alvis von Bron.*"

The other sisters all turned and stared at Freya and Alvis. They did not say anything, which made it even harder for Freya, but she could tell from their looks that they were not happy to see her. Their stares told her they felt hurt and betrayed. Freya could not blame them. She had trusted Alvis and tried to convince her sisters that they could still trust him, too, when he showed up at their bedroom door. Instead, Alvis betrayed them and had claimed she was in on the betrayal, a lie her sisters clearly had no trouble believing.

"I need to speak to them alone," Freya pleaded, turning to Alvis.

"I'm afraid I can't do that, Freya," Alvis replied. "At least not until the crews come in to make sure those passages are sealed for good. We don't know how many more there could still be or where they are, and we can't risk you running away before the big day."

"Please," Freya begged. "There are no passages here. We only found the one in our room. Please, just a few minutes."

Alvis was unreadable as he looked at both Freya and her sisters, eventually uttering a short sentence.

"Two minutes."

Alvis backed out of the room, observing the eleven of them carefully until he stepped out of the room and closed the door behind him. Freya watched him until the door closed behind him, turning around to receive a slap in the face from Will.

"That's for trusting and going with that HY bastard!" Will barked. Freya did not even try to refute her, she believed getting hit by them was the *least* she could do. "And this is because you're all right."

Will wrapped Freya in the tightest hug she had ever given. The other nine sisters quickly joined in and gave Freya a group hug so powerful it left her confused and gasping for breath.

"But why?" Freya choked, trying to get the words out. "Last night, just now, I thought you thought I betrayed you. That you hated me."

"Not you, you big doofus," Rita explained. "It's that HY bastard Alvis we want to tear apart."

"Agreed," Marianne stated. "I'll admit we were all surprised and confused last night. Especially after realizing we left Wanda behind. If that made any of us give you the impression that we thought you had turned on us, we apologize. But we all know better than to trust *anything* that comes from the mouth of an HY cadet."

"Then, you don't think I betrayed you?" Freya asked, choking on her words as they came from her mouth.

"No," the sisters answered in unison.

"But your hair?" Freya wondered, gazing up at each of their now bald heads.

"Is that all you're worried about?" Maud laughed. "Don't be. Personally, I think the Nazis did us a favor by shaving us bald. We've all hated that our blond hair marked us out to be 'proper little misses.' Now, it's gone, and I can't tell you how liberating it feels for it to be gone, even if it is just for a while, much more liberating than when Will and I attempted to dye it."

Will and the others nodded in agreement, big genuine smiles appearing on each of their faces. Freya realized they were telling the truth, not only did they not blame her for what happened to them, but they also loved the fact that they were now bald. In trying to punish them, the Nazis had done them a favor.

"Now that all of that is settled between us, what's our next plan?" Will asked.

"The next plan is our wedding plan," Alvis announced, walking back into the room, and quickly gaining a scowl from everyone present. "It's time to go, Freya. I've already given you more time than I said I would. Any more, and people will get nervous. It's time to start planning our wedding. As for the rest of you, I imagine you all want to be bridesmaids. I'll arrange to have a sufficient number of groomsmen available as well as plenty of dresses and wigs for you to choose from."

"So, all you want us to plan on doing is show up, look pretty, and be part of *your wedding*?" Will sneered.

"Well put, Will," Alvis answered. "Just plan on being there. Come along, Freya."

Alvis took Freya's arm and pulled her out of her sisters' room, closing it behind her, leaving her wondering how they were going to escape this mess and if there was a way to escape it.

"I know you must hate me for this, Freya," Alvis mumbled. "You must think I'm a monster. But this is the only way to protect you and your family against the Nazis. You *must believe me*."

I don't know what to believe about you anymore. Freya mused, not bothering to respond to Alvis's comment. *I don't know what the Nazis did to you, or showed you, that made you sell us out—and that's assuming you hadn't sold us out long before that, but what I do know is that I never knew you at all. The boy I* did *know, Frankie, turned out to be just a character you were playing. The real you is someone else. I'm just glad Wanda isn't stuck in this mess. Wherever she is, I hope she is alive, safe, and free.*

| 33 |

"I know they will help me," Wanda mumbled to herself as she crept through the town. The air raid had left its mark. Buildings were destroyed. The streets were filled with people and soldiers attempting to clean up the debris, collect rations, and avoid "volunteering" to help reconstruct the zeppelin plant—the main target of the air raid.

"I just wonder how they'll react once they see me?" Wanda said.

Wanda was making her way toward the Lake Constance Swing Club's B site. Since it was built inside of a bomb shelter, she knew that any club members inside it would have been safe from the raid. Despite what Wor said, she still believed in the other club members and was sure that they would help her rescue her sisters.

"There it is." Wanda smiled, relief washing over her as she found the B site still intact and waiting for her. *Now, to see if anyone is inside or around.*

Just because Wanda was happy to be back at the Swing Club, it did *not* mean she was not being careful. Alvis had already betrayed them. And while the papers said that they had all been captured, there was no way to tell how the other members of the Swing Club would react if a "captured" member of Swing 12 suddenly showed up at their front door. Taking her time, Wanda checked behind her to make sure she was not being followed or tailed. She circled the entire B site until she was sure it was not being watched and that no one was following her before making her way inside.

"Old Kludge, J. B.!" Wanda exclaimed, finding two members of the swing club huddled in the shelter and sharing a drink together. They jumped the moment they saw Wanda enter the club.

"Don't get scared," Wanda reassured them. "The papers lied. I wasn't captured, nor am I being followed. I never made it back to Linden Academy last night. But now I need your help, yours and the other members of the Lake Constance Swing Club. We have to rescue my sisters from Linden Academy. So, where is everyone? We have to move now!"

Instead of moving, however, Old Kludge and J.B. turned back to their drink and poured themselves another one each.

"Guys, come on." Wanda pleaded, surprised by their apathy. "Let's get the club members and get going!"

"Winnie, it's over," J.B. finally said, pouring another drink and placing it on their table. "After the air raid, the Nazis raided here and the other party site. These weren't the local party members we've been able to fool around with but full adult members, some even coming back from the War. They were the ones who told us the twelve of you were captured and started rounding the rest of us up like cattle. Old Kludge, myself, and a few others managed to get away, but the others were not as fortunate. Where they sent them, and what's happening to them right now, God only knows. What I do know is that I can't face that fear again and that we can't win against them."

"What do you mean we can't beat them?" Wanda asked, shocked over J.B.'s statement and hearing Wor's words echo in her mind. "We *have* been beating them. We've stolen food, fed the hungry, painted the town with our message, and liberated all of those Christmas decorations to use at the party. We got the best of them every time."

"That's because until now, they really didn't consider us worth the trouble," Old Kludge countered. "Let's face it, your sisters didn't even want to start Swing 12 in the first place. Before now, we were lucky. Just a bunch of dumb kids who did realize they were messing with adults. Now the adults have finally stepped in and shown us what will happen if we keep messing with them. I don't know what kind of deal Frankie made with the Nazis, but I'm certain it must be the best one to ensure your sisters' safety. The best thing you can do now is to share a few final drinks with us and then turn yourself in. That way, at least, you'll be reunited with your sisters."

Wanda did not sit down. Instead, she backed away from J.B. and Old Kludge, both of whom had returned to drinking, and made her way out of the B site, finding Wor just outside the door.

"Did you hear?" Wanda asked, disheartened.

"I did," Wor answered.

"This is what you meant by 'playing the part.'" Wanda continued. "That groups like ours have 'ground to a halt from just one real hit from the Nazis.'"

"It is," Wor confirmed. "Until now, they thought to play the part of American swingers and/or rebels without genuinely understanding *what that meant.* Even after witnessing the terror of *that night*—and believe it or not, I have seen far worse—they still never accepted what happened then can and *would* happen to them now. They never realized that in this kind of fight, you *will* get hurt or worse. Especially if your opponents are the Nazis."

"I thought they did know," Wanda sobbed. "When I first came here, I thought this club was a wonderful place full of music, expression, and free of the Nazis' control. And when we started doing more with it, I thought that the other members, including my sisters, were happy to help and knew what they were getting into and understood the risks."

"I doubt any of them really knew or understood the risks," Wor countered. "They knew they were getting into trouble, and they were having a fun time doing it—which they needed because of this restrictive regime. But they didn't know or understand just how much trouble they were getting into, or the consequences. Once they did, it was too late, leaving members like Old Kludge and J.B. the way they are now."

"So, all it takes is a little genuine fear, and they turn coward, just like that?" Wanda spit.

"I wouldn't be too hard on them," Wor added. "The Nazis are experts at using fear and terror. I witnessed *that night* two years ago, too. I personally don't think it was just meant to be an attack on the Jewish population, it was also a scare tactic. A way for the Nazis to tell everyone in the country that 'if you cross us, you'll be next.' And anyone who witnessed *that night,* even if they were safe, I bet is terrified of reliving it and being on the receiving end of it. Old Kludge and J.B. simply had a taste of that end and are now trying to drown their fears instead of facing them. Personally, however, I'm more concerned about what you are going to do."

"What I'm going to do?" Wanda asked.

"Yes, what are you going to do, Wanda die Fürstin?"

"I'm going to go get my sisters, and we are leaving this town, this country, for good," Wanda answered, marching off in a huff.

"And how do you plan on doing that?" Wor asked, walking up behind her. "You can't just march up to the doors of Linden Academy and demand that they hand over your sisters to you. All you'll accomplish is handing yourself over to them. Nor can you use your secret passage. By now, the Nazis are watching it in case your sisters try to escape through it, or if you or someone else tries to sneak in. All alone, with no sisters, no club members, no plan, what are you going to do? What *can* you do? All alone, you couldn't even take on a few HY cadets. If it wasn't for your sisters coming to your rescue, they would have..."

"I *know* what they would have done!" Wanda snapped, turning around to face Wor. "I know, I have nothing, but that doesn't mean I have to *do* nothing. Two years ago, on *that night,* Mr. Cohen told us, 'No matter what happens, *never* stop protecting your family.' It was the last thing he told us before a bunch of SA thugs raided his home and hauled him and his brother out into the night. Now I have to do something to protect *my* family. If I have to climb the walls overlooking Lake Constance to break open a window, sneak into the school, and wear a BdM uniform to blend in to find them, I'll do it. If you're just going to stand there and lecture me, then just get out of my way and go back to whatever hole you were cowering in because I don't care what you have to say. All I care about is rescuing my sisters. Good-bye."

Wanda walked past Wor and away from the B site. Truthfully, she did not know what she was going to do once she returned to Linden Academy. All she knew with certainty was that she would do something, anything, if it brought her one step closer to rescuing her sisters and getting them all out of Germany.

"Wait!" Wor called, catching up to her and cutting her off. "You're only going to get yourself caught or killed if you go charging in there with no plan. I'll help you."

| 34 |

"I don't believe it!"

Wanda was skeptical about Wor's decision to help her after talking to Old Kludge and J.B. He took her back to the basement where he had been living and introduced her to the old woman who had been giving them shelter; Sister Crispin, the old nun from Linden Academy. It turned out she was full of information.

"Believe it, child," Sister Crispin answered. "I cared for Linden Academy since before it was even a school. It is far easier to sneak into and out of than you or those blasphemous Nazi fools think. Did you or any of your sisters ever ask yourselves why a servants' passage, unused since the days of the monarchy, was so clean and in good repair when you found it?"

"No," Wanda admitted, "I always thought my eldest sisters found it and cleaned it out, so I never asked them about it. You really have been maintaining them?"

"And *mapping* them." Sister Crispin smiled and handed a document to Wanda. "That's a map I've drawn. It shows where all the entrances and exits to the servants' passages in Linden Academy are and how to navigate them."

Wanda took the map and held it like an original copy of "American Swing Music" written by the artists themselves. It was all there, the door in their bedroom, the path to the grotto, and all of the other routes they never explored, and the places where they came out.

"There are entrances in the chapel, the cafeteria, the kitchen, dozens of other rooms," Wanda mumbled, barely able to take in what she was seeing.

"And instructions on how to open any of the passages if they are sealed," Sister Crispin continued. "And I should know, *I* sealed most of them in the first place."

A mischievous smile crept on both of their faces, they realized—if for a moment—they had found a kindred spirit in each other.

"And these will help us get back into Linden Academy," Wor added, dumping an armful of clothing between them. "They'll also help us get your sisters out of there."

Wanda looked at the clothing. They looked no different from the same overalls and streetwear she had seen dozens of people in labor camps and construction sites across Germany wearing. She could see where Wor was going with his plan.

"You're doing exactly what we did by disguising ourselves in Swing clothes to make us look older," Wanda said. "Only this time we're going to be dressed up as the construction crew that's *supposed* to be sealing the servants' passageways."

"Exactly!" Wor smiled.

"But what will we do if someone asks why there are only two of us instead of the main construction team, or if I'm a girl for that matter?" Wanda asked.

"Here," Wor replied, tossing Wanda a small can of black shoe polish. "Rub a little of that on your face, pin your hair up and tuck it under a large cap, put on a baggy pair of coveralls, and don't say a word or make eye contact. I've seen other women pull the same trick to get work outside of the home. Trust me, it works. As for the main construction team, we don't have to worry about them. While you were sleeping, they received stamped instructions from the newly formed 'Department of Reconstruction and Demolition' or 'DRD' to turn in their construction clothing. Then proceed to the destroyed zeppelin factory in three days to receive recompense and new work assignments in rebuilding the factory."

Wanda noticed the mischievous way Wor smiled when he told her about what happened to the construction crew. She was beginning to realize that there was a lot more to him than she had thought possible.

"You decided to help me get my sisters out of Linden Academy since before I woke up, didn't you?" Wanda said. Wor merely answered by smiling happily.

"Why?" Wanda asked. "Is it because I would just be killed otherwise? Do you think we are a bunch of helpless girls who need a man's protection? Or do you have some ulterior motive? I can tell you right now that neither me, or my sisters, have really thought about you in the past. So, if you're harboring anything..."

Wor erupted into laughter, the sight causing Wanda to look at him more strangely than ever before.

"First of all, Wanda, as it stands, you would be killed if you tried this yourself, and the twelve of you really are just a bunch of helpless girls." Wanda scowled for a second, knowing that Wor was correct, as he continued, "However, I do *NOT* think you need a man's protection. I've already seen that the twelve of you can take care of yourselves just fine. I already told you that I've only spotted a few groups that have actually possessed the genuine spirit to stand up to the Nazis. You have that spirit. And you inspire it in your sisters. I've seen it in action."

"You've seen it in action?" Wanda asked skeptically.

"Yes," Wor explained. "If it wasn't for you, none of your sisters would have tried to stand up against the Nazis, or genuinely want to leave the country."

"Shows what you know," Wanda corrected. "We always planned to go to Switzerland. Even before forming Swing 12."

"That's only what your older sisters have been telling themselves," Wor said. "I've been watching them since your eldest sisters first walked into the club. They've claimed they were going to leave Germany, but not once have they ever tried to watch the boats to find out when they could. They just kept deluding themselves on the fantasy that they needed everyone and were waiting for the right time when all they were really doing was dancing their time away. If you didn't inspire them to start Swing 12, they would have kept dancing until they graduated and then told themselves they never had the chance when they never tried to make one."

"Humph," Wanda grumped. "If you can tell so much about them, then why haven't you tried inspiring them?"

"I have tried inspiring people before," Wor explained, "but I don't have the gift. Every time I've tried, people just thought I was crazy, too good to be true, or had some kind of secret agenda. That's why I focus on being a helper, or the one who helps the helpers. Especially since the paradox of the helper is that the one person they usually can't help is themselves. So, if I don't help you, I *know* I'll regret it. Especially since you *need* it. Is not that a good enough reason for me to help you?"

"Good enough for me," Wanda agreed, glad that she now had a reason for why Wor was helping her. "So, we have clothes and a map. What do we do next?"

| 35 |

"You must let me see them," Sister Crispin argued at the gate of Linden Academy. "The eldest die Fürstin sister needs spiritual guidance before her marriage so she will become a good and faithful wife. Plus, the remaining sisters also need to be prepared to accept a new brother into their family. I must perform this work. For the good of the Lord, and the good of the Folk and Fatherland."

"Very well, Sister," the guard at the Linden Academy gate replied. "Come this way."

"Bless you, good sir," Sister Crispin replied. *And bless you for being a foolish Nazi. One that I just have to mention "good of the Folk and Fatherland" to for you to do whatever I want. May the Lord forgive me for the deception. But for our plan to work, we need to know where Freya and the others are being held.*

Reconnaissance was the next step in the plan to free the die Fürstin sisters from Linden Academy and get them all out of the country. While Sister Crispin's map of the servants' passages would let Wanda and Wor move through the walls of Linden Academy, it did not tell them where they were being kept or which passageways were closest to them.

"*That's easy to find out,*" Sister Crispin had told them. "*I'll go back to Linden Academy and find out where the others are locked up. I can tell them I'm getting them ready for marriage and to accept a new brother into their family. After all, it's not like either of you can go walking up to the school until your plan is in motion.*"

Wanda and Wor did not like it, but Sister Crispin was right. She was the only one who could find out where the others were being held, and they needed that information for their escape to be a success. As she was being led through the familiar passageways of Linden Academy, she silently thanked God for the Nazi's lack of originality.

When the Nazis converted this place into a boarding school, they kept using a lot of the original bedrooms for dorm rooms. If we keep going in this direction, we should get the section of the academy with the largest bedrooms that were originally reserved for visiting royalty. That section of the Academy is also one of the most easily guardable parts. I expect I'll see a lot more of these Nazi goons soon.

Sister Crispin was not disappointed. She was taken exactly where she expected and found the halls swarming with guards. It was clear they did not want anyone sneaking around or trying to get out of the school. The way the guards looked at her sent a chill up Sister Crispin's back, but she did not show it. Instead, she kept on walking until her escorts led her to a door.

"This is where the ten die Fürstin sisters are preparing themselves for the wedding."

"Thank you, gentlemen," Sister Crispin replied, trying to sound as gracious as possible. "I'll take it from here."

"I'm afraid that's not possible, Sister," one of the guards proclaimed. "We have orders to watch you at all times. We cannot permit you to be with the die Fürstin sisters alone."

"Excuse me, gentlemen," Sister Crispin shot back, a note of challenge in her voice. "But there are things that I need to discuss with the die Fürstin sisters that can only be done 'woman to woman.'"

"You'll need to make an exception then for us. Or if you like, we can find some female guards to take our place."

"It is not only that," Sister Crispin challenged. "Part of my duties is to offer the sacrament of Reconciliation to these girls, and I can't do that with outsiders watching."

"But you can do that with the other die Fürstin sisters watching?" The guard challenged.

"I planned on using material in the room to set up a divider to allow each girl privacy," Sister Crispin explained grumpily.

"Then you can still do it with us present in the room," the guard finished. "We'll even set up a divider for you."

Sister Crispin realized the guards were not going to be persuaded otherwise. Opening the door, they walked into ten bald girls huddled tightly together on the floor in one corner of the room until they realized they were no longer alone. They all jumped up then and began watching Sister Crispin and the guards closely as they took blankets, drapes, and pieces of furniture from the room to partition a section of it off from the rest of it.

"Should that suit your needs, Sister?"

"Yes, gentlemen," Sister Crispin replied.

"Then we will sit by the door and watch as you execute your duties."

As the guards walked to the doors, Sister Crispin approached the die Fürstin sisters. It was clear that they recognized her from when she attended the chapel at Linden Academy, the puzzled looks on their faces said that much. But none of them dared express those feelings with words. Instead, it was Sister Crispin herself who broke the silence.

"Good morning ladies, my name is Sister Crispin and I am here to prepare you for your sister's marriage."

"Freya is NOT marrying that traitor, Alvis!" Will shouted, a sentiment equally shared by the other sisters.

"Now, let's not be like that," Sister Crispin replied, trying to play the part of a Sister who was encouraging the marriage. In truth, she understood and agreed with the die Fürstin sisters' position completely. "I am sure Master Alvis von Bron is a good soul and will make a wonderful husband to your sister and a brother for you all. You should be happy that your sister has found someone like him."

"Happy?" Rita spit in confusion. "Happy is not how any of us would describe this."

"Then perhaps we can all talk, one-on-one, about how you would describe this. I am also here to give each of you the chance to receive the Sacrament of Reconciliation. Would you like to go first? You can say whatever you want to me."

"Why I would love to, Sister," Rita answered sarcastically as she walked behind the partition to where some chairs and a table were set up and was soon joined by Sister Crispin. "Now let me tell *you* something, Sister..."

"Please, speak *very softly* and *don't get excited,*" Sister Crispin instructed as she reached into her habit and pulled out a note. The words on it almost made her jump up and shout.

"I'm alive. Sister Crispin is a friend helping us to get you out. Trust her. Wanda"

"Now is there anything you want to tell me?" Sister Crispin asked. "Any sins you wish to confess, doubts you may have, questions about your sister's marriage. Please take *as long as you need,* and speak *as softly as you can.* This is supposed to stay between us."

Rita nodded at Sister Crispin's instructions and started mumbling gibberish softly so that no one would be able to tell what she was saying. Meanwhile, Sister Crispin acted like she was listening to a confession while she pulled another note out of her habit.

"It is good that you are telling me this," Sister Crispin said for the guards on the other side of the curtain while pointing to the note and its instructions.

"On the night before the wedding, Silent Night and I are going to come for you. We have a way to get to you. We will come and escape together. Forgive me for being vague, but we need to be ready in case this letter is intercepted. I'll tell you more of the details in person. Wanda."

"Do you think *we can be free* after all we have done?" Rita asked, making it sound like she was asking for redemption but really asking if she thought Wanda's escape plan would work.

Sister Crispin turned and looked at a corner of the room, Rita following her gaze. There did not seem to be anything special about it, but Sister Crispin kept her focus on that spot.

"In the words of the Gospel of Saint Matthew," Sister Crispin began, "'Ask, and it will be given to you; seek, and you will find; *knock*, and it will be *opened* to you. For everyone who asks receives, and the one who seeks finds, and to the one who *knocks* it will be *opened*.' The *door* to your salvation might be closer than you realize."

Rita's eyes opened wide when she realized the hidden meaning in Sister Crispin's words, her own eyes darting back and forth between both the wall and Sister Crispin.

There's another servants' passage in here! Rita struggled just to keep herself from jumping up and shouting it out. *Wanda and Silent Night are going to use it and we are going to escape through it as well. I can't wait to tell the others.*

"Rita, it would seem my work, for the moment, is done," Sister Crispin announced, standing up. "Perhaps you would like to send one of your other sisters in. I am sure they would also love a chance just to *talk to me* before your sister's wedding. And once I'm done with the ten of you, I can also go and speak with your other sister, Freya, as well. I think they would all like that, don't you?"

"Yes," Rita laughed. "They certainly will."

Sister Crispin spent the next half hour telling the rest of Wanda's sisters present in the room that she was alive, coming for them, and indicating that there was another servants' passage in the room that they were imprisoned in. Some of the sisters reacted a little more exuberantly to the news than others. Sister Crispin almost had to fight Will, Maud, and Vita to keep them in their seat and stop them from trying to open the servants' passage themselves. By the time she was being led out of the room to see Freya, all of the sisters were more energized and excited than before she had arrived. It was making the guards nervous.

"What did you say to them?" one of the guards asked.

"Just what they needed to hear," Sister Crispin honestly replied. "I let them see that the coming wedding day is going to be the best day of their life. Now, if you'll lead me to Freya die Fürstin, I would like to complete God's work with her. No one wants a sad bride at a wedding. Do you?"

"No, I suppose not," The guard coughed, clearly uncomfortable with the idea he could disrupt the wedding as he and his partner led Sister Crispin into another room nearby where Freya was arguing with several other women.

"I will *NOT* put that dress on!" Freya screamed.

"But Lady die Fürstin, this is your wedding dress. You must try it on to see if it fits you."

"*NO,* I will *NOT!*"

"Maybe you should let me speak with the bride," Sister Crispin interjected. "I might be able to help her see the wisdom to her coming union. Gentlemen, could you please partition that corner of the room so I can give penance and speak with Miss die Fürstin privately?"

The guards nodded and proceeded to set up a curtain in one corner of the room just like they had done before. Freya watched, confused as the room was rearranged and Sister Crispin beckoned her behind the curtain.

What is Sister thinking? Freya wondered as she stared at her. *I remember the day she left Linden Academy, the pain and sadness in her face over the chapel's desecration. I can't believe she would just walk back all happy just to convince me and my sisters that the wedding is a good idea and to offer us the Sacrament of Reconciliation.*

Freya's curiosity only grew as she watched Sister Crispin sit down behind the curtain first, leaving her with the stares of the guards and the handmaidens, both of whom were waiting to see what she would do next.

"Fine," Freya fumed. Walking behind the curtain she found Sister Crispin writing on some paper and eagerly awaiting her arrival.

"Look, Sister," Freya began. "I don't know what you are up to but..."

Freya paused mid-sentence as Sister Crispin held up the first note from Wanda plus a second note she had hastily scribbled.

"Keep talking! Be as annoying as you want. We can't let these Nazi bastards find out what we are REALLY up to."

"Excuse me," Freya apologized, faking a cough and clearing her throat. "But there is NO WAY you'll convince me that this wedding is a good thing for me or ANY of my sisters."

Freya smiled as she screamed "no way" and "any." Sister Crispin also smiled. They both knew these were Freya's genuine feelings, but they also knew they were playing with the Nazis now, and that was something both women could seriously enjoy.

"There now, my dear," Sister Crispin began, "let's just talk and see what is revealed between us."

The next few minutes were a rave of insults and curses from Freya that most of the handmaidens on the other side of the curtain could not believe that a proper young lady would even know, let alone use. Even the guards felt embarrassed listening to her as the torrent flowed from Freya's mouth and left the rest of them wondering how Sister Crispin could handle being with such a woman. Sister Crispin, though, had to fight to keep herself from laughing. It is not that she did not think Freya's rave was genuine, she knew it was real and completely agreed with it; but as she told her about Wanda, relayed the escape plans instructions, and pointed out another servants' passageway in her room, Freya broke out into a goofy smile *while raving* that could make almost anyone laugh. By the time they were done, and Sister Crispin parted the curtain to let the guards and handmaidens see inside, they found a slumped over Freya exhausted from screaming but smiling so brightly it was clear she was overjoyed for whatever was going to come next.

"I think you'll find Miss die Fürstin will be far more cooperative from now on," Sister Crispin said with a smile, walking away from the handmaidens and back to the guards who were now looking at her with a new sense of awe.

"You are a wonder-worker," one of the guards whispered, unable to believe she sat with Freya and that both of them came out smiling afterward.

"I am merely doing what is right," Sister Crispin answered honestly. "Now if you could please show me out, I have to get back to town. There are other members of the Folk who need my services just as much as these girls."

"Of course, Sister, right this way."

Sister Crispin was quickly led out and soon was on her way back to town. She had all the information she needed for Wanda and Wor and had successfully passed on Wanda's message to her sisters. Now came the next part of the plan, actually getting the eleven of them out of Linden Academy. Upon returning home, she found both Wanda and Wor busy planning that move until Wanda noticed she was back, stopped what she was doing, and came over to talk with her.

"How did it go? How are they? Did you talk to them and tell them our plans?" Wanda rambled questions faster than Sister Crispin could hear them.

"If the Nazis suspected me of anything, they didn't show it," Sister Crispin answered. "I was able to talk to all of them. With the exception of Freya, they've all had their heads shaved as 'punishment' for their Swing 12 activities. Beyond that, I didn't notice any other signs of physical punishment. And every one of them is ready to fight tooth and nail, or to do whatever they need to do, in order to make sure this sham wedding *does not* happen."

Wanda breathed a sigh of relief when she heard her sisters were all right. The fact that most of their heads were now shaved did not faze her.

It's just hair. Wanda thought. *Will and Maud have hated the fact that the Nazis gave us special treatment for so long because of our blonde hair that I'll bet they are glad to be rid of it.*

"All eleven of them know the plan and are being kept in rooms that also have servants' passages in them," Sister Crispin continued. "They'll behave themselves and try to get the Nazis off their backs so they can slip away when you come to get them. It's all up to you now."

"Perfect, so what's next, Wor?" Wanda asked, smiling as she turned to Wor in anticipation of his answer.

"Phase 2," Wor replied.

-

| 36 |

"Phase 2" took the entirety of the night and most of the next day. While the town slept and worked, Wanda weaved through the streets with Sister Crispin to prepare their escape into Switzerland.

"We are going to need boats, disguises, passes..." Wanda murmured, reviewing key aspects of the plan with Sister Crispin.

"We have plenty of disguises back at my place," Sister Crispin replied confidently. "And Wor has already taken care of our pass problem. We just need to focus on the boats."

"Yeah, you got that right," Wanda whispered, her eyes rising, remembering when Wor showed them *how* they were going to deal with the problem of passes.

***

"You have a 'birdie,' how did you even get your hands *on* a 'birdie.'"

A "birdie" was an official stamp from the Reich Headquarters of the Foreign Organization of the NSDAP. It looked like the eagle emblem of the Nazis and was vital for anyone creating international passes.

"Wanda," Wor smiled, "you would be surprised what I have gotten my hands on while traveling as I scavenged through buildings that were either destroyed or abandoned during air raids, real or drills. I've been saving this jewel for when I was ready to cross into Switzerland. I didn't want anyone to know I had it until now. I hope you can understand."

***

If any of us knew you had a "birdie," Wanda mused, scouring the piers with Sister Crispin. *Freya and the others would have been mobbing you at the least to try and make sure they could use it. At worst, I'll bet you were wor-*

ried someone in the Swing Club might kill you for it, a justifiable fear. I wonder how things are going for Wor right now?

"More trucks and cars are coming in for this wedding than I thought," Wor mumbled, watching Linden Academy from a distance.

While Wanda and Sister Crispin worked in town prepping their escape, Wor was observing Linden Academy since he knew no one would recognize him. The day's activity was more than he expected.

"They are really making a show out of this wedding; seats in the parade field, an alter/stage set up in its center, places for 'special guests.' I wouldn't be surprised if the 'festivities' begin with a full-blown parade before the actual wedding ceremony, complete with proper introductions of both the bride's and groom's entire families. They'll probably include a long dictation about how Alvis's marriage to Freya is just as much a triumph of the 'Folk and Fatherland' over 'foreign influences' as it is a marriage between 'a proper son and daughter of Germany.' One that will help 'pave the way for new generations of Folk for the Fatherland that will lead it to 'greatness' before even mentioning any feelings of love.'"

Wor felt ill about all the pomp and circumstance being put into this sham wedding. His own tongue felt dirty just talking about how the ceremony was being turned into a big propaganda stunt for the Nazis. Yet the extensive preparations did create their own problems for Wor's and Wanda's plans.

With this many people coming to see the wedding it will be easy to notice someone leaving it, Wor thought to himself. *Once we connect with Freya and the others, part of our initial escape from here depended on being able to slip away quickly and unnoticeably. But with all these vehicles and guests showing up, it is going to be challenging to do that. What are we going to do?*

Wor already knew the best idea would be a diversion, something to draw everyone's attention so no one would notice their group sneaking away. The problem was coming up with one big enough for the job.

We can't fake an air-raid drill, Wor mused, running back to Sister Crispin's place while trying to come up with diversionary ideas. *Nor can we start a fire or some other commotion in or immediately around Linden Academy. Doing that would only draw attention to the academy and make it more unusual for someone to be leaving. I wonder if Wanda might have any ideas? She and her sisters have been coming up with distractions since they formed Swing 12.*

Wor laughed at his own remark as he made his way back into town. But he also knew he was right. Wanda would be the best person to talk to about a big diversion. The only experience Wor had in dodging the Nazis relied on being anonymous and hiding in plain sight. Big and flashy stunts and activities went against how he managed to survive and outwit them.

I wonder if she and Sister Crispin managed to finish all of their preparations, Wor fretted, knocking on the door until he heard the words, "Come in," echo from inside. Walking in, Wor's mouth nearly fell on the floor in shock.

"Your idea worked," Sister Crispin laughed.

"Yes, it did," Wanda agreed.

Wanda's hair had been cut short and messy so that it almost resembled a working man's haircut.

"What did you do to your hair?" Wor finally whispered.

"You didn't think that after hearing about how ten of my sisters were shaved bald, I wouldn't cut my hair short, too."

I honestly never thought about it, Wor mused, staring slack-jawed at her new look. "It's true I thought you could disguise yourself better if you had short hair instead of long hair, but I was never going to suggest it. I always thought we would just tuck your hair inside of a cap."

"The look on your face tells us all we need to know." Wanda and Sister Crispin laughed. "Now, why don't you tell us what you found out."

Wor told them what was happening at Linden Academy, how they were turning the parade grounds into a mock chapel for the wedding, that more cars and people were coming in than Wor originally thought, and that leaving would now be more difficult because of all the guests. He knew that a diversion would be their best chance to draw attention away from the school when they escaped. Unfortunately, he could not come up with ideas for a diversion and hoped Wanda might have one.

"Actually, we won't need to plan that big of a diversion from the sounds of it," Wanda happily replied.

"What do you mean?" Wor asked.

"The Nazis themselves are creating the 'big diversion' with their grandiose ceremony," Wanda explained. "Think about how many people are going to be watching the parade field and the school on the morning of the ceremony. With so much focus there, it should actually be easy to slip away. Think about how it worked for us when we walked around in swing attire. We made a scene in our outfits, but people ignored us because they were completely focused on following the Nazi rules and standards. It was only when we did something big that couldn't be ignored that we got attention. This will be the same. We slip in, get everyone, and then drive out while everyone is focused on the parade grounds."

"I'll remember to count the seconds," Wor joked.

"Haha," Wanda mocked. "Anyway, once we are away from the school, we pull off the big surprise to get everyone's attention while we make our final escape into Switzerland. We have our plan, we know where everyone is, and we know when we are going to start. So, what more do we need?"

"Another truck and a bunch of dummies," Wor answered, thinking about the rest of their plan.

"We've already taken care of the dummies," Sister Crispin explained. "And I'll make sure you have another truck. It will be there at the rendezvous, just like we planned."

"Then I think it's finally time for Swing 12's final performance to begin," Wanda said. She walked into the side room to change and prepare herself to begin the biggest challenge of her life; recusing her sisters and escaping to Switzerland.

| 37 |

"Is that another truck coming?" a guard at Linden Academy's gate asked.

"I don't know why you're surprised. With all of the trucks that have been coming in and out of this school today, what's one more?" a second guard answered.

"I'm just surprised because of how late it is. Light's Out was only half an hour ago. Everyone is asleep now getting ready for that big wedding ceremony first thing tomorrow morning instead of the parade," the first guard said.

The two guards looked on with curiosity as a covered truck pulled up to the gates of Linden Academy. Its driver, a filthy-looking person in sunglasses, hopped out and handed one of the guards a letter.

"You're here to seal up those tunnels the die Fürstin sisters were using?" The guard asked, staring at the official letter and the man before him, who was nodding in affirmation. "What's with the sunglasses? And why aren't you talking?"

The man pulled out a pad, scribbled a note, and handed it to the guard.

"So, you can't talk because you were cleaning up bomb damage, and the dust made you lose your voice?" the guard asked.

The driver nodded "yes" in response.

"As for the sunglasses, you have overly sensitive blue eyes, and you don't want to risk damaging them?"

The man scribbled another note and handed it to the guard.

"Would you want to risk a pair of blue eyes that I can pass down to the next generation of Folk for the Fatherland." The guard, reading the note, said aloud, "No, I wouldn't, I have blue eyes myself. Here is a spare set of keys. Just get going and try to be quiet and finish before morning. The bigwigs want this ceremony to go off without any hitches tomorrow."

The man nodded, taking the keys, and hopping back into the truck and driving into Linden Academy, his partner staring at him intently.

"What?" Wor asked, driving away from the guards.

"I'm just amazed at how easily that went," Wanda admitted, a fact Wor was a little surprised about also.

"Take the luck when you get it," Wor replied.

"Also, is that really why you wear sunglasses?" Wanda asked, realizing she had never seen Wor once without them. Do you really have eyes that are *that* sensitive?"

"Sensitive, yes, but not that sensitive," Wor explained. "I've found while traveling that if people can't see my eyes, it makes my face harder to remember and lets me blend in easier with my surroundings. Just one of the many tricks I've learned while traveling to keep me alive."

"Like how to hot-wire a truck," Wanda joked. She was still slightly amazed from a few minutes ago when Wor hot-wired the truck they were now parking near the kitchen of Linden Academy.

"Exactly," Wor laughed. "When we make it to Switzerland, I'll be sure to teach you and your sisters a few tricks, too."

Wor and Wanda climbed out of the truck with a set of heavy bags slung across their backs. Using the keys to unlock the door, they walked into the kitchen, and from there quickly made their way back to the chapel where they would reenter the servants' passageways.

"This is where Sister Crispin said we would find a servants' passage entrance," Wanda whispered, examining a point behind the altar. "We need to find...*THIS!*"

Wanda tapped her finger excitedly on a crack between two bricks, the point Sister Crispin had told them was actually a secret keyhole for the servants' passage lock.

"Now, let's put this key to good use this time." Wanda eagerly reached into her pocket and pulled out the key that Sister Crispin had given them. Inserting it into the crack, she heard it fit into the keyhole and click as she turned the key, the wall next to them popping open, revealing the passageway behind it.

"Let's go," Wor proclaimed, taking out the map and a flashlight to find their way quickly through the passageways.

Wanda and Wor raced through the servants' passageway, closing the chapel's entrance behind them. They did not want anyone to know they had reopened the one that was in there. Moving through the walls, a sound quickly made them stop at an intersection, one that Wanda recognized instantly.

This leads to the stairs that head down to the grotto, Wanda realized, listening to the voices echoing up from the passageway.

"How long...Tides...Miss the ceremony...Construction crew gets here?" a broken conversation echoed up to them.

Those must be guards the Nazis stationed in the grotto in case the others escaped and tried to leave that way again, Wanda surmised. Wor thought the same thing, putting his finger to his lips in a gesture indicating silence, before leading her to another path heading toward the room where everyone but Freya was being held.

"Do you hear anyone in the room?" Wanda whispered.

"No," Wor answered, his ear on the door. "It's safe to go in."

Sister Crispin had already told the others that if anyone was watching or with them when Wanda and Wor arrived, they needed to make as much noise as possible. That way, they would be aware of the complication and could ready themselves for a fight. Thankfully, the room was quiet as Wanda and Wor opened the door, suddenly being pulled out of the passageway by Will, who fiercely hugged both of them.

"You're alive," Will whispered happily. "You are alive!"

More hugs and similar welcomes soon followed. Wanda noticed that none of her sisters was asleep. And they had barricaded the door leading out of their bedroom. Most of the furniture was used on the door, with the rest setting up a perimeter around the servants' passage doorway, waiting patiently for their arrival.

"I'm glad to see all of you, too." Wanda gasped, losing air from the constant hugging. "But we're losing moonlight. I need all of you to strip and change now."

The die Fürstin sisters felt the situation becoming awkward. Not only did Wanda, who they thought was dead, just ask them to strip, but to do it in the presence of a boy who they were now only realizing was there.

"Now is *not* the time to be shy," Wanda declared. "We need each of you to change into these." Wanda opened her bag and started to pull out clothes similar to what she was wearing. "We can't have you all walking out of here dressed in nightgowns, school, or swing clothes. The guards will be watching for that."

The sisters looked at themselves skeptically for a second but then started stripping and changing quickly. Wor did his best not to notice the spectacle, focusing on the door in front of him and the passageway behind him. He wanted to make sure that if anyone started following them through the passageway or forcing their way against the door, he would know about it. Once everyone was changed, they followed Wor and Wanda into the passageway, locking it behind them so no one would know they used it or could follow them through it.

"Now, let's get Freya," Wanda proclaimed. Her sisters, nodding in affirmation, agreed and started following Wanda and Wor through the passageway leading to Freya's room. However, once they reached the door for Freya's room, Wor put his hand up to stop everyone. Not that they needed the indication. The noise coming through the door was so loud they could hear it clearly.

"I told you, get out of my room!"

"And as I told you, I can't. My superiors ordered me to stay with you the entire night. They feel it will look better if you are moving beyond your past and toward a brighter future."

"You mean the bigwigs don't even want to wait until this sham wedding is over and done with. They've ordered you to sleep and impregnate me, and I am *not* going to let you do that to me!"

Wanda, Wor, and the others recognized the second voice alongside Freya's voice immediately; it was Alvis.

"What are we waiting for?" Will whispered, pushing her way to the front of the group. "Let's bust in there and give that traitor what he deserves."

"I agree," Maud added, coming up alongside her sister. "More than a few of us would love to leave our mark on his hide."

Neither Wanda nor Wor doubted Will or Maud. The looks they were getting from the other sisters told them the same thing.

They are ready to throw caution to the wind for a chance at payback, Wanda mused, seeing the looks in her sisters' eyes. *They only need the key. Not that I blame them.*

"Come on," Will pleaded. "Open the door, and let's go in and give that traitor exactly what he deserves."

"Shush," Wanda whispered. "Not so loud. We can't move just yet."

"What?" several of Wanda's sisters asked at once.

"Wanda's right," Wor agreed, suddenly gaining all of their attention. "If we bust in there now, Alvis will be able to call for help, and then we'll have an entire troop of Nazis on our tail. Your sister knows we are coming, that we might be listening through the wall right now. Don't you trust she'll figure out a way to subdue him?"

Will and the others did not know what was surprising them more, that "Silent Night" actually talked to them, what his voice sounded like, or that he and Wanda made excellent points—ones the others should have already figured out.

"Fine, we wait, but don't expect *me* to wait too long. I am dying to give that Nazi bastard what he deserves."

And you'll get your chance, Will, Wanda thought, wanting to beat up Alvis just as much as the Will and the others. *Just don't do anything rash until the right time. Freya, I don't know what you are doing but move it along in there.*

| 38 |

What am I going to do with this bastard?

Freya had been walking the room, dodging Alvis's advances, ever since he surprised her a few minutes before Light's Out. She knew by now her sisters must be on the other side of the servants' passageway door. She hoped they were smart enough to stay put, especially Will and Maud, until she could figure out how to subdue Alvis.

It's not like I still can use the sleeping drops, Freya realized, trying to think of a solution. *They took the sleeping drops away from us when we were captured. Besides, Alvis* gave *them to me, he would be expecting that. Nor can I simply try to seduce him. I've already said more than enough to prove I have no interest in that. What am I going to do?*

"Okay, I'll admit it," Avis confessed, "while my superiors didn't exactly order me to sleep with you, I could tell that's what they were implying when they ordered me here for the night."

"Ha!" Freya shouted. "You really are as disgusting as your bosses. And to think, there was a time I might have actually gone to bed with you. Looking at you, at that face, I just can't help but be reminded and think about how stupid I was and how much I hate you."

Freya knew she *should* have been focusing on getting rid of Alvis instead of lamenting over her own mistakes and dwelling on her anger toward Alvis. But she could not, and she knew that weakness was costing them precious time. Something needed to be done now.

"Well, if looking at my face is a problem, I think I have a solution for that," Alvis announced, pulling a hood from his back pocket.

"You are *not* putting that over my head!" Freya recoiled as she imagined herself with a hood over her head and Alvis free to do whatever he wanted to do to her.

"It's not going over your head." Alvis corrected, taking a chair and placing it next to the bed. "It's going over mine."

Alvis sat down on the chair and put the hood over his head. "While I know what my superiors wanted me to do, this is what *I* want to do." Alvis declared, looking like he was getting ready for an execution. "You once trusted me, and I still want you to trust me, even if only a bit. I also think I do deserve a few hits from you. Now, I can stay with you all night long, and if you do anything to me, I can honestly say I didn't see anything."

"So, you *can't see anything*?" Freya asked.

"Not a thing," Alvis answered. "And you don't have to be so loud about it. My hearing's fine. I just can't see now."

"And I can do whatever I want to you?" Freya asked again, greedily this time.

"Whatever you want. Have at me for all I care," Alvis replied.

"Good."

That was the last word Alvis heard Freya say to him before he suddenly found himself assaulted by several attackers. He did not know where they came from. All he could remember was the assault and pain before blacking out completely.

***

"Who needs an idea when you got sisters and dumb luck?" Freya mumbled, changing into the new outfit Wanda handed her. After Alvis covered himself, and Freya announced he could not see anything, the others stormed the room. Freya, Will, Maud, all of the die Fürstin sisters took a shot at Alvis for turning them in before tossing him on the bed, tying him up, and tacking a "Swing Heil, Swing 12" note on the back of his uniform. Afterward, several of them looked down on him and imagined what other types of punishment they could give him.

"I think we should dress him in Freya's wedding gown," Will suggested.

"No, let's strip him and shave off *all* his hair," Maud chuckled evilly.

"Ladies!" Wor whispered, trying to get everyone's attention. "While I understand your desire for revenge, it's time for us to get out of here. The longer we delay, the greater the chance is that we're going to get caught and miss our opportunity to get to Switzerland."

"He's right," Wanda agreed. "We need to go now."

"Silent Night and Wanda are both right," Rita added, walking alongside them. "We already missed one chance to escape to Switzerland because we wanted to enjoy ourselves at the swing Christmas party. And don't even get me started on how many chances we *could* have had if we actually *tried* to plan an escape. If we miss another chance now because we want to take our time on vengeance, then none of us really want to escape the Nazis at all. Please do *not* tell me I'm right about that."

Wanda, Wor, and Rita's argument won out as Will, Maud, and the others hovered over Alvis's unconscious body. They left him on the bed and crowded back into the servants' passageway. Unfortunately, shortly after entering it, an echo stopped them cold.

"Tell me again why you want to walk through these tunnels?" a man's voice asked.

"Because the tide is coming in down in the grotto and exploring these passageways is a lot more fun," another man answered.

"Oh."

They muffled themselves and hustled back the way they had come. Turning down two branching paths to avoid the approaching voices, they soon found themselves in a very familiar part of the academy.

"Quick, open this door," Wanda instructed.

Wor did, and the group entered the die Fürstin's bedroom, emptied after everything that had happened.

"Now, what do we do?" Karma asked, muffling her voice so it would not echo to the guards.

"I say we take them," Maud suggested. "We have numbers on our side."

"But not space or time," Wanda reminded them. "And if they're armed, and I'll bet they are, then they have superior firepower on *their* side."

"We have to keep moving," Wor finally said, examining the map. "We can still double around them and get out. But it's going to take extra time. I also think we should stick to the passageways. The academy's halls were patrolled at night during *normal* circumstances. I do not think we should chance them now."

The sisters nodded in agreement. There was a good reason why they always used the servants' passageways, and they knew that reason had not changed.

"Worst case scenario, I'll try to confront them and tell them I'm working on sealing the passageways, so the rest of you can get out of here. But I'll need help in case they don't buy my mute act; I can't let them hear my voice. Can any of you imitate a man's voice?"

"I can," Vita replied, her voice instantly changing as she said the words.

"Then I need you to stay close to me," Wor explained. "Here's the plan."

After explaining the plan, the others slipped back into the servants' passageway and began winding their way through the corridors, their ears alert for any sign of the Nazi guards now sweeping them.

I feel like I'm in a mousetrap, Wanda fretted, listening for any signs of the guards. *Only we're the mice, the guards are the cats sneaking through here looking to catch us, and there are no dogs around to scare them off.*

Wanda knew her sisters felt as tense as she did. There was tension among all of them as they took a winding path leading back toward the chapel. Several times they had to stop and double back because they heard the guards approaching and saw their torches shining in the dark. Each delay cost them precious time to get out of Linden Academy before everyone woke up. Finally, they made it to the chapel door and started emptying back into the chapel. It was also where the guards found them.

| 39 |

"Hey, who are you guys?" one of the guards screamed, his light shining on Wor's face as Wor shielded the sisters as they entered the chapel.

Get ready, Vita, Vita told herself. *This is going to be your greatest performance* ever!

Wor and Vita walked up to the guards while Wanda slipped out of the door with her sisters. Taking a pre-prepared note out of his pocket, Wor handed it to the guards.

"The two of you are members of the construction crew meant to seal up the servants' passageway doors?"

Wor nodded, pulling out the fake orders which he held up in front of the guard and handed another note to the second guard.

"You also lost your voice while cleaning up bomb damage, so you want us to be patient with you while you write out your responses."

Wor nodded again.

"What about this one?" The first guard asked. "Can he talk?"

"Just fine," Vita answered in her gruffest male voice.

"It's just the two of you?" the second guard asked.

Wor took out a notepad and wrote down his response, handing it to the guards when he was finished.

"We were going back out to our truck for more supplies when you stopped us," the guard read aloud. "This job is bigger and tougher than we thought. The rest of our crew is waiting for us right now."

"Well, if that's the case, allow us to help," the second guard volunteered, causing both Wor's and Vita's eyes to pop at the complications.

"Yeah, anything is better than going back down to that grotto. Don't tell anyone I said that," the first guard added, immediately conscious since he had just admitted to Wor and Vita that they were willing to disobey orders.

"In that case," Vita laughed, "head back down the passage you came from, but don't go to the grotto. Take the other tunnel, go up two flights of stairs, and start checking locks. We found that those swing girls unlocked more of them than we originally thought, that's why we need more supplies. You can help us to see if any more doors are unlocked in the passageways—for the Folk and Fatherland."

"For the Folk and Fatherland," the two guards replied before turning around and heading in the direction Wor instructed. Once their backs were turned to Wor and Vita, they turned to each other and silently mouthed a single word, "Run."

***

"Where are they?" Freya whispered, peering out from the truck's cover and looking again for Wor and Vita.

"Relax," Wanda replied, standing alongside the truck and trying to look like she was working on it. "It hasn't been that long since we left them. Now, get back to hiding and wait. They will be here."

Wanda kept telling herself that, but she was nervous, too. The longer she waited, the greater the chances were that someone would walk up to them, ask her what they were doing, or look into the truck, and then it would be all over. The fear had only been growing since she finished hiding her sisters in the truck. Wanda noticed more cars had been steadily filling the parade grounds. It was only a matter of time before the sham wedding was expected to commence.

You should just take everyone and meet up with Sister Crispin at the rendezvous point, a doubting voice in Wanda's head whispered.

No! Wanda countered. *I already know what the fear of being left behind feels like after the air raid. I am not subjecting Wor and Vita to that.*

But Vita and your sisters already left you behind once before, Wanda's doubts said again. *What makes you think they wouldn't do it again to save their own lives? You really should just abandon them. Then there is Wor. Why you are trusting a man for help you know almost nothing about? You saw all those fake identities he had. How do you even know "Wor" is his real name. Who names a child, "Wor"?*

This was not the first time Wanda had heard these doubts in her head, and she knew a few of them, especially the ones about Wor, carried some weight.

It's true my sisters already abandoned me once, Wanda confessed to herself. *And Wor has been an enigma from when I first knew him as "Silent Night," a fact that hasn't changed at all.*

You see! Wanda's doubts screamed. *You can't trust him; you can't trust any of them! All those different names, identities, how do you know if anything he was telling you was the truth? All you do know is that he seems to be a master thief. How do you know if he is really helping you and your sisters get to Switzerland to start new lives? For all you know, he could be planning to steal you all away and sell you into slavery.*

I don't know, and none of it matters! Wanda mentally screamed to herself, silencing her doubts, which were now running away with themselves. *My sisters left me behind by accident. Not one of them meant to do it, and I know that if they had a second chance to do it over, I'm positive they would make sure I wasn't left behind. And even if they did leave me behind again, that just means I'm free to do what really matters. And right now, it's that I protect my family, no matter what. As for Wor, yes, he might still be a big mystery to me, and there is a lot I don't know about him, but let me tell you what I do know about him. He is the guy who risked his own life and safety to save me during the air raid, regardless if it meant exposing some of his secrets to me. And he is the only one who said he would help me rescue my family when he could have easily turned me down and escaped on his own. I don't know what he might really do after this is over, but right now, I know all I need to know about him, and that is enough.*

The doubting voice in Wanda's head was quiet after that much to her relief, and gazing back toward the school, she saw something that made her heart skip. Vita and Wor were running toward the truck as fast as they could.

"You made it!" Wanda beamed.

"In," Wor and Vita replied in unison as Vita jumped in the back with her sisters, and Wor hopped into the driver's seat to start the truck. Wanda was right behind him.

"What happened between you and the guards?" Wanda asked.

"We sent them running through the tunnels expecting us to be back soon with supplies," Wor explained. "When they realize we are *not* coming back, we will have everyone on our tails. We need to leave now."

"Then go!" Wanda exclaimed.

Wor did not need to be told twice. Starting the truck, he began driving quickly toward the gate. Approaching the exit, a security guard walked in front of them and signaled them to stop.

"What are you doing?" Wanda asked, seeing Wor slowing the truck for the guard. "Just go. He will jump out of the way."

"And he will immediately call every police car in the area afterward," Wor countered. "And if he doesn't move, and we hit him, it could still damage the truck in a way that could strand us here. Let me do the talking, just keep nodding once I start talking."

Wanda did not know what Wor had in mind, but she already decided to trust him, and with her family hiding behind her, it was too late to make any last second change of plans. Watching Wor stop the truck, the security guard walked up to the window.

"And where are you going?" the guard began before Wor cut him off.

"We're done with the work," Wor quickly explained, Wanda nodding the second the words left Wor's mouth. "We have been ordered out of here as quickly as possible. The superior party members don't want us around for the wedding; they want it as pristine as possible. For the Folk and Fatherland."

"Very good," the guard replied, stepping away as Wor quickly hit the accelerator and sped through the gate. Driving away from Linden

Academy, more cars steadily approached the school. One car in particular, and its occupants, quickly caught Wanda's eyes as Wor drove them.

"*Goodbye, mother, father,*" Wanda said to herself as she watched their car drive up to Linden Academy. She knew that her mother and father were expecting to see Freya's wedding, but instead would find them all gone.

"Hey, are we clear?" Will whispered from the back of the truck.

"Yeah," Wanda replied, giving one last thought to their parents, seeing no other cars around them, and watching Linden Academy quickly becoming smaller behind them. "We are all clear."

All at once, the eleven die Fürstin sisters in the back let themselves forget they were still in Germany and began cheering about how they finally escaped.

"We're finally out!" Will shouted.

"Those schemdricks and smucks can eat our dust," Vita rhymed.

"We should have left sooner," Rita reflected, still happy to be out of there as the rest of her sisters. All of them were shouting similar cheers and praises.

"Hey, keep it down back there," Wor chastised them. "We are still in Germany and not safe yet."

"Wor is right," Wanda agreed. "Save the cheers for when we are in Switzerland and *really* out of the Nazis' reach. You don't want to be caught and sent right back to Linden Academy, do you?"

That question shut them all up. All eleven faces turned down with shame, realizing Wor and Wanda were right.

"So, now that we are out of Linden Academy, how will we get to get to Switzerland?" Freya asked.

"You'll see," Wanda laughed as a smile crept onto Wor's face. "It's time to put the final phase of our escape plan into action and give Alvis, the students of Linden Academy, the rest of those Nazi bigwigs, and their guests the swing show of their life. The time has come for Swing 12's final performance."

| 40 |

"Get up!"

Alvis's next feeling was of cold water dumped onto his face bringing him back to full consciousness as he struggled to sit up. He fought against bindings holding his arms and legs.

"Get him up," an outraged voice ordered, a voice that Alvis instantly recognized as hands lifted him up, pulled something off his back, and pulled the hood off his head to reveal his father, Tyr von Bron. Several other Nazi bigwigs also stood over him with disappointment radiating from their eyes.

"Father," Alvis gasped, trying to remember what happened last night. "What are you—"

"You, your bride, and the rest of the die Fürstin sisters should have been on the parade grounds for the wedding *thirty minutes ago!*" Tyr exclaimed.

"Thirty minutes ago," Alvis repeated, his voice now trembling in fear.

"Yes, so these other party members and myself came up here to find out if something was wrong," Tyr explained. "Instead, we find the die Fürstin sisters *gone*, their rooms locked from the *inside*, and my son, a proud member of the German people, bound and rendered unconscious with a hood over his head and *this* stuck to his back."

"Swing Heil, Swing 12," Alvis read aloud, an ever increasing dread falling over him with every syllable spoken.

"So, *Cadet* von Bron, since the guards we had posted in the grotto and servants' passageways claim to have seen nothing, do tell me, and these fine gentlemen, just what happened last night and where your bride and future sisters-in-law have disappeared too?"

Alvis did not want to tell his father, or the other party officials, anything. In truth, he did not know either. But he *did* have a good idea.

I remember now what happened last night, Alvis feared, looking at his father and the others as they waited for his answer. *I put that hood over my head myself and dared Freya to do whatever she wanted to do to me. The next thing I knew, I was attacked by a group of assailants. Freya's sisters must have found another servants' passageway entrance in their room, made it to Freya, and escaped. But how could they find another one that quickly? Know how to get to Freya's room, and escape? I was told that the other entrances were being sealed, so how...*

"We are waiting, Cadet," Tyr said, interrupting Alvis's thoughts, not that he wanted to answer his father anyway.

I can't tell my father I put a hood over my own head, Alvis realized. *And I asked for Freya as my wife to protect her and her family. If they think I let them do this to me then it's over. What do I tell them?*

Alvis did not have to worry about telling them anything for long. Familiar music began echoing up to the school, quickly gaining everyone's attention.

"Who is playing that, 'Jungle Music'!" Tyr screamed, running to a window along with the other party members. They could see down to Lake Constance as several motorboats raced across the water, each one carrying a group of girls in flamboyant clothing with a turntable playing swing music. "It would seem your *bride* and *family* are making one last disgraceful show of themselves. And this time in front of their family and all the members of the party present. Well, this time, we do it *our* way. Call the boats! Capture those swing girls. Let's see if some time at the pig farm at Auschwitz might change their disposition."

"NO!" Alvis screamed, quickly gaining the attention of everyone in the room.

"You are *against* the party's orders?" Tyr asked menacingly.

"Never," Alvis lied. "It's just this isn't like them."

"And what is that supposed to mean?" Tyr pressed.

Alvis thought fast. He was *definitely* against sending the die Fürstin sisters, or anyone else, to the "pig farm" at Auschwitz. He remembered the horrors he witnessed there, that he was forced to partake in, that his father and the other Nazis present were able to carry out. It's what convinced him that the only chance he and the die Fürstin sisters had of surviving the Nazis rested in joining them. However, he *was not* lying when he said what they were doing now was not like them. In fact, it reminded Alvis of something else.

"Whenever Swing 12 wanted to draw the police and local HY troops away from them, they would put on a big swing party elsewhere," Alvis explained. "Those boats are decoys. Go after them, and they will slip away and make us all look like fools."

"And I should trust someone so easily captured by them?" Tyr scoffed.

"Father, I'm telling you, they are not in those boats."

"Call the boats," Tyr ordered again before pulling Alvis to his feet, taking a knife out of his uniform, and cutting Alvis's bonds. "We shall see, *Cadet* von Bron."

***

Alvis and his father rode in a private motorboat up to a trio of patrol boats. They had intercepted the die Fürstin sisters' boats as they played their swing music and made their way to Switzerland. During the entire boat ride, a single thought screamed in Alvis's head.

"Please let me have been wrong. Please let them be on the boats."

While Alvis did not want to see anyone sent to the "pig farm" at Auschwitz, he also did not want his father and the other party officials to look like fools. Alvis knew where they would direct their anger.

"The moment of truth, son," Tyr snickered, climbing onto the boat.

"Yes, sir." Alvis quivered, following his father.

"Well, where are the girls?" Tyr barked, looking for someone in charge.

"Well, sir," a nervous boat officer began, "we stopped the boats and silenced the music. But as for the boat's passengers, well, see for yourself."

The boat officer led Tyr and Alvis to the center of the boat. Twelve straw dummies, all dressed in swing clothes, were lying on the deck.

"I told you it was a diversion," Alvis mumbled, immediately regretting it afterward. He saw his father's eyes turn dark with fury onto both the dummies and to him.

"The boats were all rigged to sail toward the border," the boat officer explained. "This letter was also found with the dummies."

Tyr snatched the letter from the officer and quickly read it before turning angrily to Alvis and shoving the letter into his hand.

"Why don't you read it?" Tyr instructed. "*Aloud*, for everyone to hear."

Alvis trembled, scared at what he was about to say with all eyes now watching him, and began reading the letter.

"Dear Alvis von Bron a.k.a. Frankie, I'm sorry, but my sisters and I are unable to attend your wedding today. But since it would be rude to leave you standing at the altar, please accept these gifts to serve as our replacements. They should work perfectly for a Nazi like you. They came from 'a good stock,' won't talk back, and you can do whatever you want with them; dress them up to look like the proper young ladies that a proud son of the German people needs in order to make them fit in. All for 'the Folk and Fatherland.' Enjoy life, your fellow swing kid, Freddie, and her sisters."

Tyr ripped the letter back out of Alvis's hand the instant he finished it. The fury on his face, and the faces of the other party members who had joined them during the reading, radiated together so brightly Alvis thought it was making him sweat.

"So, *Frankie*, that's why you seemed to know so much about how Swing 12 operated. *You were one of their swing boy followers!*"

"It's a lie," Alvis lied, trying desperately to divert his father's anger. "The die Fürstin sisters are making this story up to turn your attention on me while they escape. I'm sure we can still find them."

"And what makes you think you can still find them?" Tyr asked. "Unless you really are a swing boy yourself?"

"No!" Alvis barked. "Never would I willingly subject myself to that 'Jungle Music.' When Freya warned me about the sleeping drops, she also told me about other swing boys who often aided them in their plans. I can interrogate to find out where the die Fürstin sisters are hiding."

"And just who are these swing boys?" Tyr asked greedily.

"Klaus Klingemann, Johan Becker," Alvis replied, giving his father the real names of both Old Kludge and J.B. "She told me about others, too. Just give me one more chance. I will show you and the party that I am a proud son of Germany and that I am willing to give my all for the Folk and Fatherland."

"You will," Tyr replied greedily. "Because you are going to lead Klingemann, Becker, and the other names you have for me on the next campaign at the Eastern Front."

Russia! Alvis gawked internally. The realization froze him as cold as the air he knew he would soon be breathing.

"You say you are a proud son of Germany. That you and are willing to give all for the Folk and Fatherland, to do me and your family name proud. Then take these swing boys to Russia and do what your brother couldn't. Take it for the Reich."

"Yes, sir," Alvis muttered, realizing that saying anything else would be foolish and futile. *Russia, that's practically a death sentence,* Alvis thought to himself, remembering what happened to his brother and more than familiar with the stories coming back from the Eastern Front. *If the Russians, or the weather, don't kill me, Old Kludge, J.B., and the other swing boys* will *for not only ratting them out but conscribing them to fight with me in Russia. I might be better off just drowning myself now and getting it over and done with. That or I'll need to figure out how to desert and defect to Russia. Either way, it's over for me.*

In the distance, Alvis could hear a train's whistle echo across Lake Constance while he contemplated attempting suicide to escape going to the war, facing the other swing boys he had betrayed, or taking the chance with them and then trying to defect to Russia. He knew his chance at staying safe with Freya and the other die Fürstin sisters was gone. As his boat rode back to town across Lack Constance, one lingering thought passed through his head before being cast out of his mind.

Could we have escaped the Nazis and hid in Switzerland?

The image of the "pig farm" at Auschwitz quickly changed his mind.

No. Even if we made it, Switzerland would only give us temporary safety. I don't know where you and your sisters are right now, Freya, or who helped you, but you'll never be completely safe.

| 41 |

"Can I see your passport and papers, Father," a customs officer asked at the Kreuzlingen train station. A tall priest handed him the material, which the officer looked over cautiously. "Father Dismas, traveling to start a new church in Switzerland along with the Sisterhood of St. Crispin, traveling papers stamped by the Reich Headquarters of the Foreign Organization of the NSDAP. They must really want religious folk out of Germany, don't they? Not that we don't need you here."

"You have no idea," Father Dismas replied in a hoarse voice.

"Are you alright, Father?" the customs officer asked.

"I just have a cold," Father Dismas explained. "Can we be on our way now?"

"I'll just need to see everyone else's papers first," the customs officer answered.

"Of course." Father Dismas turned to his traveling companions, collected thirteen sets of paperwork, and presented them to the customs officer, which he examined carefully.

"Everything looks to be in order, welcome to Switzerland, and forgive me if I may be bold, but it looks like the lot of you need to get some new shoes. The ones you are wearing look so worn-out they might fall off your feet."

"We will. It's just we have been walking for a *long* time," one of the sisters explained. "All trying to get to our place of rest. Now I think we might finally be reaching it."

"Then let me just say it again, 'Welcome to Switzerland'."

"Father Dismas" and "the Sisters of St. Crispin" walked out of the train station and into the open air. Kreuzlingen was swarming with refugees from across Europe. So, the group made slow progress as they made their way into a shaded alley and started stripping off the outer layer of their clothes.

"I can't believe that worked!" Vita cheered, glad to be out of the nun costume and now looking like a schoolboy with a hat on her bald head.

"I'm sorry I ever doubted you, Silent Night, or should I just call you Wor?" Will asked.

"Wor is fine," Wor answered, changing out of his "Father Dismas" costume. "And don't worry about not trusting me. You had no reason to trust me, nor any reason to still trust me, other than Wanda's recommendation and your own personal instincts. I wouldn't have trusted me either if I were in your position."

Wanda smiled, listening to her family banter with each other and Wor as they celebrated arriving in Switzerland, the memory of their escape still fresh in her mind."

***

"There is Sister Crispin with the new truck," Wor announced, pulling their truck off to the side of the road and to an old dock where another truck was waiting for them. "We'll be on our way as soon as we get the boats going."

"Good," Freya snickered. "I just finished a letter to Alvis that I want to send him via those boats. I can do that, can't I?"

"Of course," Wor and Wanda answered together, neither one of them wanting to deny Freya some payback for what Alvis had put all of them through.

During the ride, Wanda had explained to her sisters the diversion they were going to use to mask their escape into Switzerland, as well as how they were going to cross the border. Now that they stopped, all eleven of them were climbing out of the truck and heading to the boats. Twelve straw dolls—similar to those they used to hide in their beds at Linden Academy—were waiting for them along with a pile of swing clothes that Sister Crispin had collected over the years. Soon, all twelve dolls were dressed and propped up with name tags signifying each die Fürstin sister—Freya's doll carrying the letter for Alvis. The boats' rudders were fixed in place with ropes so that once they were sent on their way, they would sail right past Linden Academy on their way to the Swiss border. It needed only one final touch.

"These are the loudest turntables I could find," Sister Crispin said, placing one into each boat. "And a swing record for each one."

Wanda looked at the titles of each record. She knew she would never see them again and that she was sacrificing them to save herself and her family.

If I can ever find another copy of those records, I will *find them,* Wanda promised herself. As her sisters started the engines, the music and boats, began sailing toward Linden Academy.

"Now, everyone onto the new truck," Wor instructed. "Put the costumes in the back on over what you are wearing and no arguments. You know the plan. It's time to go to Switzerland."

Wanda and her sisters climbed into the back and started to change. Sister Crispin, already changed, drove the truck while Wor changed in the front seat. A little while later, using the fake passports stamped with Wor's birdie, "Father Dismas and the Sisterhood of St. Crispin" were on a train heading for the Swiss border. Looking back briefly, Wanda could see a collection of boats in the water in Linden Academy—quickly becoming smaller—fading in the distance.

They fell for our diversion, Wanda mused, allowing herself a brief smile. *Good-bye, Germany. I don't care when this war is over, or how long it takes for the Nazi Reich to fall, but I know I will never call this country "home" again. Good-bye for good.*

***

"Good-bye for good," Wanda mumbled.

"Good-bye to whom?" Karma asked.

"Germany," Wanda replied. "I'm just saying one last good-bye to it."

"Honestly, it doesn't deserve it," Maud added, a sentiment the others quickly shared.

"Well, it's time we get going," Sister Crispin announced. "I have a friend who has been taking in refugees since the Third Reich began. It was where Wor and I were always planning on going after we made it here. At this point, what's an extra dozen?"

The die Fürstin sisters laughed at Sister Crispin's comment and began walking with her through the crowded streets of Kreuzlingen. Their worn-out shoes flapped on the road as they walked into an unknown future.

I don't know what's ahead of us from here on out, Wanda thought to herself as she imagined everything that could go right and wrong with her life from this point onward. *This is not a happy ending, it's a happy beginning. I have my family, friends I know I can trust and count on, and* we *have each other. And for now, that is enough.*

| 42 |

Epilogue—15 Years Later

"Wow, there really is almost nothing left now."

It was the first time Wanda set foot in Insel, in Germany, since she and her sisters escaped to Switzerland. Since then, she learned a trade, married a wonderful man from Liechtenstein—and now called the country her new home. She had also watched her other sisters marry and begin families in Switzerland, Liechtenstein, and Luxembourg. But none of them ever went back to Germany. However, the news that the ruins of Insel, the town they had escaped from, being demolished in a few days, brought a wave of nostalgia. It made Wanda return to see it one last time.

"I had heard that during the War a bombing raid had all but leveled this place," Wanda said to herself, remembering the old news reports. "And that and the Allies' invasion, plus the Nazis Scorched Earth tactics all but finishing it. Linden Academy isn't even there anymore."

Not just Linden Academy, but the whole cliffside that it was resting on was now gone because of an Allied air raid. Around her, Wanda spotted other scavengers looking for anything valuable among the ruins before the bulldozers came in to completely level the remains of the town and turn it into an automotive plant. Wandering around, Wanda eventually came to the Lake Constance Swing Club's B Site, one of the few buildings still intact.

"I'm a little surprised this old place is still standing," Wanda announced before a voice from inside caught her attention.

"Wanda, Wanda die Fürstin, is that you?"

Wanda looked into the club as a figure walked out. She smiled at the familiar face and dark sunglasses she had not seen for many years now.

“Wor!” Wanda cried, running up and hugging her old friend. The last time she had seen Wor was shortly after the war ended in 1945. In the years between their escape to Switzerland and his departure, Wor had revealed himself to be older and more skilled than any of them ever thought possible. Wor all but single-handedly taught them trade skills and self-defense. When he left after the War, “to go home,” he had told them they did not need him anymore but knew he would see them again. Now, here he was in front of her.

“It’s so good to see you again. What are you doing here? Oh, and it’s Wanda Winter now.”

“Congratulations!” Wor cheered. “And I’m probably here for the same reason as you. I heard this place was being torn down for good, was nostalgic, and decided to come back for one last time and see if there was anything to pick up and bring home.”

“And did you?”

“Yeah, you. Let’s walk back to the train station, I would like to know how everyone is doing.”

Wanda and Wor walked back to the station, and she filled him in on everything that had happened to her sisters since he left them. She also told him about her own goal to become a music historian and work for a radio station. She especially wanted to focus on swing, because of its personal influence on her.

“It sounds like you’re right on the path to a future, Mrs. Winter,” Wor smiled. “In that case, I would like to volunteer these for your future radio station work.”

Wor handed Wanda a stack of records. “I found them in the bunker. You might recognize them.”

Wanda did, and she could not believe what she saw. Three were copies of the records they had used in their decoy maneuver to escape Germany, the ones she promised herself she would find new copies of. The last one was the one she rescued from the alleyway after the Nazis raided a house and threw it and the record player out of the window and had kept hidden at the club since. When they made their plans to escape, she forgot to pick it up and had long thought it was lost to her for good.

"I thought these were destroyed," Wanda gasped.

"No, they survived," Wor countered. "I think they were waiting for you."

"Thank you," Wanda smiled, also feeling that she might have been called back here for this one reason. "And what about you, Wor? Did you make it home after the War?"

"I did," Wor answered as they entered the train station. "It's a lot further up from here than Liechtenstein, but I think your train will be getting here before mine."

"Then, while we are waiting, I've always wanted to know, what kind of a name is 'Wor?' I always wondered about that. Is it short for Worthington or something like that?"

"Something like that," Wor laughed. "It's actually my first initial, and two middle initials. My name is so long that just using them to create the nickname 'Wor' is too easy for me *not to* use."

"So, that's it," Wanda replied as a train pulled into the station.

"This looks like your train," Wor said, a note of sadness in his voice. "I'll be going home later. Tell your sisters I said hello and that I will see them again someday."

"I know you will," Wanda said, knowing she would see Wor again as she climbed onto the train with her records under her arm. Sitting in an open seat by the window, she was about to close her eyes when one final shout caught her attention.

"Winnie!"

Wanda looked out the window to Wor, who was now not wearing his sunglasses. It was the only time she ever saw his face, and she *knew* she would never forget it—understanding now why he never showed it off before. Something about his eyes, the blue eyes now looking at her, told her that she and her sisters were going to be alright, and that she should not worry about him either because he was going to be alright too, and that he would always be with them.

"Good luck!" Wor cried as the train pulled off.

"Wor, Silent Night, good luck and Godspeed to you, too." Wanda cried back as the train pulled out, taking Wanda out of the last of her past and into her future.

The End